THE *NEW YOR*

R O G U E

RICHARD MARCINKO

VIOLENCE
OF ACTION

"...arcinko ... makes Arnold Schwarzenegger
...ok like Little Lord Fauntleroy."
—*The New York Times Book Review*

$7.99 U.S.
$11.99 CAN.

THE NEW YORK TIMES BESTSELLING ROGUE WARRIOR®
SERIES BY RICHARD MARCINKO AND JOHN WEISMAN

DETACHMENT BRAVO
ECHO PLATOON
OPTION DELTA
SEAL FORCE ALPHA
DESIGNATION GOLD
TASK FORCE BLUE
GREEN TEAM
RED CELL
ROGUE WARRIOR

"Excellent. . . . All of the books are outstanding
adventure stories and a short course in special
operations techniques and weapons."
—Col. Calvin G. Bass, USAF [Ret.], *Tulsa World* (OK)

AND BY RICHARD MARCINKO

THE ROGUE WARRIOR'S STRATEGY FOR SUCCESS
A Commando's Principles of Winning

LEADERSHIP SECRETS OF THE ROGUE WARRIOR®
A Commando's Guide to Success

THE REAL TEAM
True Stories from the Real-Life SEALs Featured in
the Rogue Warrior Series

Available from Pocket Books

ISBN 13: 978-0-7434-2276-5
ISBN 10: 0-7434-2276-7

50799>

EAN

The Rogue Warrior® series by Richard Marcinko and John Weisman

Rogue Warrior
Rogue Warrior: Red Cell
Rogue Warrior: Green Team
Rogue Warrior: Task Force Blue
Rogue Warrior: Designation Gold
Rogue Warrior: SEAL Force Alpha
Rogue Warrior: Option Delta
Rogue Warrior: Echo Platoon
Rogue Warrior: Detachment Bravo

Also by Richard Marcinko

Leadership Secrets of the Rogue Warrior
The Rogue Warrior's Strategy for Success
The Real Team

ROGUE WARRIOR®

RICHARD MARCINKO

VIOLENCE OF ACTION

POCKET BOOKS
New York London Toronto Sydney

This book is a work of fiction. Names, characters, places and inci-
dents are products of the author's imagination or are used ficti-
tiously. Operational details have been altered so as not to betray
current SpecWar techniques.

 POCKET BOOKS, a division of Simon & Schuster, Inc.
1230 Avenue of the Americas, New York, NY 10020

Copyright © 2002 by Richard Marcinko

Originally published in hardcover in 2002 by Atria Books

ISBN -13: 978-0-7434-2276-5
ISBN -10:   0-7434-2276-7

First Pocket Books paperback printing October 2003

10 9 8 7 6

POCKET and colophon are registered trademarks of
Simon & Schuster, Inc.

ROGUE WARRIOR is a registered trademark of Richard Marcinko

Cover design by James Wang

Manufactured in the United States of America

For information regarding special discounts for bulk purchases,
please contact Simon & Schuster Special Sales at 1-800-456-6798
or business@simonandschuster.com.

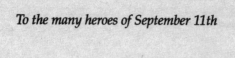

To the many heroes of September 11th

VIOLENCE
OF ACTION

1

"There are occasions when daring and risky operations, boldly executed, can pay great dividends."

GENERAL MATHEW B. RIDGEWAY, *Soldier*, 1956

THE STRANGER SLOUCHED COMFORTABLY IN THE DRIVER'S seat of his rented black Lexus, a new Panasonic DVD player perched in his lap. Outside, a cool mist had descended over the deserted, tree-lined street. Raindrops pattered a soothing rhythm against the car's roof and windows. The small, yellow flames of the neighborhood's gas streetlamps flickered weakly against the gloom. Extraordinarily expensive, they'd been selected for their graceful lines, not their usefulness. Waiting patiently, the man welcomed the inclement weather like an old friend who'd showed up unexpectedly on his doorstep. In his business, bad weather was an ally.

He studied the DVD player's miniature screen as the image of Samuel Beckstein appeared in a clip from a recent evening news broadcast. Like a conquering hero, Beckstein was vigorously striding down the massive flight of stairs in front of a marble-columned courthouse, coming to a halt before a jackal-like mob of reporters. The camera zoomed in on the civil rights attorney's face as he pontificated about his latest legal victory. It had to be said, Beckstein was not a handsome man. His weary face was riddled with deep age lines and irregular patches of discolored skin, suggesting years of overexposure to the sun. A shock of longish, ill-kept, iron gray hair sprouted from his oblong skull. For an instant, his eyes, deeply set in cavelike sockets, seemed to stare directly at the man in the car. "You're a tired old fuck, aren't you?" the man whispered to himself. The electronic file played through a few other similar video clips and then ended.

He checked his watch, a simple Swiss Army officer's model on a stainless-steel band. It was time to move. He'd dressed appropriately for tonight's occasion in a lightweight black wool suit, a black turtleneck, and hand-sewn black leather lace-up shoes with rubber soles. His powerful hands were encased in a pair of thin, black leather shooting gloves. Soft and supple as a baby's skin. The overall effect suggested a stylish, modern-day Grim Reaper. Appropriate indeed.

His right front coat pocket held a tight-fitting assault mask—a black Nomex balaclava. The mask would conceal his most noticeable feature, a nasty scar running dead center across his forehead. The deep channel was the result of an unfortunate encounter with a Russian rocket-propelled grenade during the invasion of Panama.

He shut off the DVD player, set it on the seat beside him, then slipped an S&W Model 13 .357 Magnum revolver out of the sturdy leather shoulder holster beneath his left armpit. His hand-tailored suit coat concealed the weapon perfectly. The revolver's blued cylinder was loaded with six rounds, each a 158-grain soft lead, hollow base wadcutter seated backward inside a shiny brass casing. He'd designed and tested the round himself. Upon contact with soft tissue or bone, it would reliably expand to roughly the size of a .70-caliber projectile. Satisfied his weapon was ready, he returned the revolver to its holster.

There was no one in sight on the street as he slid from the cozy warmth of the Lexus. He softly closed and locked its door behind him and began the half-block walk through the damp night air to Beckstein's home. Strolling casually along the wet sidewalk he keyed a pre-programmed number for the lawyer's private line into his cell phone. After several rings Beckstein answered.

"Yes?"

"Samuel? Ed Curry here. Still okay to drop by?"

"Ed!" exclaimed Beckstein. The lawyer's voice assumed its nationally famous courtroom drawl. "Wonderful of you to call. Yes, yes of course. You're close?"

Closer than you think, cocksucker, the advancing gunman thought to himself. "Yes, Samuel. Just around the corner. Home alone?"

"Yes," Beckstein replied. "My bodyguard is off tonight. Fucking some sweet little bitch barely over the legal age, or so I'm told."

The man in black smiled. "Some guys have all the fun. See you soon."

"I'll deactivate the security gate," said Beckstein. "Come straight up to the front door and I'll let you in."

"Shouldn't be but a minute." He didn't wait for a

response, but punched the END button on the phone and slid it back into his jacket pocket.

Reaching the house's outer perimeter, he took out the ominous black hood and pulled it over his head in one practiced motion. A subtle adjustment here and there ensured a seamless fit. He pushed open the wrought iron security gate just wide enough to slip past it. He stopped, listening and watching for anything unexpected. The rain was falling harder now. Big, fat drops of icy-cold water hammered against the top of the executioner's hood and soaked into his powerful shoulders. Sensing nothing unusual, he swiftly mounted the short flight of steps leading up to a massive front door of lustrous, dark wood. As his research had indicated, the townhouse's exquisitely restored Federal façade hadn't been marred by anything as practical as an exterior security camera, or even a low-tech peephole in the door. Why bother to employ some muscle-bound bodyguard if you couldn't take the most basic precautions yourself? he wondered. The asshole deserved whatever he got.

He eased the big Magnum revolver free of its holster and rapped its heavy, 3" barrel against the door. Moments later he heard the deadlock turning from the inside. His every muscle prepared to strike.

As soon as he felt the door open, his whole body sprang forward hard. His left hand violently pushed the door aside as he exploded into the foyer. The astonished Beckstein stumbled backward as the inside doorknob flew from his grasp and the masked intruder exploded into his home.

The man smashed the butt of the revolver into Beckstein's face, crushing his nose and producing a spray of broken cartilage and rich red blood. As the lawyer's hands instinctively flew upward to protect his now ruined nose, the gunman raised his revolver level with Beckstein's gleaming forehead and pulled its custom-tuned trigger. No explanation, no hesitation.

Beckstein's face caved in as the lead wadcutter burrowed its way through his forehead and into his cranium. The soft, wide mouth of the bullet began expanding upon contact and reached an impressive .72-caliber in diameter by the time it ruptured the attorney's brain. It proceeded to punch a massive chunk of bone out of the back of his skull. Sloppy, pinkish-red gobs of pulped brain matter were sucked through the jagged hole as the lead chunk exited, landing with a satisfying splatter on the foyer's walls and floor.

Beckstein never knew what—or who—hit him.

Keeping the Magnum on target, the killer watched as Beckstein's body slumped to the floor. Then he straddled the fallen figure and fired a second bullet directly into the oozing mass of Beckstein's face. "If you were ugly in life," he whispered, "you're a beautiful motherfucker in death!" Dropping all of his weight onto one knee, he delivered a massive crunch to the center of Beckstein's chest. The sternum-shattering blow released a harsh spray of foamy red bubbles from the man's unmoving lips. Holstering the revolver, the killer slipped a microcassette tape from his front pants pocket and placed it next to the dead man's shattered skull.

As he rose, the hollow chime of an antique wall clock began to toll midnight. He stepped over the dead attorney like he was stepping over a piece of rotten meat and silently padded through the foyer to a large, lavishly decorated reception room. Moving swiftly

across the room's glistening parquet floors and
museum-quality Oriental rugs, he made his way to a
side door that opened directly into a corner of the back
garden. Slipping past a jumble of patio furniture, he
located the rear gate exactly where he'd been told it
would be, obscured behind a thick cascade of slippery
green ivy. Once through the gate, he was in a long, narrow alleyway that allowed service people discreet
access to the grand houses that lined these blocks. He
slipped down the dimly lit alley keeping to the shadows, avoiding the garbage cans neatly stacked behind
each house he passed. His pace was cautious but even.
As he moved steadily away from the night's killing
ground he scanned his flanks and rear for anyone fool-
ish or unlucky enough to follow him, but he was all
alone.

At the end of the long alley, he found the tan Mazda
coupe that had been left for him earlier. Before opening the door and slipping into the car he checked its
backseat. More than one sorry asshole had found himself mugged by an unexpected visitor with a Slim Jim
and sharp knife. Satisfied, he belted himself into the
driver's seat and started the car. He fished the cell
phone out of his pocket and punched a speed dial
button. After three rings, his call was answered by a
clipped New England accent.

"Yes?"

"Please inform Mr. Black that I'm on time."

"Of course," replied the voice. "He'll be pleased."
The line went dead.

Thirty minutes later, the man in black arrived back
at his downtown hotel. Going directly to the luxury
suite he'd rented the day before under a false name,

he called room service and ordered a Caesar salad and a porterhouse steak, bloody rare. Sipping a glass of excellent cabernet, he stepped out onto the room's private balcony and took in the breathtaking view of the city's monuments spread out before him. Once upon a time, the gleaming structures had actually inspired awe in him, but now he could see them only as monuments to a terrible vanity. *Vanity of vanities, all is vanity.* Raising his glass, he silently congratulated his men for the night's success. They'd done well. It had been, as always, a team effort. Samuel Beckstein's assassination would be the means of delivering their message to the president of the United States and then to the world.

The doomsday clock had begun its countdown.

2

"If I appear to be always ready to reply to everything, it is because, before undertaking anything, I have meditated for a long time—I have foreseen what might happen. It is not a spirit which suddenly reveals to me what I have to say or do in a circumstance unexpected by others: it is reflection, meditation."

NAPOLEON (1769–1821)

"... TWENTY-THREE ... TWENTY-FOUR ... TWENTY-FIVE." *Fuck!* With sweat flooding my eyes and my arms quivering in the throes of self-induced fatigue, I willed—more than pushed—the thick Olympic barbell and its 300 pounds of black plate steel back up onto the bench's twin supports. Gasping for oxygen I swung myself around and sat up. *Cocksucker!* With a sidelong glance at my watch I saw I'd been in the Manor's newly refurbished gym for a little over two hours. Pain coursed through my body in sharp electric jolts. I love pain. It reminds me I'm alive. If you can't handle pain in training you'll die from it in combat. I know. I've seen it happen.

Before hitting the gym, Trace Dahlgren, Paul Kossens, and I had hauled ass on a three-mile run around my property. By the time we'd sprinted the last 200 meters I felt like I was gonna puke my guts up right then and fucking there. Jogging is for namby-pamby wimp motherfuckers. You accomplish nothing by jogging. When I run I fucking *RUN!* Bent over and gagging, I tried to focus on my watch face. Twenty-four fucking fast minutes through open country! Damn good for an older but no less tough Rogue Warrior and his two new teammates.

Yes, dear reader, you heard right. My two new teammates. You see, I'd done what the Rogue does best and raised up a new generation of looters and shooters in my own image. Shit happens, and when it does he who is flexible wins.

A little history here.

Once upon a time, Yours Truly created from scratch the purest, most ass-kicking counterterrorist force in the world—SEAL Team SIX. I got to handpick my team from the best of the best and then put them through the most intense and ongoing training in war fighting I could beg, borrow, or steal for them. When I began recruiting shooters for SEAL Team SIX I knew exactly what kind of operator I was looking for. I didn't give a rat's ass in Hell what someone had accomplished in his career as a SEAL before he came to me. Yesterday's successes are fond fucking memories. As soon as you start resting on your laurels, you begin cutting corners and taking shortcuts. You get fat. You get lazy. You want to play it safe. In my business—the business of killing people—the oxygen thieves, corner cutters, shortcut takers, and professional safety experts are the ones who will get you killed. If you're dead you can't accomplish your mission. And if the mission isn't accomplished you have fucking *failed!*

I chose men for SIX who weren't satisfied with yesterday's accomplishments. Operators who weren't afraid to risk everything they had for the greater good. SEALs who weren't afraid to try, come up short, try again, come up short, try again, and keep on trying until they got it right. Shooters who were willing to die if necessary rather than come in second place.

And I required men who were loyal. Not loyal to an abstract theory or philosophy, or to a faceless, soulless institution. I needed men who would jump out of airplanes from five miles above the earth scared to death—but more scared not to. Who would dive to depths the Navy's dive tables say are *verboten.* Who would be willing to kick in a door or board a ship knowing their next step would probably bring a hail of gunfire their way. Such men don't follow theories, philosophies, or cardboard commanders. They follow leaders. And I am a leader, the Wrathful God of War and Combat. My men knew they'd never find me *behind* them. They knew it was their job to keep up with me. And you can only keep up with someone when he's out front running point, taking fire, kicking ass, and collecting enemy dog tags.

After giving painful birth to SIX, I went on to build and lead another team named Red Cell. My mission there was to evaluate Navy security around the world, finding weak spots that terrorists might exploit. To do this I mustered the best and brightest fence jumpers, lock pickers, electronic wizards, and shooters possible. Red Cell was so successful at finding problems with Navy security that the Navy killed it, then turned its sights on me. It took them 60 million of your tax dollars to railroad me into a federal playpen for a year's worth of self-evaluation, color TV, and weight lifting. If they thought pumping iron every day at Club Fed was going to break me, turn me into some soft, apologetic former Navy SEAL officer who'd toe the company line, they were wrong as fucking rain.

Which brings us up to the here and now.

I still lead from the front. Times (and teams) change. I've taken my licks and my losses. Sure, there's been pain but it's the pain that drives me. My enemies—both foreign and domestic—haven't rolled over and quit. Therefore, neither have I. The threat to your and my country is greater and more cunning than ever. This is no time and no place for spit-shined boots and fat stock portfolios, for old war game vets and their field-training exercises where predetermined winners always wear white hats. No, this is the era of the Rogue Warrior. It's a time for guys and gals who love to kick ass and take names to get busy. My new team and I don't come bearing bouquets of pink roses. We come bearing black rubber body bags. One size fits all.

Who's the solution? I am! Me—and those I've molded into mirror images of my Rogue Warrior self—are good for what ails this embattled world. As long as the future holds the potential for natural disasters, political collapse, social disruption and violence without end, it also means I've got fucking job security! Through judicious reasoning, careful planning, thorough preparation, and aimed fire, your world and mine is going to be a safer, saner place to live and raise our kids.

I cannot fail. I will not fail. They will not beat me.

They will have to kill me to stop me. Thus saith the original 24K Rogue Warrior. But you know this already good and faithful reader. So who the fuck are Trace Dahlgren and Paul Kossens? Lemme tell you . . .

Trace joined the military after graduating from college in New Mexico. She killed her first man at the age of thirteen, when she found a drunken uncle in the process of raping her seven-year-old sister. No charges were filed. Indeed, the reservation police quietly and deeply buried both the rapist and the report to avoid public and governmental attention. Ms. Dahlgren inherited her toughness of spirit from her mother, a full-blooded Chihuahua Apache. At fifteen, Trace convinced one of her tribe's "Old Ones" to teach her the ways of the Apache warrior. She learned how to fight with blade, spear, revolver, rifle, rope, and stones. At the conclusion of her training she traveled the ancient trails with the Old One and went on to learn the Art of the Apache Mystic.

Twice married and twice divorced, once in college and again after joining the Army, Dahlgren became an intelligence analyst assigned to SFOD-DELTA. In 1993, when DELTA began graduating female shooters, she volunteered for the DELTA selection program and passed with flying colors. As one of DELTA's first female operators she took up weight lifting, running, and Bruce Lee's famous martial art, Jeet Kune Do. At 5'8" and weighing in at 135 lean pounds of pure cougar, Trace is also one helluva beautiful woman. Full figured with shoulder-length reddish-gold hair and gray-green eyes, she turns heads wherever she goes. Just don't tell her that.

She came to my current team after hearing through the DELTA grapevine that I was looking to recruit a female operator. Discharged from the Army, she nonetheless remains on Uncle Sugar's payroll, retirement benefits and all.

Paul Kossens is German-American and looks it, with his athletic build and thick blond hair. His father was with German Naval Intelligence in Spain during the Second World War. When the war ended, he was brought to the U.S. by German spymaster Reinhard Gehlen to help build the new and upcoming Central Intelligence Agency's East European spy net. He met Paul's mother when she was working for the OSS in Washington, D.C., as the executive assistant to Wild Bill Donovan. Paul came along late in his parents' lives and because of this he was raised with the benefit of the maturity and wisdom of older parents. He inherited his father's love for secrecy and special operations. From his mother he received his passionate zeal to serve a cause higher than himself—which is why he joined the Navy, his *vater*'s service during the war. Paul became a Navy corpsman and then a SEAL. He served at SEAL Team ONE on the West Coast, eventually becoming a dignitary and asset protection specialist. His talent and coolness under fire saw him selected as part of the team charged with locating and taking POW the rancid little pineapple-faced dictator of Panama, General "Manny" Noriega. Paul went on to participate in numerous special operations throughout Central and South America, including the 54-hour harbor-mining mission at Corinto, Nicaragua, courtesy of the CIA.

Like Trace, Kossens came to me after hearing I was looking for a few good SEALs who were interested in doing more than playing war games on their platoon's laptop computer. With a B.A. in business administration from the University of San Diego, and a third language (Russian, as a useful balance to his German), I couldn't pass up this eager 8492 Special Operations Technician from the Teams.

In the gym, the three of us were sweating through the exercise and weight-training routine two young studs from SEAL Team SIX had custom-designed for me eight months earlier. It was a ball-buster. I couldn't care less. Like I said, life is not fucking easy and neither is staying in SEAL Team shape. I saved the bench press for last knowing it was the meanest bitch in the program. Twenty-five joint-creaking, muscle-wrenching reps at 300 motherfucking pounds of unforgiving steel plate—I love the challenge! Sheer pain lightly wrapped in animal willpower. Give me an impossible task any day of the week. As I pushed through the routine, Trace and Paul each worked out at their own pace. We left each other alone, except for the occasional wisecrack now and then as we taunted and pushed each other to do one more rep or add an extra twenty pounds to the stack.

Finished on the bench, I grabbed a towel from the black rubber gym floor and sopped rivers of sweat from my face and neck. Then I grabbed a basketball and sank a nice three-pointer from mid-court. Yeah, the Rogue was physically feeling damned good these days, fuck you very much.

Which is as it should be.

I'm 240 pounds of muscle strapped to a stainless steel frame. I'm running eight-minute miles and every other day I swim 2000 meters at a nearby pool. Besides helping me set up a new gym full of the best workout equipment and designing a twenty-first-

century fitness routine, the shooters—MY shooters—
from SIX spent a weekend at the Manor doing their
best to educate me and *the girls* about nutrition and
the fucking evils of alcohol (as if I couldn't have edu-
cated *everyone present* on *that* subject!). When we said
our good-byes on Monday morning and the boys
from SIX hit the road back to Virginia Beach, I had to
admit one thing: the new kids now running with the
Devil at SEAL Team SIX are all right.

Wait a minute, you may well ask. How is it the
Rogue Warrior, bane of the United States Navy and
scourge of its elite SEAL Teams since being railroaded
through not one but *two* show trials at the American
taxpayers' expense, can now freely hang out with the
ultimate in counterterrorist units, SEAL Team SIX?

Good question, grasshopper. Sit and let an older
and wiser Rogue explain it to you. You may recall that
the government had last required my unique brand of
service in the pursuit of two darling Irish terrorists,
William and Gerry Kelley. They went to their watery
graves, courtesy of Yours Truly, during my tour with
Detachment Bravo in jolly old England.

After submitting my carefully sanitized after-action
report pro forma I found myself under furious attack
from every direction. My unilateral decision to play
the adult version of Sink or Swim with Mrs. Kelley's
murderous sons hadn't gone over (under?) too well
with the gutless wonders at our State Department.
Their whining alerted some of my still-powerful enemies at the Pentagon and Navy, enemies who orches-
trated a call for my head to be put on a spike. It seems
there are *rules* governing the care and feeding of those
who make careers out of murdering the innocent
among us, and drowning them is not found in the

State Department's official handbook. I'd played by *my* rules and the Irish bastards had gone down to Davy Jones's locker—hook, line, and fucking sinker. No loss to the world and certainly no loss to *moi*. Trials are too expensive these days. When you send me out to kill Tangos, then that is what the fuck I do. You'd best expect the mother-raping bastards to die and die damned hard where I find them. I—pay close attention here—*will not* bring a terrorist back alive. My version of the old Wild West wanted poster reads WANTED: DEAD OR MOTHERFUCKING DEADER!

Make a fucking note here.

You'll find this in the Rogue Warrior's updated and abridged rulebook on whacking Tangos. The Rogue says drowning terrorists is perfectly fine and dandy. Gutting the bastards and using their innards for chum is okay, too. Although I hate punishing a good shark by feeding it trash like the Kelley boyz. I have an affinity for sharks.

Within a week of my return from England I began hearing nasty rumors about congressional hearings and criminal charges with me in the bull's-eye. Been there, done that. If there's one thing I've learned over the years it's when to fight Stupidity with Fire. With all the lovely money I've made from my best-selling books I no longer have to rely on limp-dicked, court-appointed Navy JAG lawyers whose careers are at the mercy of the very judges who hear their cases. I called my outrageously expensive civilian junkyard dog attorney, a former SEAL teammate who'd decided it was more fun to make big money and fuck with people using the law than it was to kill them, and explained my plight. Within days a flurry of extremely hard-assed letters were sent out to All Concerned.

They basically said I wasn't talking to anyone and no one was going to talk to me unless it was through my lawyer. In other words, BLOW ME!

Next I made some not so discreet phone calls around Washington, as in "Bite-My-Sack-D-fucking-C." As an up-and-coming naval officer with a talent for intelligence work, I'd learned that knowing shit—really good shit—about people, places, and things is a must if you want to wage Rogue war on the world at large. Some of the voices calling loudest for my decapitation were also the subjects of long-held and informative little entries in my personal database. After crashing through the various security firewalls my tormentors had built around themselves at their offices and homes I set about enjoying a few short but immensely *productive* conversations with my detractors. Chats with those whose own questionable behavior and peculiar habits I'd carefully logged while coming up through the ranks. "You fuckee-fuckee me and I'll fuckee-fuckee you bigger, harder, and faster!" I told each suddenly squirming goody-goody two-shoes at the other end of the line. One by one they got my message and—would you believe?—the self-serving chest pounding lessened up on the Hill and down at the Pentagon.

Blackmail, you say? No, just Washington power politics at their most pure.

Once this initial round of chitchat was over, I moved on to a few face-to-face meetings with some old-and-not-so-dear friends who'd smelled my blood and were clamoring to get on board the "GET DICKIE" bandwagon. One such fan, a former SEAL officer I'd nicknamed "The Little Ensign," made the tactical mistake of accepting my invitation to meet for lunch at the posh O-Club at Fort Meyers next to Arlington National Cemetery.

We hadn't cottoned to each other during our earliest days on the Teams and our dislike of each other had only intensified as we were each promoted up the Navy ladder. My personal intelligence network informed me my old nemesis was rattling his tiny little saber again. Old rivalries never die. I've made my fair share of enemies over the years and they never tire of taking cheap shots whenever an opportunity arises. I'd offered one such "officer and gentleman" the chance to fight me fair and square, man to fucking man, on the beach during a SEAL Team reunion in Little Creek, Virginia. He declined. Then he whined to anyone who would listen that I was crazy to challenge him. The fucking pussy was as yellow as the piss that flows out of my prick after a half case of good German beer. He couldn't handle the ass whipping he knew he deserved and would have gotten. In the land of the Rogue Warrior, there are straight shooters and there are back shooters. I've noticed most of my enemies prefer the latter role.

Anyway, The Little Ensign showed up for his free lunch looking awfully smug; no doubt he thought I was down-and-out and planning to ask him for some sort of favor. His South Carolina drawl had only gotten thicker over the years and the Citadel ring on his finger glinted every time he moved his hand. We shot the shit over the meal, each of us probing the other for those openings where you can shove a fucking knife in and hit something vital. I'd first learned the Art of Diplomacy during my tour as an embassy-based naval adviser in Cambodia during our nasty little war in Vietnam. When I went to Washington (as in D.C.), higher-level table-turning and informed statecraft were taught to me by the very best in the business. If I say so myself, I've only improved with age. The beady-eyed little bastard sitting across from me was about to fucking find this out the hard way.

With lunch over and a crisp hundred dollar bill fresh from my wallet sitting atop the politely delivered check, it was time to take the safety off my weapon. I mentioned to The Little Ensign that I'd been hearing some disturbing things lately. Things with his name attached. Things having to do with me.

"Why, what in the world do you mean, Dick?" he drawled, his palms upturned, an oily mask of phony innocence plastered on his bulldog ugly mug.

"I mean just what you fucking heard me say, cock-breath!" I replied. "You never had what it took to join SIX, and you're still pissed as all hell that I wouldn't look the other way and let you come to the party anyway!"

I could see in his eyes that I'd nailed it. Yeah, the rat-bastard remembered his interview with me as vividly as I did. He'd waltzed into my office thinking he was going to bamboozle me with his family pedigree and all the bullshit he'd managed to pull off during his career, but he'd ended up limping out the door with his gold trident shoved sideways up his ass. He never figured out if you wanted to make it on SIX you had to run the gauntlet—MY gauntlet—and come out the other end bloody but still standing. SIX was my command, my responsibility, my job, my fucking life. The Little Ensign may have been a dandy SEAL elsewhere, but he wasn't Team SIX material and never would be.

"Suck my dick, Dick." He sat back, arms folded

across his chest, his plump little belly rolling down and over his silver SEAL Team belt buckle.

"No can do," I said. "You're the only cocksucker at this table. You're gonna walk out of here with my dick in your mouth, and you'll remove it only long enough to call your people and tell them what a wonderful time you had with your old pal Marcinko. You'll tell them how clever you were, getting me to trust you after all these years. You'll tell them I confided in you that I'm considering taking legal action against some powerful and influential individuals—as yet unnamed. The allegations will include defamation of character, slander, and even libel once the evidence I have gets into my lawyer's greedy little meat hooks.

"Then you'll do what you always did when you were kissing ass in the Teams. You'll pound your little tail on the deck and yap loudly about how important this information is and how you're going to 'cultivate' our new relationship. You'll say that you and your friends can really fuck me over by your passing on to them all the nasty old secrets I may tell you. But in reality, asshole, you're going to keep me briefed as to what the fuck is on their agenda. That's what good little informants do. They rat on anyone who is stupid enough to trust them."

I stopped and waited, letting the realization of what was now happening to him sink in.

"Fuck you, Marcinko!" His fists balled up and for an instant I thought the little cocksucker was actually going to take a swing at me. He'd thrown the dice and they'd come up snake eyes. Now it was time to blow him out of the water.

Over the years I've learned the key to effective diplomacy is to let your opponent's theatrics and emotions sail past you without comment. You deal strictly with his actions, with the facts. So I let my lunch guest vent his rage but I didn't respond in kind.

"I appreciate your position," I offered politely. "However, let's be frank with one another. I know about the federal judge you were pushing to go after me a few years back and the totally illegal surveillance you've had placed on the Manor."

His face paled. I noted with satisfaction how his hands began to tremble slightly. I had him by his fuzzy little balls and I was now about to squeeze them *velly velly* tight. And tightly squeezed *cojones* are painful. I know this because my own nuts have been tightly squeezed a time or two . . . and not by somebody sexy initiating foreplay on the way to the main course.

"I also know you went a little 'rogue' yourself upon retirement." This revelation hit home like three rounds of high velocity 9-mm ammunition coming out the business end of my favorite Glock. "That anti-government bullshit won't play well with your pals on the Republican side of the aisle, not to mention the yogurt stirrers on the Democratic side. Especially now with the war on terrorism and all. They *hate* anything remotely tied to your brand of patriotic—or should I say racist—fervor.

"There's not much about you and your little scams that I'm not aware of," I said in the most matter-of-fact voice I could muster. "But let's not waste our time belaboring the point." I sat back in my chair, palms flat on the table, my diplomat's face now given way to the warrrior face I'd worn as a career killer for the United States Navy.

"Dick," he uttered so quietly I had to lean forward

to hear him. "That shit's over. I'm doing okay now. Good job, good contacts. You know how it is . . ."

Fucking-A, I do.

He was mine.

"You tried to fuck me, son," I growled. "You came here thinking you'd break it off in my ass . . . on my time . . . on my dime. You were wrong."

He looked me dead in the eye but I could see he now understood how bad a hand he'd played. He could only hope to get out the door with some dignity left. You never crush a man when you've got a use for him. It was time to close the deal and send The Little Ensign off with his little white sailor hat held tightly in his hands.

"What do I gotta do?" he murmured.

"Anything aimed my way you'll report back to me. At the same time you'll stop-all-engines any of the bullshit you've hatched on your own. If any of our other 'colleagues' from the bad old days in the Teams ring you up and want to play *Fuck Marcinko*, you'll string them along and then report it to me immediately. Anything less and I'll put a Limpet mine beneath your hull and sink you in place. Any questions? Good. You're dismissed."

As I watched him shuffle out of the dining room I reminded myself I had a few more such meetings to hold with other detractors. Meetings meant to douse the fires being fanned against me by my own kind. I didn't figure on hearing much from The Little Ensign. He was lousy informant material. I figured the little bitch would find a way to drop out of the political ballgame and that was good enough for me. One less enemy on my flanks meant I could concentrate on my front where the real fighting takes place.

Up front and personal.

Make a fucking note. The best defense is a hard-assed offense. I *never* fight fair. I fight back. And when I go to war it's all or nothing. The bottom-line strength of your commitment is what often carries the day in war or in business. I've never questioned my commitment to anything once I've given it. My enemies have learned this the hard way. My friends—and I've damned few of those—know never to worry about their six if I'm on it. I've grown older, wiser, and a damn sight meaner with age. I'm a gray-backed Grizzly with whom *you will not fuck* unless you're bound and determined to get your ass punched, kicked, bit, and shoved into the dirt. The Rogue Warrior's Rules on Taking Prisoners: *Don't*. Truth is, I don't have to hate you to kill you.

After sealing the watertight doors behind me and leaving word with my attorney I was not to be bothered, I hit the road. Taking a chunk of royalty money out of the Rogue Warrior® bank account, I bought a Dodge RAM and camper and had both custom-painted in SEAL Team gold and blue. I outfitted the Beast, as I named my new all-terrain war wagon, with the luxuries of home and set out with map in lap and a fresh bottle of the good Doctor Bombay at my side (on ice, of course!). Along with my favorite Glock 26 and a half a dozen extra magazines of 9-mm brain busters, I threw in for good measure a new Stoner .308 battle rifle with a 4-power Leupold scope attached. America hasn't been a safe place for a man or woman on the road for some time now. Properly armed and willing to be dangerous is an American tradition and I'm all for tradition when it comes to keeping my frog-man's ass in one piece.

There was another reason for my locking down the Manor and getting the fuck outta Dodge. I'd spent the best years of my youth and most of my adult life fighting my country's wars without question or complaint. As a result, my body as well as my mind had been beaten up, fucked over, messed with, and generally hammered to the point where every damned thing hurt, ached, or haunted me when I woke up each and every damn morning. Teammates had come and gone. Friends were few and far between. My love life sucked—and it had been months since my cock had been. Legal battles, first with the Navy and then with parasites in the civilian world, had dangerously drained what financial independence I'd managed to rebuild for myself after graduating from Federal Pen University *Momma Cum Loudly*. On top of *that* bullshit, the hundreds of missions I'd spent getting the shit kicked outta me while chasing down the enemies of my country, cutting off their fucking heads, and then shitting down their bleeding throats, had taken their toll.

Fuck. Wouldn't you buy a damned truck and drive off into the sunset yourself?

I knew I needed to fall back, regroup, and rebuild before I could put together a new team. Then I'd return to the fray bigger, badder, tougher, and more dangerous than ever. I wasn't going searching for myself like some fucked up tea-drinking do-gooder in an orange skirt. No sir, I was an old, beat-to-shit war dog on the road to heal his wounds and learn as many new tricks as possible along the way.

I spent a week heading west, driving eighteen hours a day. When I stopped it was either for gas and a quick meal in some shithole along the highway, or for a quick swim and bath in a river or stream I'd found on the map. Whenever someone thought they recognized me from my books or a past television appearance I'd blow them off with a curt nod and then fire up the truck and get the fuck back on the road. Life was simple. Eat, drive, drink, and sleep wherever and whenever I felt like it.

When I reached Utah I swung off the main road and headed up into the mountains. After two days of exploring the broken crags and peaks overlooking the flat fucking wasteland of the Mormon Prophet's paradise I found what I was looking for. For the next week I lay still as a corpse on a tiny sun-blasted rock ledge with my Stoner in hand. Peering through its scope I mentally designed a killing ground 700 meters deep and 500 meters wide. For the first two days I watched and recorded every living creature that made its home on my range. The larger animals I would let live. The smaller ones, however, I considered good training aids and therefore fair game.

On Day Three I began killing from a distance. The Stoner's harsh bark bounced up and down the ravines and gullies every time I spotted a racing rabbit or curious ground hog. Coyotes became my favorite and most difficult shot. Wary and sensing that a new predator was operating in their backyard, the wild dogs made every effort to outsmart me. They'd slowly crawl on their bellies through the sage and sand, trying to reach the rotting carcasses of my earlier victims. Naturally camouflaged and wonderfully cunning, they made the game that much more challenging.

On Day Four I started killing the winged carrion eaters that came to feast on the dead. Blowing the fuck outta them was a special joy to me. I've always hated vultures, human or otherwise. I'd let each one get his fill before sending a high velocity round crashing through its body. Payback is a motherfucker. Gun control means hitting the target.

I spent Day Five cleaning the rifle and its optic from stem to stern. If anyone had heard my shooting they never came out to investigate. The Stoner was zeroed to perfection and gave me no mechanical problems. Even better, my natural shooting ability with a long gun was again up to Rogue standards. I could hit anything that moved and was the size of a coyote or smaller. I'd hardened myself to the rigorous demands of a sniper and weathered the bleaching hot days and bitter cold nights of the Utah desert. By the time I'd repacked the Dodge and made my way back to the highway, I was feeling much, much better. Shooting to kill has always had that effect on me. And I've always hated cute little furry animals anyway.

I swung up into North Dakota where I attended a yearly SEAL reunion in Minot. For three days about sixty of us ate, drank, and swapped war stories. I met my teammates' wives and kids, at least those who were lucky enough to still be married (though not necessarily to the same woman they'd started out with). I met a waitress named Roxanne at the local diner my first night in town and we ended up fucking each other silly for the rest of the weekend. She was a leggy, blonde former airline stew who'd burned out on flying the friendly skies and getting hit on by middle-aged pilots whose wives thought their husbands were cockpit commandos ever since September 11, 2001. Rox had come to Minot to visit family the year before and ended up staying just for the fuck of it. It was easy to tell she'd been bored to death by the hometown cock monsters. Every night I gave her free play with the Rogue's royal ten inches and happily let her work out her wildest fantasies. Every day we enjoyed the company of good friends and good booze.

By the time I left Minot, Rox was swearing like a SEAL and could fuck, suck, and drink nearly any stud in town under the diner's tables. Me? I felt centered again after being among my own kind, and better yet, I didn't feel the urge to jack off every time I saw a Brittany Spears music video on the Ram's onboard television!

Four days later I was in Tacoma, Washington. I'd heard about a street-fighting motherfucker named Kelly Worden from some of the operators on SIX. They said the guy could hurt you just by smiling. After getting lost driving around the fucking city I finally stopped a cop and asked if he knew where the fuck it was I could find Worden. Turned out he did. All I had to do was sign an autograph. I linked up with Mr. Worden and spent the next two months living out of my truck on a small beach across the Narrows Bridge. For the next two months, five days a week, five hours a day, I trained with Worden at his home. It cost me $500 a week to learn Worden's *Natural Spirit* method of close-quarters combat. But what I'd heard was true—the bastard could hurt you just by looking at you. Then when he touched you, the pain *really* got intense! At first I tried to fight him with everything I'd learned on the streets as a young punk who'd brawl with anyone he met. Then I tried all the down and dirty shit we'd learned in the teams and that I'd introduced to both SIX and Red Cell.

The fucker just laughed and proceeded to beat the

crap outta me with his fists, his feet, his fucking head, and anything else that came to hand.

Remember what I've been telling you about pain? I lived in a constant state of pain for those two months. My bruises had bruises. My joints felt like they'd been torqued with a jackhammer. My muscles were beaten, battered, and pulped. But in time I began to learn a new way of fighting. And I loved it. The pain was teaching me well.

I'd learned how to properly fight and kill with a knife. The Emerson CQC-7 tactical folder I'd picked up at a local knife show now complemented my new skills. Along with slicing and dicing with cold steel I could also beat a man to death with a rolled up *Newsweek* magazine; strangle someone to death with triple-reinforced dental floss; and break nearly every bone in an opponent's body as easily as wiping my ass. My speed and power, blow for blow, had been magnified tenfold. I'd mastered the art of deception and could strike like a cobra without giving my intention away with an inadvertent glance or twitch. By the beginning of the second month I was Worden's *uke*, or silent training partner. He'd gotten a contract to teach his unique brand of combatives to the First Special Forces Group's Green Berets at Fort Lewis and I was rolling with Kelly's punches well enough that I could help him instruct.

With my martial arts training came additional studies in the healing arts. Worden introduced me to a couple of true masters who'd come from China and the Philippines to settle in the Pacific Northwest. In turn, they shared with me how to use herbs and the natural properties of the body to cure injury and illness. Worden, a master healer himself, worked on the wreckage of my battered body using his inner *Chi*. Old pains faded and new ones quickly disappeared. Soon I could treat myself. I was now not only a Master Destroyer but a capable healer. The balance suited me more than I'd have ever expected.

When I left Mr. Worden's school for modern-day warriors I was physically, mentally, and emotionally fit. Better yet, my close-quarters fighting skills had been taken to a level well beyond formidable. I was no longer a brutish brawler with a thick skull and quick fists. I had attained a **master's ability** to destroy my enemies with perfect **timing and effective** technique.

For the next several months I went wherever the road or my mood took me. To San Diego and the Silver Strand to visit and learn from my brothers at SEAL Teams 1 and 5 at Coronado. To Mexico where I spent a month training Mexican naval commandos in ship-to-ship boarding operations to help stop water-borne drug smugglers working the Pacific Coast between Mexico and the states. From Mexico back to the United States, where I made the rounds of America's finest shooting schools, beginning with Clint Smith at Thunder Ranch in Texas. Along the way I met up with my old friend and fellow Tango hunter Danny O. Coulson, the founder and first commander of the FBI's famous Hostage Rescue Team. Coulson brought me up to speed on what was happening real time in our war on both foreign and domestic terrorism. Danny is the only motherfucker who could get me to wear a cowboy hat to a bar and enjoy doing so.

Fuck you very much, Danny!

It was in the middle of all this, while doing a little job down in El Salvador, that I happened to meet up with a couple of fire-breathing, whip-smart military punks named Trace Dahlgren and Paul Kossens. After what we went through down there, I recognized them as the foundation of my new team and they were just crazy enough to join me.

A few phone calls to my attorney revealed the heat was off in Washington. Dead terrorists were now good terrorists. And how they died didn't matter. My detractors had been muzzled and my absence had helped take the edge off their self-serving need to see me sidelined during the current fray. I was fit, fucked, and ready to go to war again. From the ashes of the old Rogue Warrior had been born a new and more deadly version of my Self. It was time to return home, time for me to go operational once again. Meaning? New Demo Dick, new team, and new bad dog attitude for anyone stupid enough to get in my way.

My blue cell phone began ringing its ass off as I toweled dry my hair. The gut-busting workout had left me feeling refreshed. "Marcinko here," I barked into the cell. Five minutes later I punched off the line with my brain in overdrive. It hadn't been the Avon Lady calling.

Our presence in Washington was requested. Make that *required*. Karen Fairfield at the Office of Internal Security Affairs, or OISA, was sweating right through her pretty panties over reports coming in from the D.C. cops about a murdered attorney, a terrorist threat, and—oh, yeah—a missing nuclear weapon. All Hell was breaking loose in the Oval Office and Karen wanted us on the road *yesterday*.

Did I forget to tell you? After my return to the Manor I'd been invited—*invited*, mind you—to attend a meeting at the State Department proper. It seemed there was a renewed need for the Rogue Warrior and his special brand of counterterrorism. We cut a nice financial deal as security consultants under purposefully vague contractual terms through State. Our credentials and badges (yes, *badges*) were issued through the U.S. Department of State's own Bureau of Diplomatic Security by the authority of its chief in charge of the Coordination Center and Special Projects / Office of Overseas Operations, or CCSP/OOO. Then we were seconded to the new outfit called OISA, which reports directly to the president of the United States.

I am once again sanctioned to kill my enemies wherever I find them.

After briefing Paul and Trace, I began packing my overnight bag. It was the bit about the missing nuke that made the hair on the backs of my hands stand up on end. If a Tango, or Tangos, had gotten their nasty mitts on such a thing, there wasn't a city or citizen in the United States that was safe. OISA was sending an NSA chopper to pick us up and move the new Rogue Warrior and his team most ric-tic to the murder scene where the cassette had been recovered.

This was Big Dog time. Tactical nuclear weapons. Who the fuck knew how to get their hands on this kind of heavy shit other than me and a handful of my operators from Red Cell? I guessed that was why they were bringing us in. It was a dirty damned job and dirty deeds done cheap have always been my specialty. I zipped the black bag shut and slammed a fresh magazine into my Glock. Trace was downstairs yelling for us to move our asses. The chopper was coming in.

3

"I may be accused of rashness but not of sluggishness."

NAPOLEON, 6 MAY, 1796, to the
Executive Direction, *Correspondence*,
Vol. 1, No. 337 (1858–1870)

A HUNDRED MILES OUTSIDE LOS ALAMOS, NEW MEXICO, the glare from the early morning desert sun was already intense enough to turn the infrequently traveled stretch of highway into a shimmering river of black and silver. The black-clad figure in the middle of the highway completed his task quickly and then gave a quick thumbs-up to the unseen shooter he knew was covering his back. He trotted away from the spike strip he'd positioned across the two-lane blacktop highway and scrambled back up to the firing position where he'd left his RPG and its two olive drab–colored high explosive grenades. Glancing toward a nearby shallow rise in the road, he slid the first rocket-propelled grenade into the launcher's tube. Within just a few moments he heard the sound he'd been anticipating—

the hum of the engines of an approaching convoy. Lowering himself into the gritty sand of his makeshift shooting platform he flicked the launcher's safety to the OFF position but kept his right index finger well away from the weapon's trigger. An accidental discharge was not part of today's game plan.

Three hundred meters to his south and one hundred feet higher on the crest of a small hill, the team's hard-target interdiction specialist could also hear the telltale rumble of the approaching target. Snuggled comfortably into his right shoulder was a .50-caliber Barrett M82A1 rifle. Its 10X Leupold & Stevens Mark IV M-1 scope easily allowed him to track the progress of the two U.S. government vans as they traveled at a steady fifty-five miles per hour through the wide open New Mexican desert. The lead van topped the gentle rise and began picking up speed as it headed down toward the nearly invisible spike strip, but it was the fate of the second van that was his personal responsibility this morning. Taking into consideration both the environmental and meteorological factors for the morning's shoot, he'd chosen his firing position with enormous care. Shooting platform and body position were critical when it came to employing a heavy gun like the Barrett successfully against enemy personnel or vehicles. Having frequently made use of the big .50 during covert operations in Afghanistan and deep inside Iraq during the early months of the so-called war on terrorism, the well-concealed sniper was supremely confident of his ability to take out his target—and anyone in it—rapidly and with a minimum of expended rounds. To terminate the chase van, he'd selected the Raufoss .50 BMG M903 sabot round and its spin-stabilized Penetrator slug. The Raufoss's slug could easily penetrate the van's reinforced windshield, leaving the driver vulnerable.

The sniper's secondary mission was to provide real-time information to his colleagues positioned farther down the highway about the progress of the lead van, whose tires would be severely damaged after running over the spike strip at fifty-five miles per hour. The specially designed spikes would have no trouble ripping through the safety tires' Kevlar-belted layers. Simulated practice runs by the team indicated the van would lose at least two of its tires, and possibly all four, once they rolled over the razor sharp prongs of the spike strip. The van's driver could probably nurse the vehicle at least another half-mile down the highway regardless of how many tires went down, but the vehicle's speed would be dramatically reduced, allowing the two intercept vehicles positioned a mile down the road to meet it head on and set up a secure blocking force across the highway.

Rocket Man watched with growing anticipation as the first van crested the hill and began to pick up speed on its descent. He adjusted his position so he could bring the launcher up to his shoulder in a single, easy motion.

Despite the lead van driver's high-tech, custom-made sunglasses, the dazzling morning sun prevented him from noticing the slender strip of razor sharp spikes spanning the highway until his van was nearly on top of it. Swearing loudly, he'd hardly even begun to brake when he felt the vehicle's two front tires exploding. Punching the accelerator, he grimaced as the rear tires were similarly damaged. Holding onto the steering wheel for dear life, the driver tried to maintain as much speed as he could as the van rumbled clumsily down the road. It took all his strength to control the vehicle given its additional weight and gutted steering.

Three van lengths back, the driver of the chase vehicle had an extra half-second of reaction time. Shouting a warning to the heavily armed operators riding with him, he slammed on his brakes to avoid the spike strip's gleaming steel teeth. An experienced emergency vehicle driving specialist, he was able to bring the van nearly to a complete stop, though not before the front tires ran over the strip. The armed point man for the rapid response team in the rear instantly reached for the door of the van so he could investigate the cause of the damage. The driver gave a small sigh, relieved that he hadn't smashed into the lead van.

That feeling of relief was cut short when a .50-caliber sabot round's stabilized slug exploded through the driver's side of the windshield and blew a gaping hole through his Level III soft body armor and his chest. He was already dead when a second slug slammed into his body an inch below the first. The sniper's precision marksmanship was aided by the fact that the driver's body remained anchored firmly in place, thanks to a specially designed safety harness he wore, similar to those used by professional race car drivers.

Almost simultaneously, two more gaping holes appeared in the passenger side of the windshield and the team leader riding shotgun on this morning's run to California met the same fate as his driver. Behind him, six uniformed men desperately struggled to disengage themselves from their safety belts, secure their weapons, and exit the besieged vehicle.

The sniper had done his job perfectly, now it was up to his colleague, Rocket Man, to take over. The shouts of the men in the rear of the van could be heard by Rocket Man as he knelt into a good firing position, the RPG firmly grasped in his hands, its dull gunmetal black launch tube resting atop his right shoulder. The rocket-propelled, armor-piercing grenade would arm itself in flight. He'd carefully computed the necessary standoff distance between where he estimated the van would come to a stop and his firing position, but he knew it would be a tough shot given the physical constraints of the ambush site. Still, he was considered the best man with an RPG on the team and he was intent on maintaining that hard-won reputation.

Pressing the launcher's thick trigger he felt his body jerk back as the fin-stabilized grenade swooshed toward the van's open side door. A great belch of smoke and flame erupted from the rear end of the tube as the grenade was released. Not waiting to judge the effect of his marksmanship, Rocket Man snatched up his second grenade and deftly inserted it into the empty maw of the launcher. He felt a wall of scorching hot air hit his masked face a millisecond before the sound of the grenade exploding inside the van hammered his ears. Looking up he watched as one of the van's team fell to the ground, rolling around on the highway in flames. Even as the man was trying to beat out the flames consuming his head and shoulders, the dull *craaack-THUD* sound of a firing Barrett .50 rolled over the desert. With grim appreciation Rocket Man watched as the steel penetrator round brought an immediate, if rather messy, end to the burning man's agony.

Raising the launcher up a second time, Rocket Man

took an extra moment to carefully fix his sight on the burning van. Nothing appeared to be moving inside the gutted vehicle. Anyone who might have managed to escape through the far windows, rear door, or driver's side door would have been taken care of by the Barrett. The crackling of the flames and the sickly sweet smell of frying flesh filled the air as the vehicle began to burn more fiercely across from him. Satisfied that his target was aligned, Rocket Man released the second grenade. It slammed into the passenger side door of the van, ripping the entire front end off the vehicle and scattering body parts from the two corpses up front out into the desert.

Setting down the launcher, Rocket Man swung his black Colt M4 carbine up from where it was hanging across his chest on a three-point black nylon tactical sling. He moved the lightweight assault rifle's barrel up and down the kill zone searching for anyone unfortunate enough to have survived the twin blasts of the grenades and the Big Fifty's heavy-ass high velocity slugs courtesy of his partner. Nothing moved. With a light wave he signaled the "All Clear" to his teammate.

He knelt, pulled a canteen from its pouch on his combat harness and took a long, deep swig of cool water. In the distance he could now hear the strident rattle of automatic weapons fire and he knew the rest of his mates were taking down the lead van. It was now his and the sniper's job to engage any vehicles coming down the highway from the north. Cradling the M4 he checked the M203 40-mm grenade launcher attached beneath the carbine's barrel. A single high explosive round was resting in the tube, its rounded copper-colored nose capable of easily stopping anything made by Dodge, Honda, or Jeep. Any civilians who had the bad timing to come along now would be considered collateral damage. Unfortunate casualties of war. He knew his God would overlook such trivial matters. Small sacrifices made in the preparation of the ultimate sacrifice yet to come.

Inside the first van pandemonium reigned. As the driver attempted to maintain speed and control, the security team in the back were shouting instructions at each other and readying their gear. The sharp *RACC-CCK!* of German-made MP-5 10-mm submachine gun bolts echoed in the air as the men jacked the high velocity rounds into their weapons' hungry chambers. The radio operator responsible for maintaining communication with the chase van and the command center at Los Alamos gave up entirely on the chase van and began calling for an airborne response team to launch out of Los Alamos immediately. Glancing out the heavily tinted back windows of the van he saw a plume of dirty white-gray smoke rising up from the base of the hill. So much for those poor bastards, he thought to himself. Who the FUCK is crazy enough to hit *us*?

The driver saw two civilian SUVs hurtling toward them side by side down the highway and shouted a warning to those in the back. By now his vehicle's ruptured tires were flat, the van's speed was a pathetic twenty-five miles per hour and it couldn't maneuver worth a shit. Powerless except to keep the vehicle crawling forward, he watched as the SUVs spun sideways on the highway about 200 meters in front of him, blocking the highway. The side doors of the SUVs slid open and four men, all clad in black BDU uniforms, jumped out in unison.

The operator could guess from his antiterrorism training what was coming next. Slamming both his feet hard against the brake, he fought to bring the van to a stop and shouted the order to evacuate. Before anyone could heed his command, four modified M60 light machine guns firing 7.62 NATO ball ammunition sans tracer rounds began chewing the van apart. Inside, the security team and their driver were flailed alive by hundreds of incoming copper-jacketed steel-core rounds.

On their leader's order, the assault team began walking forward in a line, sending a continuous rhythm of alternating, well-aimed heavy fire into the van as they approached it. When they reached the van they ceased firing and listened carefully for the slightest movement or moan, any hint of life coming from inside. Nothing.

One of the attackers grasped the mangled handle of the passenger side door and yanked it hard. As he wrenched the door open, a blood-soaked form sprang out at him in a blur of arms and legs, landing almost directly on top of him.

"Fuck me!" he cried out and fired a round directly into his assailant. Only then did he realize his attacker was a corpse that must have been leaning against the door. The mutilated body now lay on the highway at his feet.

"Easy boys," muttered the team leader. "No use wasting good fire on dead meat."

Then he called, *"Positions!"*

The men quickly arranged themselves in a tight half-circle around the front part of the van.

"Breacher up!"

At this command, a fifth operator who was pulling

rear security at the SUVs came sprinting forward. Simultaneously, one of the M60 gunners turned and ran back to man the roadblock. There, he rested his hot-to-the-touch and freshly reloaded machine gun atop one of the SUV's hoods, pointing its smoking barrel south. With the .50 available to cover both ends of the ambush as well as anything that might try to fly overhead, the kill zone was now effectively sealed.

The breacher ran to the van and under the attentive guard of his security team clambered into the gutted vehicle. He climbed over the freshly butchered and bleeding bodies to where the secure storage compartment was located on the port side of the rear cargo area. There he placed and armed the explosive charge specially designed to open the compartment. Satisfied, the breacher slid back into the driver's compartment and called, *"Fire in the hole!"* The trio outside the van kneeled and turned their faces to one side as the breacher squeezed shut the clacker of a Claymore antipersonnel firing device. With a soft *WHOOMPH!* the compartment's titanium door was blown free.

Coughing slightly from the smoke inside the van, the breacher retraced his slippery path to where a metal-clad, medium-sized suitcase was now exposed. Reaching inside the reinforced compartment he grasped its handle and tugged the 30-pound case up and out onto the floor of the van. "GOT IT!" he yelled.

"Let's move!" shouted the masked assault team leader. "We're on the fucking numbers here!"

The breacher exited the van with his newly acquired trophy and the group turned and ran for the SUVs. Once inside they pulled past the destroyed van and drove at a high speed toward the north end of the kill zone. As they approached, the sniper worked his way down to the highway, Barrett .50 in hand. Rocket Man, too, was standing by and ready for extraction. Minutes later the team was heading northbound at a law-abiding sixty-five miles per hour.

"Call the Colonel and tell him we've got it," ordered the commander. "And let's get out of these costumes. Halloween is officially over!"

As the call was made using a secure cell phone issued to them by the ever-trusting folks at Fort Bragg, the men pulled their tight black masks from their heads and stripped down to the khaki shorts and obnoxious T-shirts they wore underneath. Laughing and backslapping each other as the SUVs roared past the first civilian vehicle they'd seen on the highway since the hit, they looked like a typical band of off-duty servicemen heading for a few days' leave in Las Vegas, nothing more dangerous on their minds than gambling, drinking, and screwing. Within two hours they'd reach a small private airstrip and board a waiting private plane. From there they would take their just-acquired treasure to its new (though short-lived) home.

It was an odd sort of prize they'd killed so many men to obtain, one whose true power could only be released in the course of its own destruction.

4

"It is even better to act quickly and err than to
hesitate until the time of action is past."
MAJOR GENERAL CARL VON CLAUSEWITZ,
On War, 1832, tr. Howard and Paret

OUR CHOPPER FLIGHT WAS FAST, FURIOUS, AND WITH LITTLE
conversation. The LZ turned out to be the fairway of
the eighteenth hole of a very posh country club near
the dead lawyer's house. A police squad car was
standing by to take us to the crime scene and our
driver, like the NSA flight crew, was a somber, serious
bastard. I liked that. It meant they weren't fucking
around wasting my precious time.

I'd dressed as inconspicuously as possible—a pair
of stonewashed blue jeans, black turtleneck, a pair of
lightweight clutter boots, and a dark blue sports coat.
Trace and Paul were likewise casually dressed. Less
typical was the hardware we carried under our
clothes. All of us were toting our favorite shooters.
Mine was a Glock 26, an Austrian made 9-mm compact pistol with night sights. It's small, lightweight,
extremely accurate, and damn near impervious to the

elements. I'd further outfitted my little bastard with a titanium drive rod and enhanced recoil spring plus an extended slide release. These simple accessory modifications made an already super-reliable close quarters battle pistol even better. I'd thrown a spare magazine for the pistol in my coat pocket and clipped my freshly issued Bureau of Diplomatic Security badge onto my belt, left side front. If I was going to be tromping around a crime scene, I figured I'd best look like part of the investigating team, not one of the criminals.

Trace favors a Kimber Compact .45 auto. Where she hides such a cannon on her trim figure I'll never know . . . and don't want to. Kossens leans toward the tried and true H&K USP .45 compact. I've seen the kid shoot. He's Rogue class with the German auto and carries it in a Galco shoulder rig with two spare mags. It was a ten-minute drive from the makeshift helipad to the spot where the dirty deed had been done. Even though he was famous for his civil rights work, Beckstein must have charged somebody some seriously hefty fees for keeping their ass out of jail, judging from the neighborhood we were driving through. To the northwest of D.C., almost in Maryland, this was seriously expensive real estate. When we got near the crime scene, I was impressed to see whoever was in charge had shut down the entire vicinity. Police cars, their overhead emergency lights flashing, had been parked to form barricades at each end of the wide street. Uniformed officers, some carrying black AR-15 carbines on assault slings, were checking and identifying anyone trying to enter or leave the area. For the moment, this community had been sealed off from the rest of the city. As we were allowed to drive through the barricade, I noticed a few pairs of hard-nosed cops knocking on doors up and down the street. They were going house-to-house, notebooks in hand and scowls on their faces. Because my international security company, SOS TEMPS, trains cops, I've gotten to work with quite a number of them over the years. Trust me, these guys were not happy campers. House-to-house interviewing sucks anytime, but in this zip code it was probably torture. Most people in D.C. who can afford to live in digs like these don't expect to be asked a bunch of seemingly pointless questions by some cop on the beat. Instead of wanting to help find their neighbor's killer, they'd probably just be pissed that Beckstein's murder was making them late to their fucking tennis match. A black Lexus parked at the curb was being carefully photographed inside and out by a crime scene team. A little farther down the street, our cop driver turned through an open black iron gate and came to a stop in the middle of a semicircular driveway.

"Here you go, sir. Ask for Captain Barrett, Homicide. He's expecting you."

"Captain Barrett? Not Danny Barrett . . . big tall motherfucker?"

"Yep, that's Captain Barrett. You can't miss him, sir. Big as a fucking house."

The patrol car slid away from the curb leaving us standing outside one impressive son-of-a-bitch mansion. "*Be it ever so humble. . . .*" I heard Paul half-singing under his breath.

Sure as shit I knew Captain Danny "Big-As-A-Fucking-House" Barrett. We'd first met many moons ago when he was a young Marine captain in Vietnam working the CORDS program as an advisor. Like me, Barrett was a mustang officer who'd come out of the enlisted ranks with a full head of steam and a burning desire to kill as many Communists as possible before the war ended. His work with CORDS was impressive enough to catch the attention of the spooks at the CIA. They'd convinced the Corps to second him to their organization as a *summa cum laude* counterinsurgency expert. Danny Barrett played hard and fast in Vietnam. The Viet Cong put an impressive bounty on his head that they were never able to collect. Barrett finished the war as a highly seasoned and decorated major. I'd heard through the grapevine he'd retired a Lieutenant Colonel after twenty-five years of honorable service. What the fuck he was doing as a D.C. homicide detective I couldn't imagine. But if Danny Barrett was in the AO it meant I wasn't going to get jacked off by some no-nuts gumshoe that didn't know nookie from a nukee.

With the kids on my six I headed toward the mansion's front door.

"If it isn't Richard-Motherfucking-Marcinko!"

And there was Danny Barrett, towering above me, just like I remembered him. At 6'8" and 310 pounds he remained the largest man I'd ever laid eyes on. The retired Marine officer was massive, and every ounce of his bulk was well-tuned muscle and sinew. He came down the front steps two at a time, his big paw outstretched. "Dan," I replied as we shook hands, "How the fuck are you?"

"Good, Dick. Damn fine, actually. Unhappy as hell about what we've got here, though. Take a walk?"

I turned to Trace and Paul. "You guys start hunting. Check the backyards between here and the end of the block. I'll catch up to you," I told them. They nodded and went on their way.

Barrett draped a big arm around my shoulders and steered me across the wet grass. "Yours?"

"Yeah, new team," I replied. "They were with me when I did the Salvadoran a few months ago. First trip together. They're shit hot."

"I'd heard it was you who pulled our ambassador's daughter out. Nice work. Been a while since I've been to El Sal. Anything changed?"

"Yeah," I chuckled as we reached a quiet spot around the side of the house, "there's about twenty fewer guerrillas alive to disturb the peace!"

Danny lit a cigarette, inhaled deeply, and blew a long funnel of smoke past me. Then, shaking his big head back and forth like a hound that's temporarily lost the scent, he said, "I heard the bullshit about the problem you had in Ireland. Also heard you leaned hard on some folks recently to get back in the game. You're a real cocksucker with the Beltway crowd." Barrett eyed me carefully. I noticed he still held his cigarette low, a life-saving habit picked up in Vietnam.

"Fuck 'em," I replied. "What about you? I'd heard you'd retired. Is the Marine Corps retirement program so bad these days that you hadda go get another job?"

The homicide detective laughed, the sound coming from deep within his thick chest and erupting in sharp bursts. "The Crotch treated me good, Dick. But I wasn't hardly out the door before some fella called me from the P.D. and said they were *creating* a spot just for me as a captain in Homicide. When I asked why they thought I'd be interested, the guy mentioned the Agency. You know how they work. I suppose they figured it would be nice having me on-call and wearing a badge, given our long and prosperous association over the years."

I nodded. The Agency likes to keep its operators close by, retired or otherwise. "Dan, OISA sent an NSA bird out to the Manor to haul our asses here. They mentioned something about nukes. What the fuck is going on?"

Barrett sighed then took another long drag from his cigarette before answering. "This lawyer—Beckstein— took two rounds in the face from an arm's length away sometime last night. We've recovered one of the slugs. Custom round. A man-killer.

"Door was unlocked, security system off. The shooter just walked in and blew Beckstein away without missing a beat. This is no random killing or a home burglary gone sour. We got no witnesses and Beckstein's bodyguard has an airtight alibi. He was across town screwing the drawers off of the victim's seventeen-year-old daughter. Politically this thing is hot. Beckstein was well connected on the Hill. My boss is screaming for results yesterday."

"What about nukes?"

Barrett's eyebrows arched hard and his face went cold. "I'm getting to that. Let's go inside," he growled.

The lawyer's corpse was lying on the floor where he'd fallen. I looked the dead man over. I've seen plenty of dead bodies and, percentage wise, Beckstein's looked better than most. Yeah, he'd sucked up two rounds to the pumpkin and half his skull was gone, but other than that he was whole and could be identified by his next of kin. Better treatment than some of my SEALs had gotten.

"Captain Barrett?"

I turned and saw a thin Hispanic man, bald as a billiard ball. Barrett introduced us. "Leo, meet Dick Marcinko. Dick's with me."

He stuck out his hand and said, "Pleased to meet you, sir." His attention immediately shifted back to Dan. "Captain, I found a partial shoe print on the living room carpet not far from where there's a door to the backyard that's unlocked. We've got an unsecured servants' gate going from the yard to an alley in the back that runs parallel to the street here. Looks like the perp walked in the front door, shot Beckstein twice, then went out the back."

"Get the lab working on that shoe print. Anything else?"

"Yeah. Beyond the gun shots to his head, Beckstein also took a helluva blow to his chest—his sternum was shattered. I'm guessing bone splinters punctured the heart. Whoever did him was *not* fucking around."

"Thanks, Leo. Stay with it." Barrett gestured for me to follow him up the beautifully carved teak stairway to the second floor. At the top of the stairs he turned right into a handsomely furnished but very messy private library. "Grab a seat, Dick. We need to powwow."

I sank into a luxurious leather club chair. Every available surface in the room was piled high with books. Legal texts, novels, history, biography, philosophy, science—a crazy jumble of subjects and authors. And I sensed these books weren't for show—from their well-worn condition, they'd obviously been Beckstein's close companions. Looking around his office I couldn't help but be impressed. His "I Love Me" wall was studded with pictures of him posing with some of America's most notable celebrities and power brokers. This guy had definitely gotten around. No wonder Danny was feeling heat from on high. Still, all of Beckstein's powerful connections weren't worth a rat's ass when it came to keeping his brain inside his skull. Everybody's the same in front of a loaded gun. "So what's up, Danny Boy?"

"We found a microcassette next to the body. The message was short and not so sweet."

"So what does this asshole want from us?"

"Sounds like it's not one guy, but a whole team, Dick," replied Barrett. "And it's not what they want, it's what they're going to do to us, to this country, if you don't get to them first."

"I take it this is where the nukes comes in." Bad images were running through my mind. Whoever hit Beckstein was using him as an attention getter. "When can I hear the fucking tape?"

Barrett fixed me with a stare as warm as a glacier. "It's already gone to Karen at OISA. These bastards may have gotten their hands on at least one suitcase nuke. Word is a NEST team was hit this morning in New Mexico. All KIA. No sign of the nuke they were carrying, from what my source is telling me."

The big cop shook the last remaining cigarette out of a pack and crumpled the plastic wrapper in his fist. Fuck me! This was a worst-case scenario from my days at Red Cell. We'd proven to the Navy that our nuclear program and its weapons were vulnerable to terrorist attack. Hell, we'd not only proven we could infiltrate the sites where nuclear weapons were stored or pre-deployed, we'd proved we could actually steal the goddamn bombs. Apparently someone else had balls as big as my Red Cell operators. The thought made my gut go sour. Rogues are one thing, renegades are another.

I damn sure wanted to hear the fucking tape.

"Soon as I played it and realized what was on the damn thing I called one of my contacts at the Agency.

They sent a courier to secure it and get it to Karen. Then I heard you were inbound."

"Where do we go from here?"

"Not we, Dick. You." Barrett snubbed his half-smoked cigarette out. "I'm to run you and your crew back to the helo. As soon as you've seen this kill zone, Karen wants your undivided attention. You'll get your marching orders from her."

"Well fuck, let's roll. But I charge extra for recovering stolen nukes!"

"Same old Marcinko," the retired Marine laughed. "You'll be a fucking pirate 'til the day we bury your hairy ass."

"Don't count me out even then, buddy!"

With my brain running various unpleasant scenarios involving mushroom clouds and killer radiation, I went downstairs again and started looking for Trace and Paul. I headed out the back gate into the alley that Leo had mentioned, figuring that was where the kids would probably be snooping around. Sure enough, I saw them, or rather heard them, but they weren't exactly snooping. They were sprinting a fucking hundred-yard dash! Both went flying right past me down the alley and then I realized they were in hot pursuit of somebody making tracks about half a block farther down. Trace hollered, "Dick! On us! On us!" She was about a half-step behind Kossens who was burning up the asphalt with his long-legged stride. Fuck! They must've spooked somebody worth talking to. I saw the distant figure they were chasing dart left, disappearing into somebody's back garden. I figured he had to be heading for the street and a better escape route than this narrow alley.

I tore back through the house and grabbed Danny in the foyer. Must have been the look on my face because he didn't stop to question me, just ran to his car, an unmarked Crown Victoria parked out front, and we both jumped in.

"Danny, go!" I yelled, and in seconds we were hauling fucking ass down the street toward the barricades. Ahead I saw a few guns being drawn, but the startled cops didn't seem to know exactly what to do as the foot chase passed them right by. There were too many people milling around to allow any indiscriminate shooting. Even a trigger-happy D.C. cop would know that, right? We cleared the barricade just as I saw Trace disappearing around the street corner. "There!" I yelled to Barrett. "Left at the corner!"

As Danny wheeled the powerful cruiser around the corner we stopped just long enough for Trace to throw her tight little ass into its backseat. "Get this guy!" she spat out as she gulped to fill her tired lungs with fresh oxygen. "We spotted him . . . in the fucking alley . . . after you'd . . . gone in. Looked like he was checking some sort of listening device . . ."

"There's Paul, to the right! Turn fucking right!" I yelled.

I braced myself hard against the padded dash as Danny swung the car around the corner. Kossens was about halfway down the block, the man he was chasing was almost at the next corner, and the gap between them seemed to be widening. We were heading for a busy intersection of some sort. As Barrett slid the Crown Vic past Paul, Trace kicked the right rear passenger door open for him. I felt Paul throw himself inside and slam into the backseat.

"GO!" he yelled.

Barrett managed to maneuver us through the intersection's heavy traffic and I thought we were gaining on our prey when I suddenly lost sight of him. A moment later we came to a screeching halt as the driver in front of us slammed on his brakes. In the blink of an eye the entire street was a snarl of unmoving traffic and the obnoxious blare of car horns became deafening. Traffic. What a bitch.

A silver Mercedes-Benz SUV about fifteen cars in front of us looked to be the source of the problem. OK, I could play traffic cop. I jumped out and hit the pavement, determined to get this fucking car out of the way one way or another. Glock in hand, a fat little Federal Hi-Shok jacketed hollow point nestled in its chamber, I slipped by the cars in front of us, ignoring the frozen, frightened faces of the drivers as they saw me passing. I approached the stalled SUV ready to read the driver the riot act. Behind the wheel, a pretty black woman in a form-fitting white tennis outfit sat stock still. And no wonder. There was a fresh bullet hole right through the center of her forehead. The guy we were chasing didn't pull any punches.

I took up a security position at a 90-degree angle to the dead woman and scanned the area for our running man, but I hadn't a clue where our mysterious marathon runner had gotten to. Uniformed cops were suddenly all over the place. Great timing, boyz. I immediately holstered the Glock and grabbed my State Department badge, holding it up high where the street officers could clearly identify it. A big, ugly, unknown motherfucker with a beard and ponytail holding a gun is not exactly what a cop wants to see when he pulls up on a shooting scene.

"He's with me! He's a cop!" yelled Danny as he

rushed over to where I was standing like a statue while a cop pointed his big steel six-gun at my head. Barrett flashed his badge and jerked a big thumb toward the dead woman in his car. "Give us a hand with the victim!" The officer in my face nodded, holstering his weapon and turning away without a word. I went back to the car.

Danny was giving a report to the cops when I heard a call about our missing snoop come over the police radio in his Crown Vic. "Barrett!" I hollered to him. "They got the motherfucker holed up, maybe with hostages! Let's roll!" I jumped into the passenger seat as Danny shoved himself behind the wheel. He turned the siren on and we worked ourselves free of the traffic and found open road. Trace and Paul were ahead of us in a patrol car heading for the location.

"Damn, Marcinko," Barrett yelled so I could hear him above the siren's piercing wail, "you still attract trouble like cow shit attracts flies!"

Like I said, Danny and I go way back.

We drove into a part of town that seemed light years from Beckstein's white-glove territory. It was all strip malls, fast-food restaurants, and weed-filled empty lots. Danny came to a stop next to several other police cars across the street from a nondescript, single-story office building that looked like it hadn't been touched since the 1950s. A mostly empty employee parking lot bordered it on one side, surrounded by a tall chain-link fence. There were uniforms crawling all over the place. As I got out of the car I spotted Paul and Trace. We married up. "So what the fuck?" I asked.

"He's inside," explained Paul. "Cops say maybe hostages, but they don't know. We should have gotten him back in the alley, we just couldn't quite close the distance."

Trace nodded in agreement. I could see both were pissed at themselves. "First, I figured him for a reporter trying to get a scoop on the murder, but the way he slipped through our fingers when he saw us coming was too damned slick. He practically had a sign on his back that said 'Professional.'"

"I'm sure the lady with the bullet in her head back there would agree—you definitely weren't chasing the *Post* society page reporter," I said. "Whoever he is, he's in this thing up to his fucking eyeballs. You two did great. Now let's finish the job and go get him." I looked over at Barrett. He nodded. Whoever this asshole was, we wanted him and wanted him first. I had a feeling. And I always trust my gut when it tells me I'm right.

It took Barrett less than a minute to tell the uniforms to hold the perimeter. "I'm going with you," he said upon returning to our little group. "Let's introduce ourselves to this fuckup."

With Trace on point we made our way to the northwest corner of the squat office building. Once there, I looked around to make sure everyone was ready. In most situations like this you back off and wait for SWAT. Or, if you were lucky enough to be on SIX or with Red Cell, you'd have the necessary time to gear up and rehearse an entry plan. That wasn't going to happen here. It was hey-diddle-diddle-straight-up-the-middle time. We needed the cur inside and we needed him now. If he was part of the crew that hit Beckstein then he was part of the crew that was now in possession of one U.S.-made tactical nuclear weapon. I didn't want him exercising any rights other than the right to talk to me or have the crap beat out of him. After that, the cops and ACLU could bandage up whatever was left and make sure it got the best legal help since O.J.

"Trace," I hissed. "You low-crawl the window and take up opposite! Paul, you follow her."

Trace nodded. She slipped her Kimber out of its custom tactical holster (NOW I know where she carries that thing!) and in an instant was shimmying along the concrete on her belly. Kossens followed and seconds later we had both sides of the entry point covered.

"Danny, you still the fucking strong ox I remember? See that big garbage can? You're gonna throw it right through the fucking window on my say-so. As soon as it goes through, I'm going through behind it. You've got our six!"

Barrett nodded. Holstering the massive .41 he turned and grabbed the steel garbage can I'd pointed out. Filled with all sorts of shit, it must have weighed an easy hundred pounds. The big bastard lifted the container by its handles with ease. He slid past me and lined up just out of the line of site of the window. Dahlgren and Kossens were in position and ready to spring after I did.

I checked my Glock to make sure it was secure in its holster at my side. With a few deep breaths I readied myself for what was to come. I'd have to follow the can through the window, draw the Glock once I was in, and hope like hell I didn't get my ass cut to ribbons by falling glass. Trace and Kossens would follow right behind me and together we'd move through the building as quickly as possible in search of our target. I knew neither of my team was wearing their ballistic vests and I never wear one. Why? They can drag you down if you wind up in water; they get in the way when you're breaking through doors and windows; and most of all they give you a false sense of security that can inhibit your best instincts and reduce your reaction time. Shoot first and fast has always been my personal motto. Our goal was to get this bastard alive and in one—more or less—piece, if possible. However, if he as much as pointed a weapon in our direction I knew one of us would take him out to protect the others.

I looked over at Danny and nodded once. Showtime!

Barrett took three short steps, swinging the big can hard and then let it fly. I watched as it hit the plate glass window, smashing through it with a crash that was loud enough to make a deaf man crap his pants. Thousands of shards of safety glass exploded inward and I was right behind them, burrowing my face as deeply into my chest as I could. I cleared the low wall and tumbled into the room, rolling as I hit something that gave way beneath me. A beat-up desk chair. I was up and on the balls of my feet, Glock in hand.

ATTACK! ATTACK! ATTACK! I heard Trace and Paul coming in on my ass as I moved forward. Across the room I saw a door being pushed shut and instantly threw myself right at it, yelling at the top of my lungs for the team to get with me. The door gave way as I slammed all 240 pounds of Rogue into it and I heard a startled yelp of pain as it smacked into whoever was on the other side. I burst into another sparsely furnished office and saw the little blond fucker we'd been chasing over half the city. He began to raise a chromed pistol toward me. I rushed him, using my own weapon to smash his aside, and punched him hard in the face with my free hand.

He staggered backward with a grunt. I'd busted his nose wide open and bright red blood was gushing down his face. As I closed in on him once again he lashed out with a low-line kick, catching me hard on my right shinbone. *Fuck!* I ducked as he swung a fist at my head then realized the other one was coming up hard and fast from below my line of sight. It connected beneath my jaw and stars exploded inside my skull. Great, I thought, a badass who actually knew how to fight!

I felt another kick and my left knee buckled. Then he had me by my neck and I could feel one of his knees slamming into my lower ribs. I burrowed my head down and fought to stay upright. My elbows were now tucked in tight to protect my ribs from serious damage. I had to punch my way outta his grasp or this silly little fucker was going to beat the holy shit out of me! I felt him trying to twist me to the right and down so I just relaxed and went with his energy. Oldest trick in the book. The sudden absence of resistance caught him off guard and I felt him slip a bit. I pushed forward with both hands and yelled as loudly as I could right in his eardrum. A gap opened up between us and I filled it with a series of hard punches to his face and body. I backed him up against the far wall and just as things were looking up for Yours Truly, I got kicked square in the balls.

Forgive me, I stand corrected: *that's* the oldest trick in the book.

For a moment I thought I was going to black out. I fought it and somehow managed to land a wild left haymaker against the side of Blondie's skull. As I was grabbing my nuts and lurching sideways I watched him trip and fall hard against the corner of a cheap-ass desk. I felt a wall at my back and my knees buckled beneath me. I couldn't breath. I could feel puke rising up from my stomach. As I slid down the wall I blew chunks. Fuck me! This was *not* how I'd planned things.

I managed to open my eyes long enough to see Trace swinging her Kimber at Blondie's head. With a *thwack* the all-steel pistol slapped him upside his skull and he hit the floor like a dead man. A second stream of vomit lurched up outta my guts and all over the cheesy light green carpet I was hanging on to for dear life. Dickie's balls were on fire. They hadn't felt squeezed this tight since I'd gotten my divorce papers from my ex-wife's shark of a lawyer.

"Skipper? Hey, Skipper! You okay?"

Finished puking, I raised my eyes to where Trace was squatting beside me. I nodded weakly. Actual tears were running down my cheeks and I could smell fresh vomit in my beard. Yeah, I was fucking-A fine. Never better, thank you very fucking much!

Paul helped me up off the floor and he and Trace eased me into a chair. I watched Danny do a quick search of the asshole who'd probably ruined my sex life for the next six months. The big cop then cuffed Blondie and yanked him to his feet. I grinned as I saw his eyes rolling around in his head like loose marbles. Trace had scrambled his brains good.

"I'll put him in the car. You two get Dick outta here, and find his fucking gun before you leave!" With a smile Barrett nodded to me. "Nice plan," he said. "I especially liked the part where you got your nuts kicked outta the ballpark. I've gotta remember that one."

"Fuuuck you," I wheezed. "Where we taking him?"

"OISA," he replied. "If we can tie him to the ass-holes we think we're looking for he's outta my jurisdiction and into yours. Whatever you do from then on is your business."

I nodded. Trace handed me my Glock and I shoved the little pistol into my coat pocket. Standing without anyone's help I jerked my head toward the open door. "Let's get the fuck outta here," I snarled.

"You okay?" Trace asked.

I nodded in the affirmative. However I didn't pull away when she took me gently by the arm. Time like this a man needs all the help he can get.

"How's the old nut sack hanging, Skipper?" I heard the hint of laughter lurking in her voice and almost chuckled myself.

"It's about halfway up my ass, Dahlgren. Wanna see?"

"Maybe later. In the meantime hold what you got."

"You do the same, Dahlgren."

We both managed a laugh at that one as she guided me out of the building and to Danny's car.

Teammates. You gotta love 'em.

5

"The ancients had a great advantage over us in that their armies were not trailed by a second army of pen-pushers."

NAPOLEON, ed. Herod, *The Mind of Napoleon*, 1955

THE NSA CHOPPER DROPPED US AND OUR VERY QUIET NEW friend at an isolated concrete pad I recognized on sight. I'd used it frequently during my last formal command that was based near Dulles Airport. At that time I'd been ordered by Vice Admiral James "Ace" Lyons, then deputy chief of naval operations for Plans and Policy (OP-06), to create Red Cell for the express *overt* purpose of evaluating the vulnerability of U.S. naval installations worldwide to terrorist attack. In reality, Red Cell was tasked with conducting *covert* counterterrorist missions. We were given the job of waging preemptive strikes against terrorists and their organizations *before* they could mount operations against the unsuspecting, the unprepared, and the innocent. This meant my operators would find 'em, fix 'em, and then kill 'em without warning or mercy.

Ace Lyons knew our allies in Israel and Great

Britain had long practiced this form of covert warfare. International law states that terrorists are equal to criminals and therefore not subject to the same rules of engagement extended to the uniformed armies and even to recognized guerrilla militaries. By the mid-1980s America was just entering the business of taking out Tangos before Tangos took out targets. Red Cell was to specialize in the overseas infiltration, penetration, and elimination of identified terrorist cells. I selected fourteen balls-to-the-wall plank owners for Red Cell, three officers and eleven enlisted operators. Thirteen of these men came from SEAL Team SIX, that nasty bunch of motherfuckers I'd created in my own "Kill 'em all and let God sort 'em out" image. The fourteenth came from the Marine Corps' ultra-elite Marine Force Reconnaissance teams.

The chaotic, confusing area surrounding Dulles Airport had been the perfect place to headquarter Red Cell. You could hide half the regular Army in the sprawling maze of its terminals, storage areas, commercial warehouses, and runways. And from Dulles we could fly to anywhere in the world anytime, using specially prepared false passports and I.D. Our equipment, including weapons and explosives, was slipped into commercial airliners' cargo holds by my operators posing as hardworking, underpaid, dumb-ass luggage handlers. And still we were within driving distance of the Nation's capitol with easy access to everything that cesspool of bullshit and self-serving, power-hungry asswipes has to offer. (Yeah, I love D.C. as much as it loves me.) Red Cell soon became an integral part of the nation's direct action counterterrorist arsenal. Like Shaft, we were *bad* motherfuckers!

It's my personal opinion that if the Navy had left

me and Red Cell alone, there very possibly would have been no Obie Wan bin Laden alive to plot the attack on September 11, 2001. We'd have paid a house-call to him and his lieutenants early on, and then begun hunting down his cells here in the United States. But that's another fucking story.

A black Ford Expedition was waiting for us at the landing pad. Not too much later we were in the bowels of the city, our driver winding his way through D.C.'s fucked up traffic circles and grids toward a fashionable business district about twenty minutes from the White House. The Expedition pulled over to drop us off in front of an austere, tidy six-story brick townhouse. Once a single-family residence, later converted to overpriced yuppie apartments, it was now the discreet headquarters for the recently formed OISA. Honeycombed throughout the building were ultra-secure briefing rooms constructed like the bug-proof bubble rooms, or Special Classified Intelligence Facilities (SCIFs), where I'd been briefed in the old days when secret shit really had to be kept secret.

Where somebody's grandma used to hold her after-noon tea parties there were now specially constructed holding cells used to carry out private conversations with those found to be less than cooperative. We'd be dropping Blondie off in one of these cold little rooms for the time being. I had big plans for that little fuck. My balls started to feel better just thinking about it.

As we climbed out of the car, the driver said, "Fourth floor, Sir. They'll meet you at the elevator." With that, he pulled away from the curb and neatly folded the SUV back into downtown traffic.

There was no need to knock on the door or look for a doorbell. An invisible surveillance system had detected our presence on the stoop and the white-painted front door opened for us with a gentle buzzing sound. We entered an oval-shaped, marble-floored entrance hall dominated by a curving staircase that appeared to ascend to the second floor. In reality, I knew the graceful staircase was a beautiful fake, leading to a door that opened onto a bricked-up wall. To our left was an elevator whose oak doors perfectly matched the hall's antique paneling. Again, there was no button to push—the doors simply slid open as we approached them. The interior of the elevator was out of another world, a more familiar one—the world of government security and no-frills functionality. I had no doubt the elevator cabin also served as a metal detector and x-ray machine. Every crevice of our bodies was probably being scrutinized during the swift ride upstairs. Hope they were enjoying the view.

The bright *ding* of the elevator's bell announced our arrival on the fourth floor. The doors hissed open and we found ourselves in front of a ferret-faced little woman in a lumpy tweed suit. The gray-haired harpy nodded curtly and motioned we were to follow her. As we made our way toward a suite of offices I observed a battery of surveillance cameras aimed in our direction. More hot shit security monkeys with guns were monitoring us. I flipped a big Rogue bird at one of the cameras and smiled. Hi. Dick Marcinko has come back for a visit. How do you like me so far, asshole?

Our escort pointed a bony finger toward the end of the hall. Apparently I was expected in the far conference room. Without ever saying a word, she turned and slithered back to her office and shut the door behind her. Where Karen hired her day help was beyond me. Did Transylvania export office workers?

"Take Blondie up to the top floor," I told Paul and Trace. "I'll talk with the boss and link back up with you."

"I got fucking rights, ya know! I wanna call my *fucking* lawyer!"

It was Blondie. I stepped in close and looked down on the little bastard. My nuts still hurt from the beating they'd taken. The Good Humor Man I was not. "Your name Miranda? No? Then you got no fucking rights, asshole. Look around. This look like a fucking police station to you?" I jerked my thumb upward and spun on my heel. I'd be seeing Blondie again in a short-short. When I did, it would be under the worst of circumstances for him. We needed information and we needed it fast. If I heard anything like what I was expecting in the next few minutes, Blondie's ass was toast.

I headed into the conference room and found Karen Fairfield already there waiting for me.

"Hello, Captain. Nice to see you again," she said, standing up as I entered. We shook hands politely. She was an exceptionally beautiful woman, a fact that always half-surprised me, given the position of genuine power she held in the administration. My own prejudice no doubt, but part of me still expected a woman of Karen's stature to look like the old crone who'd met us at the elevator.

"You too, Ms. Fairfield," I replied. "Always a pleasure to serve you. In any way I can." I tried not to lick my lips as I said that last part. When she didn't reply, I decided to jump back to safe ground. "That coffee sure smells good."

"Let me get you a cup. Black, yes?"

"Good memory." I studied Karen as she slipped

past me. She was wearing a well-cut black suit that hinted at an athletic but still full figure. I put her at 5'8" and 130 pounds. Chinese-American, her coal black hair was as long as mine. She wore it loose, like my morals. Her skin was a smooth, pale bronze. She moved with the deliberate ease and balance of a classically trained dancer. She was the product of Bryn Mawr College, Harvard's School of International Relations, and a rocket-powered career at the State Department. We'd occasionally "seen" each other since I'd been hired by State and transferred over to OISA, which Karen headed up for the president himself. Coffee in hand, she turned and smiled. That smile reminded me how many moons had passed since we'd last screwed each other silly. Down, boy, I told myself. We're here on business.

"Dick, there was another shooting . . . ?"

I gratefully took the cup and gulped down the rich, hot brew. "Yes, an innocent bystander," I said. "We've got the shooter upstairs. He's definitely connected to Beckstein's murder. He was keeping the house under surveillance and won't say shit to explain himself. Danny Barrett is handling the paperwork."

Karen nodded. Her hair fell across her face and she brushed it back with a practiced hand. She was an incredibly sexy piece of work. "Please have a seat. I'm afraid we've got very little time and a lot of ground to cover. The situation we're facing right now is exactly the kind of worst-case scenario that caused the president to establish the Office of Internal Security Affairs. This is going to be OISA's first real test. And therefore, mine.

"I'll cut to the chase. Samuel Beckstein was one of the president's most senior legal advisers and an internationally famous civil rights advocate. Whoever murdered him last night left a cassette tape next to his body with a message for the president, and by extension the entire nation and the world. On the tape, this person announces his intention to detonate a tactical nuclear device somewhere within our borders. Before you got here, it was confirmed a NEST team transporting such a device from Los Alamos to Southern California has been ambushed. No survivors. The device is missing."

I took a long pull of coffee then set the cup down on the conference table. "Whoever can take out a NEST team and bag a nuke is a serious motherfucker."

Karen was sitting directly across from me. Our eyes locked. When she spoke her voice was low, its tone unmistakably grave. "In about five minutes this room is going to fill up with some very important people, Dick. They all have their own agendas and will do everything possible to promote these, even in the face of a potential catastrophe like this one. How much do you know about suitcase nukes, Dick?"

"Long or short story?" I asked.

"I'm listening to whatever you have to say, Captain."

I stood and walked to the far end of the table. If I played my cards right and Karen came out of this bullshit meeting looking good, I just might get laid (and save a couple hundred thousand innocent lives as a bonus). I'd make this good. "First off, suitcase nukes—technically, special atomic demolition munitions—or SADMs—aren't anything new. We've had 'em since the late '50s. During the Cold War both the Russians and us used man-packed nukes as tactical rather than strategic weapons. A SADM can be precisely placed on the battlefield or behind the enemy's front lines to do specific damage to a selected target or targets. The big rocket-launched cocksuckers that everybody thinks of as nuclear weapons do too much damage and turn the world to shit. No one wants to hold ground that glows in the dark!

"Given the huge advantage in conventional forces the Soviets had over NATO at the time, they were a major part of our war-fighting plan. We, meaning the good old U.S. of A., deployed SADMs courtesy of our Special Forces people. The nukies were placed at key points along the axis of advance that our intelligence geeks figured the Russians would most likely take if and when they decided to storm Western Europe. We knew we were too few and too weak to stop them on a conventional basis. However, we realized we could temporarily shut down their forces by detonating tactical nuclear weapons along their front, giving NATO a fighting chance to reinforce, regroup, and mount a counteroffensive."

Karen nodded. "Just how small were these devices?"

"By the time I started training with them they were pretty compact. Each device weighed about 68 pounds. They were 28 inches in diameter and 30 inches tall. They could be outfitted with either a jump harness so we could parachute into the target area with them, or a flotation collar so we could deploy them from a submarine. Or you could be really bare-bones and just hump the fucker in by foot."

"How powerful?"

I didn't reply right away. Talking about man-packed nukes over coffee was something I don't normally do. Those of us trained to take a SADM in and detonate it were carefully selected for the job. Our lives became closely monitored by counterintelligence spooks. Anyone who could jump, swim, or hump an atomic bomb to a selected target and kill 100,000+ enemy oxygen thieves by simply turning a few dials and throwing a switch is someone you want to keep tabs on. At least I fucking would if I were in charge.

"If you had a first generation tac-nuke, you could take out most of downtown New York by placing it in one of the subway tunnels. You'd kill at least 100,000 people and probably twice that number considering the target concentration. I can't even imagine the kind of panic that would occur once an atomic bomb was officially identified as the cause of such a disaster. Hard headline to put across without freaking out most of John Q. Public. Chaos would reign. There'd be no reliable communications. No effective emergency medical care available. No law. No order. The National Guard wouldn't be able to do anything more than wring their hands. One device, one SADM, detonated in the heart of any major city in this country would fuck us over beyond anyone's worst nightmare. These devices are the ultimate terrorist weapons. They exist, they work, and they are available for the taking, as we've apparently just found out."

I poured myself another cup of coffee while Karen processed all this. I waited for her next question, pretty sure I knew what it would be. I was right.

"When you were running Red Cell, were you ever able to steal a nuke?"

"Yes. More than one, actually."

"*Damn it!*" Karen's eyes blazed. "NSA just told me with a straight face that we've never lost a SADM. And you've now confirmed that not only can these things be stolen, but that *you've* done it yourself . . ."

"I didn't technically *steal* it," I said. "I gave it

back . . . after a while . . . after they were really pissed."

"I want to know how you did it."

"Okay, but you're not going to be happy. I put two of my operators on surveillance. Their job was to collect information and intelligence about the immediate area surrounding the storage site. Which way did the vans transporting the devices turn after leaving the main gate? Did the drivers stop anywhere nearby to gas up, get a pack of smokes, have a bite to eat?

"I then put two operators on the perimeter of the storage site itself. They gathered intel on where the security cameras were placed, if there were guard dogs on-site, whether or not ground sensors were present, what the daily routine was for all personnel assigned to work at the facility.

"If we needed further HUMIT or shit like ID cards, I'd hire a couple of sexy working girls to dress trashy and visit the nearby bars and taverns. While the ladies were distracting our noble men in uniform with their special talents, my boyz would be lifting their wallets or going through their cars for picture ID, base passes, parking decals, and whatever else we could use to penetrate the facility.

"We only needed two operators to actually penetrate the site and grab the nuke once we'd gathered all the intelligence we could and come up with a plan. That's all there is to it."

The look of horror on Karen's face said it all. "That's *all there is to it?*" She quickly regained her composure. "But what about taking them off during transit? That's what happened today."

"You need insider information to hit a rig in transit. That's difficult to arrange and time-consuming. There's also a greater degree of compromise due to counterintelligence efforts working against you. You have to deal with the shooters from NEST, the Department of Energy SWAT guys. They escort the nukes on the road. Again, whoever hit NEST is fucking way good."

"How many devices did you and your team manage to steal, Dick? Sorry, I mean, how many did you *borrow?*"

I paused before answering her. Our success at looting nuclear storage facilities had not gone over well with the powers-that-be, especially my Navy bosses who had to endure the heat each successful penetration brought with it. They'd be thrilled it was all getting dug up again. Fuck 'em. "I got ten before they shut us down."

"Shit!"

"That's exactly what they said," I told her with a broad grin.

Karen checked her watch and glanced toward the closed door. Any minute now the movers and shakers would be arriving. I had to take a fierce piss and wanted to throw some cold water on my face.

"Gotta visit the head before this meeting starts," I said.

"Hurry back. I'm glad we have you to handle this for us, Dick." A tiny smile creased her otherwise somber face and her hand lightly brushed my shoulder as I slipped past her heading for the door.

Damn, I thought, I might just get laid after all . . .

6

"I will smash them, so help me God!"

MAJOR GENERAL ANDREW JACKSON,
1815, at the Battle of New Orleans

TEN MINUTES LATER, I SEATED MYSELF TO KAREN'S RIGHT
as the room filled with faces I recognized from past
briefings and the evening news. These were movers
and shakers. King makers and ball breakers. I received
nods of neutral recognition from some of them—and
at least one look of sheer horror. I guess that guy reads
my books.

The geek who'd turned frogman green when he
saw me at the table was probably a snitch from some
agency seconded to OISA who resented the new chain
of command. Karen Fairfield's position was a para-
dox. She was exceptionally powerful given her direct
link to the president of the United States. At the same
time she was exceptionally vulnerable precisely
because of this link. Being a woman fucked her status
in the Washington hierarchy even more. How so, you
ask? Take a fucking note! Despite the liberal bullshit
you hear about gender and job equality these days,

the women of the Beltway are prized mainly as zipper ornaments. Karen Fairfield, with her Asian ethnic roots, stunning beauty, and exceptional intelligence, was a Class-A threat to the testosterone-fueled political grinder that lives, feeds, and fucks by the Potomac. And today she had the Navy's worst nightmare and legendary motherfucker at her side.

I knew the reptilian little brain across from me was clicking off all the excuses he might use to flee the room and dial up his handler and report that Dick Marcinko was alive, well, and in D.C. again . . . fuck you very much!

"Thank you all for coming," Karen began. "As you all know by now, Samuel Beckstein was shot and killed in his home last night. A cassette tape was found next to his body by the local police and delivered to OISA. The president and I have listened to this recording. I'm going to play it for you now. It is very ugly. Afterward, your comments and observations will be welcome."

Karen pushed a button on the tape deck next to her and a man's electronically altered voice began speaking over the room's hidden speaker system. Pens poised to take notes remained frozen in place as the message played. No notes were necessary. I sure the fuck didn't need 'em.

"Mr. President," the Voice began, "in the name of Almighty Yahweh we have executed the race traitor and Jew, Samuel Beckstein.

"Your friend, the Jewish Communist Beckstein, was killed as a direct consequence of his efforts to destroy the foundation of the promised White Israel, the United States of America. We defy the cursed multiracial and godless *society that is sucking the life out of America. We are patri-ots. Patriots whose hate for domestic traitors like Beckstein resulted in his death and will soon result in the deaths of all others like him.*

"We are the Sword of the White Race. We give no thought to the soulless creatures who seek to trample our nation with their heedless pursuit of so-called diversity and the lie of multiculturalism. Yahweh's holy Word and the unaltered Constitution of the United States are the twin pillars of our battle against the degeneracy that plagues our country today.

"We will not negotiate. We will not mediate. We will not compromise. Our objective is simple. The reclamation of the America for the White race only. The inferior races have left us no choice in this matter. You, Mr. President, have left us no choice. Our cause is a righteous and just one.

"As of this moment we are in control of a U.S.-made Special Atomic Demolition Munition. We will detonate the device in a major U.S. city at a time of our choosing. The detonation of our SADM will ignite the race war in this country that must take place if all good and holy White Men, their women and their children, are to again reclaim their original birthright and Nation. Make no mistake, Mr. President. We know who is at the root of our country's moral destruction. Their wicked presence is no longer toler-able to us. It is their destruction we commit ourselves to with this act!"

When the message ended, it was so quiet you'd have thought everyone in the fucking room was already dead. Glancing around I saw some expressions of dis-belief greeting this news that a major U.S. city was about to be ass-fucked with an American nuclear weapon. But in my military mind, this band of maniacs had proved they knew exactly what they were doing and weren't fucking around with our minds for the sheer cocksucking fun of it. My face remained impassive, but inside I was scared fucking shitless. I know nukes. And just one SADM detonated as described would be one SADM too many. We weren't prepared to deal with the aftermath of a city burned down by whoever the fuck these characters were. Which was a key question, I realized. The message was clearly designed so that we'd assume we were dealing with domestic terrorists of a particularly ugly stripe. But what if all this racist bullshit was just being waved in front of our noses so the stench would distract us from our real opponents? Iraq? North Korea? Some fundamentalist ayatollah who was pissed we weren't buying enough of his oil these days? It was a possibility. All the more reason to get upstairs and have a serious conversation with Blondie.

But if these really were Americans out to change the nation's destiny and if they could get even a handful of equally crazy bastards armed to the teeth into our streets with holy vengeance against anyone other than a "good white man" on their minds . . . a race war could very well be sparked and burn the nation to the ground. Would Americans pull this kind of crazy shit? I'd stolen nukes, but only to wake up the sleeping guards and complacent generals with a good swift kick of my boot up their asses. Could some radical fringe group really pull off the same thing? Some gang of inbred white supremacists who didn't have the benefit of my years of life in the military machine? My thoughts were interrupted by a sudden outburst from across the table.

"Bullshit!" The word came boiling out of the

bearded troll in the bad polyester suit who'd been giving me the evil eye earlier. "Unsettling, yes. But surely a ridiculous threat made by some nutcase."

"Carl, please share with us what makes the NSA discount what we've just heard." Karen shot a quick sidelong glance at me.

Carl the Troll shimmied his dumpy little ass around so he could address the group as a whole. "It is perfectly obvious whoever killed Mr. Beckstein is using the threat of blowing up one of our cities with an alleged stolen nuclear device simply to distract the police from the primary crime here, which is the murder of a powerful lawyer with God knows how many enemies. Christ, people get shot in their homes every day in this city. The police just need to do their job and find Beckstein's killer without getting diverted by all this apocalyptic nonsense."

I hunched forward as the Troll spun around in his chair and fixed Karen with his beady little blue eyes.

Take a fucking note.

I've always hated real-life trolls. Theirs is a life lived each and every day under the curse of what shrinks call "The Little Man Syndrome." Never able to overcome their feelings of inferiority brought on by their tiny size, trolls take every opportunity to attack, insult, and diminish those around them. Particularly those who exert some level of control over their personal or professional lives. There was no doubt in my mind the NSA geek was a bright fellow. The problem was he used his smarts like a club to beat down any poor fucker who didn't immediately put him in his place.

"Karen," the Troll oozed, "we all know that information about SADMs is in the public domain these days. Any twelve-year-old punk with a PC can read about them on the Internet, print their research up on an ink jet and hand it out at school the next day. However, it is the position of the NSA that no international or domestic terrorist group currently has in its possession such a device. Further, no domestic terrorist organization or cult either has, or could hope to secure, the kind of nuclear device the speaker on this recording claims to have under his control."

I watched Karen purse her lips in contemplation of the line of bullshit the Troll had just fed her. *I* knew that she *knew* differently.

"Let me be sure I understand you, Carl. You're telling us there is no possible way one of these suitcase-sized nuclear weapons could be stolen or otherwise removed from their storage facilities or taken by force in transit." Karen leaned forward, her elbows on the table, hands pressed together in front of her face as if in prayer. Her fingers were powerful and slim, with carefully manicured but unpainted nails.

Sensing he'd made his point, the Troll beamed at her. "During the course of my fifteen years with NSA, I assure everyone here, there has never been a successful intrusion into one of our tactical nuclear storage or transit facilities. We've never had a device misplaced or lost, much less stolen. For God's sake, *we're not the Russians!*"

He paused here for a laugh that didn't come. Some of those around the table were scratching cryptic little notes on yellow legal pads. The Troll interlaced his chubby little dick skinners together over his bulbous belly and snuggled back into his comfortable seat. I imagined he was kicking his elf-size feet in glee beneath the table. He was the perfect NSA slug. A vicious little liar with a pencil for a prick and a soft little ass for his bosses' pleasure whenever they needed an intellectual whore to do their dirty work for them.

"Mr. Marcinko? Do you agree with Carl?" asked Karen. Before I could respond, she added, "Oh, forgive me. Some of you may not know Captain Marcinko. He's new to OISA and is with our operational division. Richard is a counterterrorism expert as well as counterterrorist. He is a retired Navy SEAL whose accomplishments include both SEAL Team SIX and the counterterrorism unit called Red Cell.

"Mr. Marcinko visited the Beckstein murder scene where the recording we've just heard was recovered. He arrived here early enough to clarify some things for me about the devices the NSA assures us cannot possibly be in the hands of the people claiming to have them. Well, Dick? Can we—and I include the president when I say we—be as confident as the NSA is on this matter?"

Showtime, motherfucker!

"Not only no, but *fuck no!*" I growled. Guess they were used to more genteel language here because eyes widened, jaws dropped, and I thought I even heard someone at the end of the table fart out loud. I pressed my advantage home.

"It is my professional opinion, even after hearing the *shit* we just did, that we're dealing with military professionals. Everything I've seen and heard so far reinforces my feeling on this. Furthermore, I'm sure our colleague from the NSA knows full well how soft our security is where SADM nuclear weapons are concerned. When I commanded Red Cell we routinely penetrated DOE and military storage facilities and on more than one occasion removed man-portable nuclear weapons without detection or intervention. *If* this bastard has gotten his lily-white hands on just one such device, I suggest the NSA should cut the crap and let the rest of us figure out how to get it back in one piece."

Carl sat still as death with only his lizardlike eyes darting back and forth as he evaluated the impact of my revelation on his peers.

"Leave it to the NSA!" said an austere-looking woman sitting next to the now silent Troll. "Always count on them to put their own interests first. This whole city could be vaporized in the next few minutes and the NSA would tell us the fallout was just snow, even while we were melting into the floor!"

"I must say, I agree with Judith," interjected Karen. Turning to me, she introduced Judith more completely as Judith Reich, senior adviser to the House Intelligence Committee and a member of the president's inner circle regarding his administration's new hard-line policy on domestic terrorism.

"Why should we take the word of a convicted felon and nationally disgraced former naval officer, not to mention a self-admitted alcoholic, whose so-called special units were little more than undisciplined gangs of misfits and hooligans?" countered the Troll from his chair next to Ms. Reich.

"Response, Dick?" invited Karen.

Looking around the room, I got a few subtle nods of encouragement, and Judith gave me an encouraging wink as well. I stood up and walked around the table, stopping when I was behind the Troll's chair. I leaned over so I was directly above the little NSA man who was now visibly shaking with anger. I had the room's full attention.

"In June of 1985, myself and Red Cell successfully penetrated the nuclear submarine base at New London, Connecticut. This was the home of our Trident- and Ohio-class subs. Up until then it was considered impregnable. The Naval Submarine Support Facility was one of several Red Cell training exercises being conducted with the full support of the Navy. The facility is responsible, among other things, for the secure storage and handling of nuclear weapons, which are preassigned to the submarines that would carry and launch them in times of war.

"After only seventy-two hours of premission planning and preparations we hit the base. On the second day of our operations we successfully infiltrated the sub piers. My operators posing as terrorists fixed simulated explosive devices on the dive planes of one submarine. We videotaped this for the record. Had the explosives been detonated, the sub would have been immobilized for months, and therefore taken out of the real-world game plan."

I paused. The Troll was sitting still. He dared not turn around to look at me. I may be a convicted felon . . . and an unrepentant gin-swilling, skirt chasing motherfucker . . . and a disgraced naval officer with a hard-on for the world and anyone who contributed to my fall from fucking grace. But right here and right fucking now I was going to chew up and spit out the Troll who'd done me dirty in front of a room full of strangers and my new boss. Take a fucking note! Whosoever fucketh with the Rogue Warrior be fucked in return tenfold.

I continued.

"We also entered the submarine and roamed through it at will. I personally planted simulated explosive devices throughout the vessel, including its nuclear reactor compartment. It was determined that if these devices had been real and had gone off, the reactor would have been breached, resulting in the fallout and contamination inherent in such a disaster."

"Good God in Heaven," someone on my right flank muttered.

"We could have commandeered the submarine and taken it to sea. My men were trained and capable of doing that. From there, using the nuclear weapons onboard, we could have wreaked havoc on any target of choice that caught our fancy. And yes, we had access to the launch codes and could have gotten them by the same means if we'd been the real-deal bad guys."

The room was silent. No one was taking notes anymore. I couldn't tell if any of the silly fuckers were even breathing. Karen gave me a nearly imperceptible nod to move on. The knife was in deep; it was time to twist it home.

"Contrary to the NSA's version of The Truth regarding the security of our nuclear weapons systems and munitions, I proved it wasn't necessary for a terrorist team to actually invade the hull of an attack sub to cause an improvised nuclear disaster.

"The most effective and nondetectable method of shattering a nuclear submarine's reactor compartment is to place what we call a 'bubble charge' beneath the sub. The charge floats below the hull of the sub and is held in place by a line or cable attached to both the bow and stern of the vessel. When the charge either detonates by using a timer, or is command detonated using any number of remote devices or techniques, the explosion creates a massive air bubble that literally lifts the sub out of the water. The vessel's weight then takes over and breaks its keel. During this process the reactor compartment and nuclear core is shaken out of its secure cradle. The result is a series of severe—and lethal—radioactive leaks.

"We determined it was easier and safer for a terrorist cell to attack a nuclear sub and its reactor using the latter method. Keep it simple, I always say. Besides, once you've seen the insides of one sub, you've seen them all."

I returned to my seat. Inside I was waiting for the Troll to fire back. He'd taken a hard hit and now the fucking NSA was in poor field position. There was no doubt in my mind this meeting would end with Karen getting the support she required to proceed with briefing the president as to the reality of what the nation was facing. That done, I'd get my marching orders to locate the missing SADM, recover it and then do what I do best. And that was to kill the motherfucker and his Tangos who'd zapped Beckstein and a whole team of loyal NEST soldiers, and were now threatening to start a holy war dressed up in some fucked up, half-baked racist bullshit.

"That was a submarine base," erupted the Troll. "We're talking about tactical nuclear weapons no bigger than a travel bag, *not fucking submarines!*"

All eyes were on me. It was time to play my trump card. "Later that year my team and I successfully bagged six man-portable tactical—or suitcase—nukes. We took them from a not-so-secure DOE convoy transporting the devices from their Concord, California, storage facility to the Naval Station at SEAL Beach, California. SEAL Beach is where the Navy loads its conventional and special ordnance munitions for overseas deployments. My operators and I had no trouble getting accurate insider information using illegal wiretaps, a couple of big-titted women, and the penetration and infiltration of the base commander's private office and safe.

"Yes, I am every bad thing the NSA says. And yes, *some* even say I'm a fucking disgrace to the starched white dress uniform of the commissioned assholes who first recruited me, trained me, and sent me to Viet-fucking-Nam. But today I'm here to tell you the son of a bitch who shot a man in the face from an arm's distance away and then has the balls to tell us he's got a fucking SADM hanging between his legs is as serious a motherfucker as one can get.

"I wasn't brought here to entertain you. I was brought here to tell you the Fucking-A Truth and then to track down and kill my—and your—enemies."

The good Ms. Reich spoke right up, asking, "You gave the SADMs back after the exercise was over, Captain?"

"I certainly did, Ma'am," I replied. "I also gave back the truck they were being transported in and all the little toy soldiers we'd taken POW, too."

No one else seemed ready or willing to ask me anything further so Karen delivered the coup de grâce. "I am not at liberty to give you specifics, but just before we gathered for this meeting I received confirmation of an earlier report that a United States military convoy transporting a man-portable nuclear device was slaughtered earlier today, just a few hours after Samuel Beckstein's murder. The SADM they were carrying is missing. There is every reason to believe this threat is real and, therefore, I'm adjourning this meeting," said Karen. Shooting a sharp look at Carl, she continued, "I know the president will be grateful for all your candor and helpful advice as we prepare to handle this situation, as well as your complete discretion. Is there anyone other than the NSA who doesn't feel Captain Marcinko is the right man for the job we have before us? If so, please raise your objections now and I'll present them to the president for his consideration."

Glorious silence.

"No? I remind all of you that this meeting was video-recorded for the official record and that everything we have discussed will remain strictly confidential until you are specifically told otherwise. On the president's behalf, I thank you all for your time and attention today. You will each be receiving your particular directives in the hours to come."

As the others stood and began to file out of the room, Karen reached over and placed a hand on my forearm. "Dick, please stay behind a moment. I want you to meet someone you'll be working with on this. His name is Clay Mulcahy. He'll be your direct link to the president and myself. Your operation is code-named 'Velocity.' The president and I determined before this meeting that once we got everyone on board we'd need to move right away.

"You're to work with Clay to assemble a team of your choosing to conduct this mission. The president orders you to locate and recover by any means necessary the missing SADM. You will also confirm who the people are who killed Mr. Beckstein and mounted this operation against our homeland. All of OISA's resources and assets will be made available to you. Once done, you are to track the terrorists down and neutralize them. Are the president's orders understood?"

As I watched poor Carl-the-Troll trudge out of the room to get back under his bridge somewhere, I nodded in affirmation of my marching orders. I'd have my chance to deliver Rogue Warrior–style justice to the bastard I'd just heard threaten my country and its people. And upon the authority of the president of the United States himself I'd gut the cocksucker or die trying!

I am the son of an immigrant family who came to America with nothing but their hopes and dreams. Whoever was behind the electronic voice was now my enemy, my family's enemy. He was all of our enemy, even Carl the fucked up little NSA asshole with his beady eyes and dumb fuck attitude. When I've identified my enemies I keep them to my front and in my sights until I've taken them down and fucking out. *Yahweh* or whatever this asshole called his fucking god could kiss my hairy SEAL ass.

It was time to get it on.

7

"Ruses are of great usefulness. They are detours, which often lead more surely to the objective than the wide road, which goes straight ahead. Animals have only one method of acting, but intelligent men have inexhaustible resources. You outwit the enemy to force him to fight, or to prevent him from it."

FREDERICK THE GREAT,
"Instructions to His Generals," 1747

CLAY MULCAHY GRIPPED MY HAND LIKE THE FORMER boxer he was. Half a head shorter than me and with a spit-shined skull that gleamed under the room's soft lighting, he made no bones about how fucking strong he was as we squeezed paws. "Dick Marcinko! How the fuck are you? Heard a lot about you, most of it bullshit I'm sure. You got the word, yes?"

"Which word in particular is that? I got the whole goddamn dictionary coming across the transom right now. Fill me in."

Mulcahy grinned. "Shut the door. We've got a call

from the president due to ring through in about two minutes."

Glancing at Karen I saw her smile. I'd heard of Mulcahy now and then while traveling the Old Boy circuit. He'd done ten years with the Secret Service as a field operative. Someone in federal service offered him a better berth with OISA and he'd jumped ship to join Karen & Company. Word was he'd climbed up the ladder the hard way, one rung at a time. A Golden Gloves fighter, he'd punched his way through college and grad school in New York and come away with fast hands and a shiny new law degree. He'd done serious time chasing bad guys for the SS and had a kill or two under his belt. His beat at OISA was managing extremely sensitive operations under the direction of the president. I'd heard it said that some hotshot with the FBI once challenged his integrity during a meeting in the Oval Office. Mulcahy, as the story went, knocked the senior agent out with one punch as the president looked on. On meeting him, I didn't have any reason to doubt the story.

I gladly dropped back into one of the comfortable conference room chairs. Fuck was I tired! And I had the sinking feeling that sleep was going to be a scarce commodity for the time being. After this phone call, I wanted to get to work on Blondie and find out what Trace and Paul were up to.

The audiotape might have been laughable if it weren't for how it was delivered. Blowing a man's brains out to send a message beats UPS any day of the week. I didn't have a lot of experience tangling with our so-called *domestic* motherfucking terrorists. Up to now my focus had been the international strain of vermin. Globetrotters and bad men with worse breath who flew in from here, there, and elsewhere to deliver bombs, bullets, and political bullshit at the expense of innocent lives and property. Homegrown religious fanatics had never entered into the Rogue Warrior's world of sanctioned mayhem. Well, until now that is.

"Clay, I've already told Dick about 'Velocity' and the president's directive," Karen said. "Also that you'll be managing the behind-the-scenes activities once Dick and his team go operational." She pulled a chair up next to me and sat. I could smell the perfume she was wearing. For a half-second I wanted to grab her, climb up on the high polished table, and do the wild thing right there.

Say what you will, I'm consistent. That's a good thing.

Mulcahy remained standing. "While you all were meeting I was trying to get more intelligence on the NEST team out of Los Alamos that got hit. I have the fucking world out there picking up the pieces but the fact is whoever did the job got clean away with the cargo. It's confirmed, no one on the NEST team survived. My guys on the ground tell me the job was completely professional using military weapons and munitions. We've locked the area down for a hundred miles in every direction but that means shit and we all know it."

I was about to ask Clay the first of about a hundred fucking questions when the phone rang.

"That'll be the president," Mulcahy said. "I'll switch us onto the speaker line."

As Clay fiddled with the phone system Karen leaned over and whispered a few additional bits and pieces of information I'd need regarding team preparation. Danny Barrett was on his way in and, if I wanted him, he would be flying out with us. Damn straight I wanted him. OISA had likewise tasked some shit-hot NGO intel operator they had on the hook to brief me on the Christian Identity Movement and its hyper-radical leadership. I'd heard of Christian Identity from my old running mate Danny Coulson when he was commanding the FBI's Hostage Rescue Team and hunting domestic terrorists around the country. Danny didn't think much of their philosophy or their activities and he'd taken down some of the worst of the "Soldiers of God" using HRT as his velvet hammer.

"Mr. President? You're on speaker, sir. Mr. Marcinko and Karen are here with me. We are secure."

Hearing the president's voice, even though it was reaching me through the room's highly sophisticated and expensive speaker system, I instinctively sat up straight, squared my shoulders, and pulled my feet together. I was now sitting in the position of attention I'd learned many years ago when I was a young buck fighting my way through Officer Candidate School (or Organized Chicken Shit, as I prefer to call it) in Newport. Here I was in the virtual presence of the commander in chief of my country's armed forces. Wasn't it just this morning that I'd been in the Manor's gym cursing the weight pile and figuring out how to get my tractor running? In the course of a single day I'd seen a man's skull splattered all over his house; seen a soccer mom's brains on the headrest of her SUV on the streets of D.C.; gotten the shit kicked outta me by some still unidentified asshole who I just *knew* was somehow involved in whatever crazy game we were now playing; schmoozed a gaggle of beltway hotshots on behalf of my *velly velly* pretty boss; listened to some fucking whacked out electro-voice tell me he was about to blow a U.S. city to Kingdom Come because everyone but him and a few self-deluded white men hated Jews and everyone else; and learned a fucking NEST team transporting a man-portable nuclear weapon had just bought the farm out in New Mexico and a fucking SADM was now AWOL.

Oh yeah, it had been one hell of a day for old Demo Dick Marcinko. And now the President of the Most Powerful Country on the Face of the Planet was holding a private landline chat with me from across town . . . or wherever the fuck he was at the moment.

I'm supposed to be retired!

"Karen? Dick? I don't have much time to spend with you and I know you've a great deal to get done. I'll make this quick, if you'll forgive me." I instantly recognized the president's distinctive soft Texas drawl and his manner of addressing people as if he'd known them for years. I have a genuine respect for the man now sitting in the White House. Second-guessed and made fun of on the late night talk show circuit, the man who I was now taking my marching orders from had surprised the nation by his forceful, determined leadership following September 11, 2001. He'd been leading a nation at war against my long-time enemy, terrorism, ever since. He had not faltered, he had not weakened; he had not softened his or the country's position on the final objective. And we were winning.

"Mr. Marcinko, or may I call you Dick?"

"Dick is fine, Sir."

"Good, I like that. Dick, Karen has told me a lot about you. She thinks very highly of you and that's why you're sitting where you are right now. And right now we need you and your unique abilities and talent to find our missing nuclear weapon before it can be used against a defenseless American city and its citizens."

The president's voice took on the hard edge I recognized from many of his past speeches. This was no courtesy call. He had Clay Mulcahy and Karen around for that kind of thing. This was personal. Between him and me. I felt the hackles on the back of my neck stand up as he continued. Adrenalin began pumping through my depleted, aching body. I was in the No Shit Zone, and I was loving every minute of it!

"Dick, America has asked you to serve her faithfully for over thirty-five years now. I've read the record. You've never failed to answer the call to duty and to do whatever it took to get the job done. You've pissed some mighty important people off along the way, Captain. And you've paid for doing things your way, haven't you?"

"Yes sir, Mr. President, I have. But I'd do it all again the same way if given the chance."

The president's laugh echoed throughout the room. "No doubt you would, Dick, no doubt you would. Listen carefully, Captain Marcinko, this is what I've done and this is what I require you to do on behalf of the country and at the direction of your president."

I felt the pressure of Karen's hand on my forearm. Mulcahy was pulling several sheets of paper from a flat black leather document carrier he'd brought into the room with him. He laid two single sheets out in front of me. I saw that both bore the Presidential Seal at the top and the president's signature at the bottom. They were dated for today. Before I could read any more the president continued.

"At Karen's request I've reviewed the circumstances of your felony conviction. In doing so I've also reviewed your service record, and your continued efforts on behalf of the country in the fight against terrorism. It is my belief, based upon the evidence provided to me during this review, that we cannot ask—in good conscience—for you to do any more than you have done unless we do something for you in return.

"I make no judgment about the criminal case brought against you, Captain. But I do find it difficult to believe we spent 60 million of the taxpayers' dollars to put a man in a federal institution for ten months . . . and needed two trials to do so. I concur with the recommendation of the Justice Department that you be granted a full presidential pardon. You have that pardon in front of you. Congratulations, Dick."

I heard myself thanking the president even as my fingertips touched the most important piece of paper I'd ever been given. A pardon. My personal and professional honor restored by presidential decree. I'd given up even dreaming such a thing could happen. But it just had. I sat rock still. If I was dreaming I didn't want to wake the fuck up.

The president continued and I forced myself to pay strict attention. Celebrations could come later. And I would celebrate this. Stand by, Dr. Bombay!

"Dick, the second piece of paper Clay has given you is my formal directive to you regarding 'Operation Velocity.' It would be absurd to ask you to put yourself in harm's way legally or otherwise after what you've just received. My orders to you and your team are very simple and clear.

"You are to use all available means and resources to

locate the missing nuclear weapon and to return it. You are to identify, locate, and destroy the terrorists who have committed this and any other act in support of the insanity being directed against the United States and its people. You have my express and specific authorization as commander in chief to do *whatever it takes* to accomplish your mission, Captain! Do I make myself clear?"

A massive smile erupted from my lips. "Fucking-A Tweety you do, sir!"

"Oh God, Dick!" Next to me Karen buried her face in her hands.

Mulcahy was too busy pulling a second sheaf of papers from his folder to worry about my lack of presidential decorum. He slid a half-inch-thick file across the table to me. "Read these first," he ordered. "I'll be your handler here in Washington. Anything you want or need you route directly through me. I'll have secure phone, fax, and pager on hand. You're good as gold, Marcinko. Just don't fuck up."

I nodded. Those were the same words the CNO used when he chose me to build SEAL Team SIX from scratch. *God, I love those words.* And fucking up was something I'd stopped doing a year ago. Fucking up was now something I did to others before they could do it to me. Fucking Up Others is an art form perfected by the Rogue Warrior and something he now teaches those who he is shaping in his new and improved image. I'd just had the world handed to me on a presidential silver platter. I would not fuck up.

"Dick? Before I go . . . ?"

"Sir?"

The room was silent. For a moment I thought the president had hung up. When he again spoke, a chill gripped me at the base of my spine. "Dick, you and those supporting you have quite a job to do. It's a job no one else is capable of getting done. You mustn't fail. You simply cannot fail. You may operate in any manner you deem necessary to ensure failure does not occur. You may do so with express guidance and authorization, or without it. As your commander in chief, I bear full responsibility for this operation, come what may. Good luck to you all. God Bless America!"

It was Mulcahy who spoke first after the president hung up. His voice was somber. "Okay Dick, it's your call now. What's the next step?"

"I got a monkey upstairs who knows something about this," I growled. "I'm going to have a wall-to-wall counseling session with him. All bets are off from here on out. I'm going to start at the bottom so we can climb our way to the top where I believe we'll find the nuke and the asshole who took it. And then I'm going to kill him. You just need to start figuring out where to bury the bodies."

I looked over at Karen as my fingers lightly touched the letters bearing the president's signature. "You did the paperwork on this didn't you?"

She nodded once. "You've earned the right to have your name cleared and the slate wiped clean. The president agreed when he saw the evidence. And he's right. We can't ask you to take this mission on and not give you something in return."

I carefully folded the letters and put them in my breast pocket. They were probably the most valuable things I'd ever received and I wanted them right where I could read them again in case I started to think all of this was a dream. Or one seriously fucked-up nightmare.

8

"I make the enemy see my strengths as weaknesses and my weaknesses as strengths while I cause his strengths to become weaknesses and discover where he is not strong. I conceal my tracks so that none can discern them; I keep silence so that none can hear me."

HO YEN-HSI, Sung Dynasty commentator to
Sun Tzu, *The Art of War*, c. 500 B.C., tr. Griffith

WHILE I WAS MEETING WITH THE HONCHOS TWO FLOORS below, Paul ran Blondie's fingerprints through the system. What came back was just one more fucking surprise in a day full of fucking surprises. Blondie was one Tony Karras. And Tony Karras was a U.S. Navy SEAL. A teammate. Thanks to OISA's pull deep inside the Pentagon, Paul had been able to pull the jacket on Karras faster than Bill Clinton unzips his pants. In a hurried conversation outside the soundproofed interview room, Paul told me that Karras had served with distinction in the Gulf War and again in Somalia. All the go-to-war shit was interesting but it was his current assignment that rang deafening bells and whistles.

Karras was currently an operator with a military team code-named Nemesis.

And Nemesis was in the business of handling man-packed nuclear weapons.

Just when the idea that we were dealing with home-grown terrorists was starting to sink in, this latest development hit me like a hammer to my skull. If the bad guys were in fact Americans, I'd just taken for granted that we were gonna turn up some sort of backwoods fundamentalist militia, an isolated sect of inbred crazies who'd learned how to steal a SADM on the Internet or some such bullshit. Now I saw how seriously I'd been kidding myself.

These were guys who had the benefit of all the same training and resources that I did. The kind of men who I might have tried to recruit for SIX or Red Cell. I'm not so fucking naive that I think every SEAL or Delta Force member is by definition a fine upstanding citizen of the Republic, but it had never occurred to me that my own backyard could be the breeding ground for this kind of sickness and evil.

I'd heard bits and pieces about Nemesis for several years since it was, in some ways, a distant relative to my own commands. Tucked away in a remote corner of Smoke Bomb Hill on Fort Bragg, Nemesis was a highly classified nuclear weapons project that involved a team of experts in the storage, transport, and tactical delivery of SADMs. You might say I tried to keep these weapons safe (or at least in our own hands) so that Nemesis could put them in play if the call to do so ever came. Members agreed to have their lives monitored by the military and NSA. Their overseas travel was restricted, and their private lives were closely watched. In essence, Nemesis operators became shadow prisoners of our own ability to wage a nuclear war.

Working in two- and four-man cells, the operators of Nemesis were the elite of the elite in Special Forces. With a single suitcase nuke and its accompanying detonation code they had at their disposal a device capable of killing upwards of 150,000 human beings. The Russians, too, had developed hand-carried atomic munitions which intelligence sources were sure had been planted in Western Europe—and by some reports the United States itself—by elite Russian Spetsnaz soldiers. The American SADMs were a better product in every respect. They were also better protected than the Russian tac-nukes, which after the collapse of Communism were rumored to have hit the black market with a price tag of $10 million per device.

This was all familiar backstory, but then Paul gave me the real kicker—no one at the Pentagon could find anyone currently attached to Karras's Nemesis team. They'd vanished the day before. Gone. *Kaput!* And with them a shitload of their high-speed, low-drag weaponry and equipment. It wasn't much of a stretch to figure they now also had at their disposal the nuke that NEST had just lost out in New Mexico. Fuck, I thought to myself as Paul finished updating me, send a pro to do a pro's job. No wonder they'd been able to take NEST out. They were better than the lads from DOE. Way better. I'd heard through the grapevine a composite team of specwar operators had been formed to handle SADM missions exclusively. It sure the fuck looked like they'd lost control of their chain dogs. It didn't take Sherlock Holmes to figure out I was now up against the first fucking string and playing by their rules.

"Find out *everything* they have on Nemesis. First and foremost, who's in charge of their operations these days," I told Paul. "I need it yesterday. Nothing held back! I know just enough about these Nemesis cocksuckers to make my dick wiggle. We're on borrowed time and let everyone you talk with know it. Karras's little friends could set the fucking device off right now and all we'd be able to do is stand here with our collective cocks hanging out and our fingers up our asses! Questions?"

Paul shook his head and took off down the hall double-time. I needed him to find this information, but also I just didn't want him around when Trace and I had our little meeting with *former* SEAL Tony Karras. Paul was blooded but he was still young in a lot of ways. I needed to be sure how far he'd go. As much as I hated the thought, I knew we were going to have to lean on Karras hard. Way hard. Rogue hard. There was no time left and no other way. He'd crossed over to the other side. I didn't know or give a rat's ass about his religious or political beliefs. From what I'd heard on the tape, they were plenty fucked-up, but that was his right. He could subscribe to any dumb-ass way of thinking he chose, but when he tried to take away the rights (and lives!) of others, he was gonna have to answer to me and my own brand of justice. I have no time for people who want to take advantage of America's freedoms and tolerance to further their own agendas of hatred and prejudice. *Take a note!* I believe in two things. One: my country. Two: me. Period. Get in the way of either and I'll take you down and out. Karras had fucked up in a big way. First, he'd become a terrorist and I hate terrorists. Second, he'd dishonored the fraternity of frogmen I belong to. Third, he'd gotten caught being a terrorist and I *hate* guys who get caught at their business!

This was going to be messy.

Trace was standing in the far corner of the sparsely furnished interrogation chamber when I blasted through the door. I ignored her and went straight for Karras. He tried coming up out of the chair he'd been sitting in but I was on him before both cheeks of his ass were off the seat. Stripped down to his Jockey shorts he was a lean, tough bit of rawhide and muscle. His cuffs had been removed. That was a good thing. I hate hitting a man who can't hit back.

And I love hitting one who won't.

He tried sidestepping my hard left hook to his rib cage but in doing so walked into an open-palm right that connected with a harsh *craaack* alongside his temple. That fucking move always puts a smile on my face. Karras weighed in at maybe 170 pounds and my rabbit punch buckled him at the knees, as intended. To his credit, he tried a half-assed head butt to my gut and to reward this last great act of defiance I smashed my right fist down hard into the small of his back. He yelped as red-hot pain surged through his kidneys and lower spine. He dropped to his knees in front of me, his hands gripping at my pants' legs as he tried to hold himself upright.

"Bastard!" he hissed through clenched teeth. "My fucking lawyer will have your convict ass for this!"

I almost lost it at this point. The image of Beckstein's scrambled brains was still fresh in my memory and now this clown was crying for a lawyer to ride in on a white horse and defend his civil rights. Sorry Charlie, I'll say it again. You wanna destroy the greatest nation on earth, you do *not* get the benefit of its protections.

I reached down and grabbed both of Karras's little pink ears. With a brutal jerk I lifted the now howling SEAL up off the floor. His hands flew to the sides of his head. I was going to rip the fucker's lobes right off his skull! When I had his feet off the floor I let go of the right ear. I snaked my hand down between Tony Baloney's legs, grabbed a mittful of nutsack, and crunched his balls together until I thought his eyes were going to explode out of their sockets. The sounds coming from his lips were loud, unintelligible, and yet were sweet music to my tone-deaf ears. I knew he'd had enough when I saw his eyes begin to roll up into his skull. Without a word I dropped him in a heap at my feet.

"Now that we're properly introduced, how about we talk, *motherfucker?*"

Squatting down beside Karras, I watched him slowly curl up into a tight little ball of human misery, both hands gently cradling his cracked eggs as he rolled back and forth on the Air Force blue carpet. "Can you hear me, Tony?" I mocked. "Everything okay, sweetheart?"

"Uhhhhhhhhh . . ."

"I'll take that as a yes," I replied. "First things first. I am officially *not* a convict as of today. Second, we no more talkie-talkie about lawyers, okay? You must love the motherfuckers because they're all you've talked about since we dragged your nasty ass in here. It's funny, given how you seem to treat them. Me, I don't care for lawyers one way or another. I'd rather fuck a geriatric whore than spend five minutes in a room with an attorney. Besides, it's cheaper to get fucked by an old whore than by a slick lawyer. So, no more lawyer talk, okay?"

Karras glared up at me. I could feel the hate coming from him like a stiff ocean breeze off the Silver Strand in Coronado. I breathed it in deep. Hate makes me strong. When someone hates me I know I'm doing my job. I feel sorry for people with no enemies—their lives must be so fucking boring. *Señor* Busted Balls could hate me all he wanted. "Marcinko!" He spit my name from his lips like cobra venom. "You got shit! You can work on me all you want! I ain't giving you *nothing!*" He closed his eyes and put his head down on the carpet. "Fuck you," he wheezed. "Fuck you."

He was sounding like a broken record and it was annoying me. I stood and turned to Trace who hadn't moved from the corner. Her face was impassive but her normally gray-green eyes were a darker shade than I could recall ever seeing them. There was a kind of scary calm about her that I'd witnessed when we'd done our first job together down in El Salvador. She'd killed a lot of hairy-assed men that night. As we'd waited on the side of a rugged volcano for the extraction bird to arrive I realized Trace Dahlgren was as serious a stone-cold killer as any motherfucking man I'd ever gone to war with. She was ice, damn near as heartless as me. I figured then it was the Apache blood in her veins. She'd make a good companion to ride the river with. Right now I needed her skills and her emotional detachment for what was to come next. Speaking loudly enough for Karras to overhear me, I told her what I'd learned from Paul.

"He's a Nemesis operator. His entire team is MIA from Bragg. A NEST team got hit a few hours ago in New Mexico. Their payload is missing and presumed under enemy control. Paul is running down back-ground for us now but I need answers. Fast. We have the president's personal authority to do whatever it takes to accomplish this mission. Whatever it takes."

Trace locked eyes with me. I didn't blink and nei-ther did she. "Tie him," she said. Pure ice.

Hearing this, Karras jumped up and bolted for the door. He hadn't taken two steps when my sidekick caught him high up on the hip and sent him slamming into the far wall. In an instant I was all over the stupid bastard. Two quick punches to the face stunned him long enough for me to take my belt off and bind his hands behind his back. Trace removed her belt and grabbed Karras's ankles. Like she was cinching up a calf at a rodeo she secured the dazed man's feet, then looped and jerked her belt up and through my own so Karras was now bent backward in the shape of a human bow.

"Got a knife?" she asked.

I took my Emerson CQC-7 from my right pants pocket. With a flick of my finger, the black steel blade popped out. Reversing the knife in my hand I handed it to Trace. "All yours," I said.

"You cannot do this to me!" Karras was back with us again. Fucking thickheaded SEAL. He wasn't stick-ing to the role I'd written for him in our little scene. At least he looked the part—that is, he looked like shit. I'd smashed his nose downtown and opened the wound up again when I'd nailed him in here. He was bleeding like a pig at slaughter time and was near buck naked. Tied like he was there was no way he could get loose. He was talking like a player, though. I had to give him that.

"Tony," I explained patiently, "not only can we do

this to you, we *are* doing this to you. I know some of the very bad things that you're involved in, but I want to know more. Your pals changed the rules on us. Fair fighting is out, and the Rogue's Rules of War are in. We're gonna get to know each other real well. Think about it—confessing your sins might do you some good.

"My friend Trace here is Apache by birth and upbringing. If anyone is entitled to a have a problem with your America for White People Only bullshit, I'd think she is. She killed her first man when most white girls were playing with their first Barbie. It's my understanding she learned the ancient ways of her people, including the skills necessary to get naked little white boys like you to sing like birds. I'm giving you to her because I want to hear you sing. I'll ask her to stop only when you've told me all you know about Nemesis, the missing nuke, and where I can find both."

Karras spit a gob of thick goo from his throat onto the carpet. Trussed up like a pretzel it was a pretty impressive, if pointless, effort. "I fuck little Indian girls up the ass," he growled.

Now *that* was an unfortunate choice of words if the Rogue has ever heard one.

"Okay, the dumb fuck is all yours," I told Trace.

As Trace squatted down beside Karras I pulled up a nearby chair. I'd seen men, women, and children tortured before. Manhandling and mutilation are time-honored skills in Southeast Asia and elsewhere. Although I'd never directly participated, I'd stood by and let the locals do their thing for a good cause. I make no judgments about such activities. War is hell. You fight wars to win. Sometimes you have to take on the devil's secret name and become the very thing you loathe. In a strange way, it can be almost spiritual when carried out in a traditional, ritualized manner.

People who claim physical torture doesn't work are full of shit. I'm here to tell you it does. But only when conducted by someone who is gifted in the art of inflicting pain for the purpose of gathering hard intelligence. Anyone can stick a knife up some dumb fuck's ass and wiggle it around. But sticking it up the same dumb fuck's ass and getting the truth out of him is a difficult, precise art.

I wasn't going to leave Dahlgren on her own to do my job for me. We are a team. She's the expert and I'm her commanding officer. We share the good times, we share the bad times. This was going to be as bad as Karras wanted to make it. If he kept playing hard-core SEAL we'd be here awhile. If Trace was as good as I was betting she was, then hard-core or no hard-core I'd soon have what I needed to get this fucking mission on the road.

Any and all means said my president. I was going to take him at his word.

Trace pushed Karras over so he was lying on his right side facing me. She slowly cut off his underwear with the knife. Grabbing his nut sack she stretched it out as far as the loose skin could be pulled. I caught myself unconsciously squeezing my own thighs together. Damn, that had to hurt like hell!

Karras howled in pain. It didn't matter. Guess he didn't get the memo about where we were—no one could hear what was going on inside the room but him and us. "You fuckers! You damn bastards, I'll kill you for this! You hear me? I'll *kill* you for this!"

Karras stopped his ranting and strained to look

down the length of his bent body at Trace. I watched his eyes go wide as he saw the knife in her left hand, his balls crunched together in her right. She was eyeing his scrotum like a curious child. Slowly she rotated her head so she was now looking directly into her victim's eyes. Karras was dead silent. His breathing was shallow and fast. He was now one scared motherfucker. I wondered if he regretted the comment about ass-fucking little Indian girls.

"Are you part of what happened to the lawyer?" she asked.

Karras said nothing. He was rock-steady still. I had to give him credit. He was tough. Stupid as dirt, but tough.

"Are you part of what happened to the lawyer?"

When Karras didn't answer Trace pushed the tip of the knife into his stretched out nut sack. With a lightning fast flick downward, she slit his scrotum open. Blood spurted from the incision, splattering Trace's hands and making a dark, terrifying Rorschach spot on the carpet. Fuck me, I thought. I'll probably get the cleaning bill for this on top of everything else.

"*EEEYAAAAA!*" Tony Karras let out a yelp so loud and primal I damn near wet myself. He began bucking and squirming in an effort to get away from the source of his pain but the two belts held firm. Yellow urine began shooting out the end of his limp prick. It mixed with the blood that was already on the floor. Take a fucking note! The pucker factor is at an all-time high once bladder control is lost. They teach you this shit in SERE school. Karras had probably attended such training in New Brunswick or at Bragg. If so, in theory he knew what was coming next. The bitch is that theory and practice are two very different things.

Most of all, theory doesn't hurt.

I thought Trace was going to ask Karras the same question again but she didn't. Instead of talking she kept working on Tony's rack and balls. Like she'd been skinning dicks all her life, she dug the tip of the knife around in Karras's now badly bleeding scrotum. A second later I saw what she was fishing for. Out popped one of his nuts, all pink, shiny, and wet. It hung in the open by a thin white fleshy tube, which Trace now neatly sliced through. The oval-shaped organ dropped to the wet carpet and rolled a few inches. As Tony's eyes and mouth opened to sizes I didn't think humanly possible, Trace speared the homeless testicle with the Emerson and held it up for all to admire.

"I suppose you can still fuck little Indian girls with one nut, Mr. Karras. But it might be embarrassing to explain what happened to your missing ball." Then, with a flick of her wrist, Trace launched the sorry little punctured nut across the room where it made a sharp *splat* as it landed against the far wall.

A foul smell erupted from Karras as he lost control of his bowels. If Trace noticed the stench she didn't give any indication. Karras had utterly given in to the horror. He'd never been here before. And he'd never imagined in his wildest dreams that he'd be subjected to such torture at the hands of his own countrymen . . . not to mention a *former* teammate. He had no rights and now he knew it. He had nothing left but the hope I wouldn't let Trace kill him if he talked. Personally, I was hoping he'd start talking like a fucking mynah bird and that he'd start right now. I decided to let Trace have my Emerson knife when this was all over and done with. Somehow using it to spread peanut butter on my favorite crackers back at the Manor didn't have the same appeal it used to.

Trace jammed the blade back into Karras's scrotum and tugged his remaining ball out into the open. His nutsack collapsed and shriveled in her right hand as its remaining occupant popped into view. The sour aroma of piss and the pungent stink of fresh, fear-filled shit was making breathing difficult in the small room. Karras rolled his eyes toward me. Tears were streaming down his cheeks. He was begging for his life—and his one remaining nut. "Skipper? Skipper? Please, please Skipper . . ."

His words sliced through me. For an instant I wanted to jump out of my chair, to push Trace away, to stop this truly evil and brutal savagery over which I was standing watch. Karras *was* a SEAL. He *was* one of my countrymen. How the fuck could I allow this to be done to him? I felt Trace's gaze. I knew if I looked at her with doubt, broke faith with her, she'd stop and walk right out of the room. I mentally reached down between my hairy frogman's legs and grabbed hold of my own nutsack for courage. "Trace," I said, "if he doesn't answer immediately and truthfully to your next question . . . cut that damn ball free and start working on his pathetic little needle dick. I'm through fucking around with this turd. As far as I'm concerned you can open up his belly and maul around inside his guts next."

Karras began shaking as if with fever. It's one thing to take a beating and quite another to be slowly, methodically cut to ribbons. There are no schools that teach how to survive that kind of treatment.

I sensed Dahlgren's gaze slipping away from me. Shit! I steeled myself for what was to come. If Karras somehow found it within himself to hold out it was going to be a long, messy afternoon.

"The Mexicans taught us how to use a knife, you know," Trace said in a far-away, singsong kind of voice as she drew a long, thin cut all the way down Tony's exposed inner thigh to his knee. He began gasping for oxygen and twitching violently. I thought he was gonna stroke on us. Trace continued as if she were telling herself an often repeated story, unaware of what her hands were doing to the man beneath her. "They would raid our villages and take the women and children captive. Many times they would play games with those who were wounded, or too old, or too sick to be of value as slaves or whores.

"They would tie them up and then amuse themselves for hours with their knives. It was the Mexicans who taught us how to scalp, and how to sell scalps for money. The Apache has beautiful hair. A scalp was proof a Mexican had killed Apache *merde*. He was paid good money for the hair of my People!"

"I never hurt no Indian!" moaned Karras.

"No?" replied Trace as she tapped the flat of the blade against the remaining healthy testicle she now held in her hand, "I thought I heard you say you fucked little Indian girls up the ass. Was that a lie, Mr. Karras? Are you lying to me? This is what happens when you lie to me!"

Well, fuck. I winced as his second nut was separated from its tiny little rappel line and sent flying across the room to join his brother. Karras went apeshit, wild-ass crazy. He tried rolling away from Trace but she leapt over him and pinned him hard with one knee on his chest. With two quick flicks she sliced off both his nipples then ran the edge of the blade down the center of his tanned chest. Blood was now flowing everywhere. Trace straddled him and dropped all her 130 pounds of she-devil on his sternum. Bent like he was, I heard joints cracking and ligaments popping under the sudden stress. I felt like I was glued to my chair. I've seen a lot of shit in my roguish life but what I was now part of was beyond anything I'd ever imagined. The demon sitting atop the bloody mass of heaving, gasping human flesh was no longer Trace Dahlgren. It was the ghost of a blood-soaked past I'd never imagined existed. I'd unleashed it. I did a gut check and bit my tongue. We were in it together. To the fucking end.

Trace began chanting in the tongue of her native people. I'd heard her do this once before after we'd grabbed a kidnapped child and were in the process of blasting our way out of a shit-hole in eastern El Salvador. It had spooked me then, and hearing it again now was having the same affect. It appeared Trace was making perfectly good fucking sense to Karras because he opened his mouth wide and let out a long, deep scream toward the ceiling.

Trace pushed the knife's blade into the upper portion of Karras's belly. It sunk in about two inches. He went silent for a few short seconds and his eyes rolled around in his skull. He coughed once, then twice. Bloody drool flowed out the corners of his mouth. His teeth were stained red. Then, hallelujah, he started to answer her questions.

I had to lean forward to hear him. The fight within had evaporated. Trace had broken him. He'd answer anything she asked from here on out and he'd be truthful. He was certain she would know if he lied and that she would make his pain that much more horrible for it. "Yes, I was involved. . . . But I didn't kill Beckstein. The colonel did. I was there to be eyes-on target afterward. The colonel killed him, not me. . . ."

"What is the colonel's name?" asked Trace. Unnoticed by Karras, she had slipped off of him and was now sitting cross-legged on the floor at his side, watching his face carefully. Her tone was soothing, consoling. She was an angel of death considering a reprieve. She was the scariest fucking thing I'd ever laid eyes on.

"Blanchard. Colonel Max Blanchard."

Fuck me. That was a name I knew from years gone by. He was a tight-assed, reclusive son of a bitch who had created Nemesis as his final assignment before retirement. I thought he'd moved to a farm somewhere a year or two earlier—seemed to me I'd even been invited to a retirement party for him. I'd first met him during my early visits to the old DELTA compound at Ft. Bragg but we'd never really taken a liking to each other. I thought he was a tight-assed prig and I'm sure he thought I was a fuckup who got allowed a lot of rope by the Brass. People aways said Blanchard was tough as nails, but he struck me as far too concerned with petty regulations and discipline to be more than a middle manager. Maybe I'd underestimated him, or maybe he'd changed.

"Did Nemesis take the SADM from NEST today?" Trace continued.

Karras weakly nodded. "Phineas Priests. The war begins with us. Needed something decisive. No more half-stepping. Blanchard is the Chosen One. We are all priests. We serve only *Yahweh*."

Trace glanced at me. I nodded. We were on a roll. "Where is Blanchard now?"

Karras balked. I saw the hesitation in his eyes. Trace caught it and in a flash she slid the knife deeper into his belly. Pulling the sharp edge out, the Emerson ripped through taut, well-worked muscle. A hard burst of bright red blood erupted from the gaping wound. Karras screamed . . . and screamed . . . and screamed some more. The screams slowly became whimpers. The whimpers turned into sobs. The sobs dissolved into silence.

I thought that we'd killed the bastard. But then his chest rose and he exhaled like a lung cancer patient giving up the ghost. He was still alive.

I sat still and let the whole scene wash over me. My humanity had been erased. I was empty. I was outside myself watching Trace skillfully field dress a human being in a soundproof room in the heart of the nation's capital. I'd never gone this far in my life. Never pushed the envelope to such an extreme. I am a rogue, yes. I am a warrior, certainly. But now I had become more than the Rogue Warrior. I was beyond whatever "he" had ever been. And I was sanctioned by my government to become this thing.

That was seriously fucked up.

But there was no going back. I was beyond whatever it was that once held me in check. I looked at Trace and I saw recognition. I saw acceptance. The circle was complete. My path was clear. I was grateful to Karras. He was the vehicle. It was a shame he would have to die.

Trace continued. "Where is Blanchard now?"

Tony's eyes flickered open. Life was seeping out of them. They were growing dim. He'd given up all hope. In his own way he was preparing for his fate. But he would tell Trace what she wanted to know before leaving. He had to. She had taken his manhood from him. She now owned him. He could only obey her. She was his master. Only she could give him release. "Oregon."

"Where in Oregon?"

"My brothers and the colonel will destroy the place where the mud people, the Jews, the queers, the race traitors, where all who are filth in Yahweh's eyes have gathered to keep His People from securing our own nation."

"Will he—will *Yahweh*—use the nuclear weapon to accomplish this?"

Karras smiled. The effort was gruesome to watch. "Yes. Yes. They must burn. Their city must be destroyed. All must see the light of Yahweh before they die. Then victory—the final victory—will be at hand."

"He's speaking in the language of his religion," said Trace. "I don't know that I'll get much more that will be useful. He's slipping into the protection his faith gives his mind and soul. It would take more time, more pain, to draw him out of that place."

"I want all he's got to give."

Trace looked at me. Her face was emotionless, impassive. She was caked in Karras's blood. Her hands and arms up to her elbows were a wet red sheen. Her features were smeared with splatters from his ruptured body. "You cannot go back," she said to me.

"I know," I replied.

Trace twisted the knife deeper into Tony's guts. He bucked weakly but made no sound. "I'll let your spirit go if you answer me," she whispered. "This is my promise to you."

Trace's words must have resonated with him,

because he finally exhaled the words I'd been waiting to hear: "Portland will be sacrificed . . ."

When Tony Karras died three minutes later, he'd given me the piece of information I needed to plan the next step of our mission—the location outside Portland where he was to hook up with two of his Nemesis pals. I'd kill the cocksucker Blanchard for making this necessary. That was *my* promise to him!

"Blanchard and his crew are way out in front of us," I said as Trace stood over Karras's corpse. "We need to talk to Karen's whiz kid about this Christian Identity bullshit to figure out what some of Karras's mumbo-jumbo meant. But Portland makes sense as a target for these assholes. It's as liberal a motherfucking Sodom and Gomorrah as you can find—outside of San Fran-Fucking-Frisco."

A hard knock at the door interrupted my train of thought. I *hate* it when that happens! "What!"

"Dick? It's Paul. We need to talk . . . now!"

I caught the Emerson in midair as Trace tossed it to me. "You get cleaned up," I told her. "Have Karen's people get you some clean clothes. I . . ."

Trace pulled her hair back with both hands. Now it too was streaked with the dead man's blood. She looked up at me. I held her gaze. "Don't worry about me, Captain. We'll get through this and come out stronger on the other side."

"Coming out!" I yelled as Paul began knocking on the fucking door again. As Trace and I left the room I jerked my thumb back at where Karras was lying in his own stew. "Get Clay in here and tell him to clean this mess up. Blondie's got to disappear. I don't care how or where. Just tell Mulcahy to bury him deep. Clear?"

Paul stepped aside and then glanced into the room. The smell was overpowering. When he saw what was left of Karras I heard him start to gag. The man on the carpet, hog-tied and de-nutted with a face full of blood and his guts hanging out, was not a pretty sight. "Holy shit," exclaimed Paul, grabbing onto the doorframe to support himself.

I stopped and spun around to face him. "You got a problem with this?"

Paul looked me dead in the eye. He was a young, tough, ball-busting stud and I liked the hell out of him. But he would either ride the tiger with me or find another berth in safer, saner waters. It was his call. Moment of Fucking Truth time. He broke eye contact with me and looked over at Trace. She stood tall. She offered no excuses. "No problem here," he said quietly.

I looked over at Trace. She turned and started down the hall. "Yeah, kid," I replied. "Good man. Get that shit in there squared away and meet us in Karen's office. Bring your ball and bat. We're heading for fucking Oregon unless these crazy sons of bitches blow it up before we get there!"

"Aye, aye, Skipper!"

I closed my eyes. For the first time in my life I hated being called Skipper.

9

"The best way to make a terrorist talk when he refused to say what he knew was to torture him . . . I was indifferent. They had to be killed, that's all there was to it."

GENERAL PAUL AUSSARESSES,
"Algeria Special Services, 1955–1957"

KAREN TRACKED ME DOWN IN BETWEEN MY TAKING A whore's bath in the men's room and attending the last briefing before we lifted off for Portland. The quick wash-up had given me my first few minutes alone since the helo had landed at the Manor and whisked the kids and me away. I needed the break in the action. Already tired and sore, the nasty session with Karras had overloaded my senses. I'd needed a few moments alone to refocus on the mission.

That came to a quick end when Karen stormed down on me, declaring, "Torture. Dick, you and Dahlgren tortured that man to death!" She was pissed and I couldn't have cared a fuck less. I was in the mission-prep mode and had no time for bullshit. Danny Barrett was in-house and in the process of getting dialed in to what had occurred since we'd left him with a ton of paperwork. With Danny along for the ride I was feeling a bit more comfortable about the shitty odds we were facing. Mulcahy had arranged for an Air Force Lear to take us from nearby Andrews Air Force Base to a base near Portland, Oregon. The most direct line of travel had been plotted and approved by those on high. We'd break all speed records getting to our anticipated ground zero, courtesy of the Air Force's best flight crew. Marine One, the president's helo, was standing by on the White House helipad to move the team and me from OISA out to Andrews. Three armored SUVs were down on the street wasting gas as we fiddle-fucked around getting our shit in order. Their mission was to get us from OISA to Marine One by the most direct route available. The clock was ticking and here I was getting a lecture on appropriate conduct when I needed to be with my team and getting gunned up.

I'd put a request in for the FBI's Hostage Rescue Team to assist in the mission. They would outload for Portland from Andrews as well. It would take their C-141 Starlifter a bit longer to make it to the West Coast than our Lear but I needed the HRT's shooters as backup. Blanchard's team were among the best. Their training and real-world experience were extensive. They were almost as good as Red Cell had been in its heyday under my command. The hit on the NEST team was a stark reminder of just how lethal Blanchard's boyz were. I knew no local police department stood a chance against his operators in a running gun battle . . . if the cops ever found them to begin with. I wanted as much firepower and expertise on the ground with me as possible once we started kicking doors and taking names. And I needed guys who know nukes. Before he'd gone on to the happy hunting grounds Karras had given us the location of the two-man Nemesis cell he was supposed to link up with after finishing his surveillance in D.C. His civilian flight across the country didn't leave until 0900 tomorrow morning. With what I knew now, thanks to Trace's handiwork with my Emerson, I figured we had perhaps twenty-four hours before Blanchard intended to detonate the SADM.

Twenty-four hours at most.

"The president said any and all means. You were there. You heard him."

Karen flared. "Dick! I highly doubt the president could have imagined that five minutes after he hung up you'd be gutting an America citizen on the floor of a U.S. government agency and using his turn of a phrase to justify your butchery!"

I was tired. I was worn down. I was pissed off and I was ready to take my people into harm's way. I didn't need a lecture on ethics or morals or any other such bullshit just now. Especially from a professional manager, and despite her talents and abilities, that's what Karen is. She sends others to carry out the policies she only puts on paper. She never gets wet, she never gets dirty, she never pulls the trigger, and she never watches those who carry out the ground wars bleed and die. She never writes the letters home to their loved ones who never halfway get the truth about how their husbands, sons, and brothers . . . and now wives, mothers, and sisters . . . serve their country and make the ultimate sacrifice for it.

That is what they pay me to do.

And I do it very fucking well, thank you.

It was time to cut this shit short. "Listen close, Fairfield, because I haven't got a lot of time to waste soothing over your outraged sense of propriety. Karras was a fucking terrorist. Sure, he had a U.S. passport and looked and talked like you and me, but he was a terrorist just the same. You think he was going to happily tell me what we need to know right *now*? He was yapping about his rights and his lawyer and the civil suit he was going to file from the moment he woke up after Trace clobbered him with her fucking .45. If I'd followed the rule book, Karras would be chatting it up with some slick-shoe mouthpiece at $300 an hour while Portland and most of its people were getting roasted on a nuclear spit!

"Take a note, Karen! Extraordinary times demand extraordinary means. I'll take the lives of half a million American citizens over the rights of one fucking lunatic any day of the week. I didn't like what we did, I didn't enjoy it, and I sure as hell hope I never have to do something like that again. But it had to be done and I did it! So either shut the fuck up and help me get this show on the road or put the cuffs on me. I can't wait to read about how the president let half a million voters be turned into black glass as I'm doing reps on my old friend the weight bench at Club Fed. It'll make for good jailhouse conversation and maybe even another Rogue Warrior best-seller!"

Karen took two steps back and looked hard at me. She'd heard me loud and clear. It was decision time. Leaders lead and overcome all odds to get the job done. Managers manage and give leaders all the wrong reasons why they can't possibly accomplish the mission at hand. I was about to find out if Karen was a dyed-in-the-wool manager or if there was hope for her in the future. When she spoke her voice was low, dangerous, and about as sexy as a jury's guilty verdict. "You know the president absolved you of any wrongdoing this afternoon. You damn well know he accepted all responsibility for whatever had to be done! You're free and clear, Captain Marcinko.

"But perhaps you've forgotten this? The president *didn't* give carte blanche to Trace or Paul or anyone else on your team. I may not own you, but I sure the hell own them. I could put Dahlgren away for life for what she did to that poor son of a bitch. And Kossens, too, as an accomplice and conspirator. Did you bother to consider *them*, you arrogant bastard?"

Actually, good reader, I had. That's what a good commander and spec-warrior does. He considers his actions and all the possibilities of how they may affect him and his teammates. That's how you hold Mr. Murphy in check. Karen was playing her management wild card to bring me back in line. However, fluffing up her comfort zone was not my problem. Colonel Mother-Fucking Max Blanchard and an AWOL nuke were my problem. It was time to bring this little *chitchat* to an end. Like I said, I had a few things to do, and being captain of the OISA debate team wasn't on my short list.

"I take my orders from the president. He gave me that authority, *his* authority. By any and all means. You want to fuck with my kids all I have to do is invoke that authority, a copy of which is now in the hands of my attorney and the original is on its way to an off-shore safety deposit box. Trace and Paul acted on my orders, and I acted on the president's. You can't fucking touch them or me without bringing down the president. We both know you won't go there. End of discussion."

Karen reluctantly nodded her assent. We were playing hardball now. She had her job to do and I had mine. "I'll tell Clay to handle the Karras matter appropriately under the current circumstances," she said with a hint of bitterness in her voice. "I believe you said—make that *ordered*—that you want him buried deep. He will be. Like all the other poor bastards you've dealt with outside the rule book the rest of us have sworn to live by. Clay is good at his job. It's one of the reasons I hired him and primary reason the president trusts him. He'll hate me for this but he'll get the job done . . . but for me, not for you.

"Good luck, Dick. One word of advice—don't look too closely in any mirrors along the way. You may discover you've become what you claim to hate the most."

In an instant she was gone, walking away both from me and from whatever it was we'd enjoyed together as lovers. I watched as the elevator doors closed behind her. I tried to put Karen Fairfield out of my mind as I turned and headed for where Barrett and the kids were waiting for me.

I came across Paul pacing in the hallway outside the room where we were planning to have our briefing. "Dick, I did what you said and Clay is taking care of Karras's body. Look, I don't want you thinking that I can't handle whatever business needs to get done. I know I don't have as much experience as Trace, but I'm a part of this team and you don't need to worry about me having a breakdown or some bullshit like that."

"I know Paul. You've proven that to me."

"Thanks. But I still need to talk to you for a sec before this briefing."

"Make it short. We've got too much shit to do and less than no time to do it."

"It's about Nemesis. I've got the sheets on Karass's Nemesis team members who went missing yesterday like you asked, and then went ahead and pulled the file on Blanchard. It's Blanchard I have to talk to you about."

"You know him?"

"Yeah, I met him when I did some early special ops training at Bragg. He really tried to take me under his wing, teach me the ropes. Kinda gave me the creeps to tell you the truth."

"Tell me more."

"Well, somehow he knew about my dad's service in Nazi Naval Intelligence during the war and about his work for the CIA in Europe afterwards. At first, his interest seemed really cool. I mean, he was like King of the Delta Force or something and I was a kid hoping not to shoot my foot off with my own gun. He knew a ton about history and was always lecturing me about how America was falling short of its destiny, how we'd lost sight of the real meaning of the Constitution. He was an incredible storyteller, a little intense maybe, but didn't seem way out there or anything. Then I noticed he'd always want to bring the conversation back to my father's war record."

"I'll bet he did."

"Dick, you know it's not something I talk about very much. I mean, why should I? I look like the fucking poster child for Hitler youth. All I need is for people to know my dad was once a card-carrying, sieg-heiling Nazi. But Blanchard said I should be proud of my heritage. He said intelligent people understood that the Nazis should be appreciated for their fight against the spread of Communism. He had this uncanny way of using all his historical knowledge to make crazy ideas like that sound sort of plausible. Then one night, after a couple of drinks, he started in on some truly scary stuff—talking about a 'White Man's religion' and how America was meant to be a homeland for people like him and me, people of pure Aryan blood. That's when I had to tell him. About my mom being a nice Jewish girl from Philadelphia and all. You should have seen the look on his face. I thought he was gonna pass out he was so surprised. He never spoke another word to me again after that night."

"Jesus. How long ago was all this?"

"Ten years ago, give or take. Like I said, I was just a pup."

"He was fucking trying to recruit you for his team. Holy shit, ten years ago Blanchard was already putting this thing together, or at least planning for something like it."

"Once Nemesis came up in the mix this morning, the whole thing came back to me. I'd written Blanchard off back then as just a racist nutcase, but I gotta tell you, when you're the focus of his attention and he starts spinning his nasty little web of half-truths and historical misinterpretations around you, it's damn hard to resist. There's something truly compelling about the guy. I can see how he'd be able to inspire a hard-core group of shooters to rally around him to pull off this fucked-up shit."

"C'mon partner, let's get Trace and Danny. Between all of us mongrels and mutts, I'm betting we've got more than enough juice to teach fucking Max Blanchard a different kind of American history."

10

"Throw the troops into a position from which there is no escape and even when faced with danger they will not flee. For if prepared to die, what can they not achieve? Then officers and men together put forth their utmost efforts. In a desperate situation they fear nothing; when there is no way out they stand firm."

SUN TZU, *The Art of War*, c. 500 B.C., tr. Griffith

"WHERE'S MY FUCKING GEAR?" AT MY QUESTION, ALL activity in the makeshift war room came to a momentary stop and umpteen pairs of curious eyes swiveled toward me. Guess I sounded a little energized. After what happened with Karras and then my chats with Karen and Paul, I was itching to get this party started. I needed to gear up, gun up, and get briefed as soon as possible. We had a plane to catch.

Danny jerked a thumb toward a pile of shit on the floor at the far end of the room. "Change of clothes, tac-gear, vest, MP-5, ammo, and assorted other necessary bullshit waiting on you. Courtesy of OISA's supply geek and the dudes over at HRT."

"You know I don't wear a fucking bulletproof vest," I growled at Danny while making my way past him.

"Dick, on this trip we all better be wearing vests. The fuckers we're going up against are mean as rattlesnakes. Just ask those guys from NEST who met up with them this morning."

"And while you're at it ask those dead motherfuckers at NEST how good their vests worked when Nemesis hit 'em! I'll bring mine along as a pillow for the plane ride. You wanna wear the fucking things it's okay by me. I'll trust in getting there with the most lead on target fastest."

Laughter rippled throughout the room. For the first time since leaving the Manor I felt at ease. I was back in *my* fucking environment. Danny Barrett was taking up half the room while adjusting a new Safariland thigh holster custom made for his .41 Magnum. He gave me a thumbs-up and then the bird when I caught his eye. Trace, cleaned up and dressed down in all-black, was talking with one of the intel geeks. The Kimber rode low in a tactical rig from John Carver out at Eagle Industries. I knew John and his work from my days at SIX. He is the prince of high-speed low-drag CT equipment and as honest a man as anyone could do business with. Paul, an HRT 10-mm MP-5 in his mitts, was finishing a function check of his weapon. Each of my operators always checked and rechecked his or her own gear before a mission. We loaded our own magazines, and chambered our own rounds. Nothing was left to chance, error, or some other guy. Like packing a HALO 'chute . . . if you fucked up, you fucked up on your own.

I pulled out a chair and grabbed my subgun off the

floor. There were ten magazines for it, and ten boxes of ammunition at fifty per box. I had another four boxes of 9-mm for my Glock, and a new .32-caliber KelTec pocket pistol with one seven-round mag to boot. This last item was my insurance policy. The little skull popper weighs less than six ounces and can be carried anywhere on the body, even on a cord around my neck. The jacketed hollow point ammunition I'd requested is specially manufactured in Texas and comes out of the barrel at over 1800 feet per second. Up close and personal it is guaranteed to ruin your day. I'd tasked Paul to get H&K 10-mm MP-5s for us. The MP-5 is easily the finest subgun made for CT work in the world and the 10-mm model is a special order item for the Secret Service, FBI, HRT, and NEST. The combination of the MP-5's reliability and accuracy, plus the 10-mm round's hard-hitting performance on bad guys makes for one tough combination to beat. I knew Blanchard was packing serious heat and that we would need all the firepower we could carry to match him toe-for-toe. The HRT would be my ace-in-a-hole. Surprises are my specialty, as my enemies have come to find out. "Let's get this show on the road!" I yelled over the chattering and buzzing in the room.

Fuckers were too damn loud!

Everyone took seats. I'd asked to be briefed on three specific subjects before leaving for Oregon. It was Clay's job to find the right brains to do the talking and I'd told him that each expert would have a maximum of five minutes to tell me what I needed to know. Putting a short fuse on this kind of shit keeps the "I'm such a smart motherfucker" posturing to a minimum. It also scares off the would-be experts and allows me to talk with no-shit professionals who don't like their time wasted by attending long, drawn out bullshit meetings. The twenty-four-hour clock before Nemesis would detonate the nuke was ticking in my head. I also knew Blanchard held the upper hand despite our breaking Karras. The colonel could go hot any time he wanted to, and Portland was only a hypothetical target based on what we'd dragged out of my man Tony by ramming a knife into him. Our mission could end five minutes from now with a breaking story on CNN. So I settled back, began breaking open boxes of 10-mm ammo, and grabbed an empty magazine from the pile at my feet. "Who's my expert on Portland, Oregon?" I asked.

"I am, Mr. Marcinko. Irene Kirby. Office of Homeland Defense."

Irene appeared to be in her mid-forties. She was short, thin like a bird, and casually dressed. Her salt-and-pepper hair was pulled back into a loose bun at the back of her head. She had a single piece of paper in her hands. I liked that. "Okay, Irene, tell us about Portland and how a nuclear bomb would affect the City of Roses."

"Yes, sir. First, Portland is actually a small, very compact city although very modern in terms of its buildings, public services, and social attitudes. Within its 132 square miles are approximately ninety distinct neighborhoods. Resident population is about 521,000, plus another 500,000 during business hours. These are mainly workers commuting from the network of adjacent cities and towns that surround Portland like a web. All total this makes for a million-plus people on Portland's streets on any given weekday.

"The city is located at the confluence of the

Columbia River and the Willamette River. When skies are clear, Mount Hood can be seen to the east, Washington's Mount St. Helens to the north, and the green West Hills, appropriately, to the west. The Willamette River literally splits the city in two with the high-end business district to the west and the industrial section to the east. It is crossed by eight bridges in the downtown area. International shipping is a major economic asset for the city and the Columbia is Portland's waterway to the world.

"The city is well laid out and easy to get around. It is crossed by major freeways linking Oregon with California and Washington State, but most of the compact downtown area is accessible on foot and the city planners do everything they can to encourage pedestrian traffic. The Portland Airport is to the northeast of the city and services international air travel. The Portland Air National Guard is located there also. The Guard can provide both jet fighter and search and rescue air capabilities, if necessary.

"It's known as a remarkably clean, friendly, tolerant city, largely spared the urban decay and unrest that plagued so many other American cities in the last several decades.

"The potential effect of a nuclear explosion on Portland and the surrounding area is not my area of expertise." Irene set her single page of notes down, folded her hands, and stared at me with inquisitive eyes.

"Thank you, Irene. Just what I needed to know. Who here is my fucking expert on what a man-portable nuclear weapon can be expected to do to a burg like Portland?"

A sallow, thin-framed man raised his hand from the

far end of the room opposite me. He was the gent Trace had been chatting with when I'd come in. The fucker looked like death warmed over and then microwaved an extra few minutes for good measure. Unlike Irene, he had no visible notes. I had to strain to hear him speak. I heard him say something about being from the NSA. Well, at least they hadn't sent that fucking midget Carl over. "Speak up, sir," I hollered at him. "I'm half fucking deaf!" I grabbed another magazine and began stuffing rounds down its throat.

"The device taken by Nemesis is a third-generation SADM," wheezed Sallow Man. "It weighs thirty pounds and is encased in a silver-colored titanium case. It features a triple-lock security system and internal homing device. The homing device is not transmitting. It ceased to transmit at the site where our NEST personnel were attacked."

"How big a fucking boom will this bastard make?" I asked the Wheezer.

Adjusting himself in his chair the NSA expert coughed harshly to clear his throat. Probably a smoker, I thought to myself. Cancer sticks and weapons-grade radiation. It sucks to be you. Wheezer continued. "The device is rated at three times the explosive power of the bombs dropped on Japan during the closing days of WW2. If it is positioned at the point of greatest tactical advantage, we can accurately predict, given the layout of the target city, the western portion of Portland will be immediately flattened and incinerated upon detonation. The eastern sections, those across the river, will likewise be incinerated and in all likelihood pancaked, too. Secondary damage and casualties of a massive nature will occur as buildings, automobiles, and so on are turned into lethal, high velocity fragmentation by the blast. The surrounding feeder urban areas will suffer varying degrees of destruction, damage, and death. It will be horrific."

"Civilian casualties?" asked Trace.

"As compressed an urban environment as the city is, I estimate there will be few if any survivors in the downtown area—depending upon where the device is positioned prior to detonation. Also, the more people on the streets or in the open, the greater the casualty rate will be. Whoever chose this particular city as his target did his homework well. Because it is so compact, it's the perfect urban setting to use such a device against, in my professional opinion."

All eyes in the room turned toward the door as Clay Mulcahy stuck his "Mr. Clean" skull into the room. "Dick? You got ten minutes max. Flights are green light and HRT just called to say they've loaded in record time and are lifting off now. You'll beat them to Portland but not by much. Their honcho tells me he's stripped the hell out of their standard deployment package and the plane is cleared direct across the country, like yours. Oregon National Guard HAZ-MAT will be at the Air Guard base outside Portland when HRT touches down. They're gearing up now."

Well, I thought to myself, things are finally fucking starting to come together. If only Blanchard stays on the predicted schedule, we might enjoy half a fucking chance at pulling the missing nuclear rabbit outta the hat. "We'll be on our way down in five mikes. Have the cars ready to receive paks. And Clay, thanks."

Mulcahy paused and give me a piercing look. I knew he was pissed about having to clean up after me, but loyal to Karen and the president and so would protect them at all costs. But I also knew he was in my

corner to the degree he could be. If anyone understood where we were going and what the most proba-
ble outcome was going to be, it was Clay. Demo Dick
Marcinko and Company were flying into what very
likely would soon become a nuclear blast site. If I
missed getting to Colonel Max and his band of merry
motherfuckers before they detonated the SADM, that
would be all she wrote. At least Mulcahy wouldn't
have to bury my nasty ass next to wherever he'd
dumped Tony K. I'd be a crispy critter, courtesy of
Uncle Sam's tactical nuclear arsenal.

"Just get the job done, Marcinko." And he was gone
without as much as a "fuck you very much." Well, I've
got plenty of fans these days. Maybe I'd send Clay an
autographed book from the Portland Airport gift shop
if me and the crew were able to nix Nemesis before
they toasted the city. If Clay didn't want to read it he
could always shove it up his ass. You can find a use for
anything if you try hard enough.

"Okay, so who's here to tell me why Colonel Max
Blanchard wants to dry-hump the prettiest little city
in Oregon for *Yahweh?*"

"I am, Commander."

I slowly turned my head to the left where the last
speaker had been sitting quietly not an arm's length
away from me. I'd noticed him when I'd sat down and
begun digging through my go-to-war shit. I put him
in his mid-thirties. He was blond with carefully
combed hair and deep blue eyes. He was fit, that
much was evident by both the cut of his suit and the
leanness of his frame. German stock, I figured. An
Aryan motherfucker with roots in the Old Country.
He and Paul could have been brothers in the fucking
Von Trapp family. "And who might you be, sir?"

A slight smile creased the man's chiseled features. "Larry Monson. I'm a contract intelligence collector and analyst for a number of federal agencies, some represented in this room. I specialize in the white supremacist movement."

"So you know who this Blanchard character is and why he's got a hard-on for anybody a shade darker than lily-white?"

Monson laughed. "Fuck, sir. There's been any number of crazy Green Berets—officer and enlisted— who've participated in the Movement. Yes, to answer your question, I know something about Colonel Blanchard. Unfortunately not enough soon enough to have prevented what we're dealing with now."

"Correction, *Larry*. What *I'm* dealing with now. Because you fucked up I got called in. And I only get a ticket to ride when the situation is FUBAR. I'm on short numbers here, Mr. Monson. How about I ask the questions and you puke the answers out for me?"

"It's your nickel, Commander. Just make sure you ask the right questions. If you fuck up in Oregon and get roasted along with your crew it'll be because you asked the wrong questions."

Cocksucker! But I like that in a man. Well, not *that* per se. Balls. I like a man with balls. FUCK! That's not right, either. Let's figure you know what I mean and leave it at that.

"Why nuke little old Portland, Oregon? Why not New York, Chicago, L.A., or even San Francisco?"

Monson sat back and tamped a well-worked briar pipe with a long, nicotine-stained finger. He looked around the room to make sure he had our attention before answering me. He was an operator. That much was now evident. I sensed he'd done more than read books and attend weekend seminars on OKC, Waco, and Ruby Ridge. This guy was paid by direct deposit and handled through cutouts whenever possible. He was a nongovernmental organization asset, or NGOA. A civilian spook. I wondered why it was he got his kicks hanging out with born-and-bred American terrorists. Guess it takes all kinds.

"The Pacific Northwest has long been identified by the White Supremacist Movement as its natural homeland. Oregon, Washington, Idaho, and Montana are where all good supremacists want to isolate themselves and create an all-white society. The major players in the movement, including Posse Comitatus, the neo-Nazi National Alliance, the White Aryan Resistance, and the infamous but martyred Order, all have deep, deep roots in this area of the country, particularly in Oregon.

"Portland is seen by the Movement as a multicultural, ethnically diverse, liberal obscenity. It is the ideal target for someone like Blanchard, who fancies himself as a Phineas Priest figure in the Christian Identity faith. By destroying Portland, the Sodom of the Pacific Northwest in the eyes of all good White Men, Blanchard will assume a very powerful, perhaps undisputed position in the worldwide white racist matrix. In doing so, he no doubt hopes to ignite a race war in the streets of America. This is what white racial holy war doctrine ordains must take place for America to be purified as decreed by *Yahweh*'s prophets to His people."

Trace spoke up. "We've heard the term 'Phineas Priest' before. What's it mean exactly?"

"In Christian Identity a Phineas Priest is the ultimate warrior. He extracts retribution for grievous sins against *Yahweh*'s teachings. He slays race traitors, homosexuals, and any others seen as an abomination to *Yahweh*. The Phineas Priest can undertake any action he believes necessary against the oppressor, who is most often referred to as ZOG, or the Zionist Occupational Government. Such priests are highly regarded in the movement. Blanchard and his followers may believe themselves to be such priests. If so, you are dealing with zealots beyond your wildest dreams. They cannot be reasoned with, threatened, intimidated, or stopped by any rational means. The fact these people are also trained, elite commandos makes their position within the Movement that much more secure. I warned about the impact of such a development several years ago. Clearly, no one was listening."

"You and me both, Mr. Monson. Anything else you can add?"

Monson leaned forward, aiming his pipe at me stem first, like a short-barreled pistol. "It is my belief that while Colonel Blanchard may be a holy warrior in his own eyes, he has no intention of becoming a martyr. He will not hesitate to detonate the device. He will position it where it will do the most damage, but where he and his team will have the greatest possibility of making a successful escape before the blast occurs. He has planned this operation carefully and well. He does not intend to be stopped. Anyone who gets in his way will die. When you think you have him, that's the time to watch your back. Make no mistake, Captain, you are in for the fucking fight of your life as soon as you walk out this door."

Well, I thought to myself, isn't that special?

I thanked the panel of experts and excused them

along with the handful of admin help that had been busy squaring our shit away since my arrival. When the door closed it was just me, Danny, Trace, and Paul. Our individual kit was stored in our own daypacks or heavy-duty gym bag. Our weapons were locked and loaded. If necessary we could catnap on the flight out to Oregon. There remained only one more thing for me to say before we hauled ass for the chopper and then Andrews.

"Anyone who wants out has my blessing," I said quietly. "This is about as close to a one-way ticket as it can get. If Blanchard knows we bagged Karras, he can and probably will fall back onto whatever contingency plan he's made for such a development. That means he could blow the nuke a minute from now, or while we're in Portland trying to get a handle on Karras's linkup with his two Nemesis pals. There won't be a single safe zone near where we'll be operating. We all know what a SADM is designed to do. Your call. Make it now."

The silence was short-lived. "We're wasting time, Skipper." It was Kossens. The kid stood up and hefted his daypack over one broad shoulder. He looked at me with an expression I'd seen on the faces of so many of my shooters before. If I'd lead, he'd follow. It was as simple as that. Or as complicated. I knew he was speaking for Trace and Danny, as well.

So that was that. I stood up and grabbed my MP-5 and my well-packed (and lethal) gym bag. "Saddle up! We got a plane to catch." Danny opened the door for us and we trooped out of the dark conference room and into the brightly lit hall. Mulcahy was waiting at the elevator, holding its doors open for us. I gave him a quick thumbs-up. He nodded in return.

"Trace on point! Kossens, up second. Then Danny. I'll pull drag. Let's get the fuck outta here!"

As I watched my team head for the elevator, I realized just how fucking fortunate a man I was right then and there. I was doing the only thing I'd ever wanted to do—leading warriors into battle. We weren't many but we had heart. And a just cause. The odds were against us, but when haven't they been? Squaring my shoulders I started after Danny "Big-As-A-Fucking-Barn" Barrett.

Hell, it was as good a day to die as any other.

11

"War is a savage business, a business where killing one's fellow men without mercy is a duty and sometimes a form of sport. Nobody enjoys killing their fellow creatures, but in war one's likes and dislikes must take second place to defeat and survival. In this book there is much killing and I make no excuse for recording cases with satisfaction and often relish, whilst on reflection one is shocked at depriving others, just as good as oneself, of their lives and for no better reason than both of us are obeying orders and performing an unpleasant duty."

COLONEL RICHARD MEINERTZHAGEN,
"Army Diary," 1899–1925, 1960

TAGGING AND BAGGING TERRORISTS IS DONE ONE STEP AT A time. Their organizations are cellular in structure with each cell operating on a need-to-know basis. It's how they stay alive in a world that is hunting their heads 24/7. I knew we'd have to climb up the organizational ladder to get to Blanchard and the nuke. Karras was our big break into the chain. It was time to start taking heads. And we'd start with the two Nemesis operators Karras was supposed to hook up with outside of Portland.

The PAVE Hawk helo we were taking to Karras's rendezvous point was courtesy of the ParaRescue unit stationed at the Portland Air National Guard base, or the PANG as they call it. Danny, Trace, Paul, and I were sitting bunched up on the aluminum plate floor of the chopper, a thick braided fast rope coiled at the lip of the open starboard side door. It was ready to be kicked once we were at the target. I had two hot-shit PJs onboard as fast rope masters for our infil. They would also provide emergency trauma medical assistance if any of us needed it once the hit went down. HRT shooters and looters were prepositioned at ground zero. That had not been an easy task. The bad guys, or BGs, were holed up in a luxury hotel called the Fitzgerald, as prime a piece of commercial real estate as can be had overlooking the mighty Columbia River. According to our hasty intelligence work at the hotel, they were in a two-bedroom suite, about a thousand square feet total. I knew the assholes we were after would have their room wired for sound and ready to barricade themselves in if they couldn't get clear of an assault team. And I knew they were holding serious firepower and were more capable than most of employing it effectively in a fight. We were up against my worst nightmare: terrorists not only trained as well as we were, but also in possession of our intellectual property regarding strategies, tactics, and the most modern techniques of Hun-busting scumbags. They knew our countermeasures and our countercounter measures. There was no room for error in dealing with these guys. It would be kill or be killed.

My biggest concern was that the bad guys were prepared to blow exit holes in all directions at once. They sure the fuck weren't going to entertain a gun battle with overwhelming odds unless forced into it. And they were unlikely to try to bust out down the main hall with all the heat that they knew would line that gauntlet. No, these bastards—if they were thinking like me—would be prepared for us with prepositioned explosive breaching charges to blast their way through walls, ceilings, and floors if necessary to save their asses. If they did so, I wanted HRT in position to stop 'em dead in their tracks. Getting innocent civilians injured or killed is not my style. We had to contain the Nemesis cell first, and then ensure it couldn't pull its head out of the noose I'd set for it once the fun began.

The HRT commander, fresh in from Andrews AFB, had done a great job of quietly infiltrating his shooters into position. Over the last hour, they'd sealed off the floors above and below the BGs and also taken up positions in the rooms on either side of the two bastards, and across the hallway. They held the rooms directly above and below the target suite. Electronic communications were being kept to a minimum for fear of being intercepted by the BGs. Fucking Blanchard had looted the Nemesis war locker and his team was in possession of some extremely sophisticated electronic wizardry. All of which I had to assume was being used against us at this very moment. It was back to the basics for the Rogue. Hand and arm signals, written notes passed between those needing to know, and hard-line phones for final coordination.

Take a note! An expert is someone who does the basics better than anyone else.

And my expertise is in taking out Tangos. No one is better at it than *moi*.

"ONE MINUTE!"

The warning came from the pilot of the 'hawk as he put the agile helo hard to port and started his run for the target. My soon to be new best friends had taken a room facing the river, one floor below the penthouse. HRT owned both the penthouse and the roof of the building. I had snipers covering all four corners of the upper decks from adjacent buildings. On the ground floor there was a second team of HRT shooters just in case these crazy fucks tried to BASE jump the balcony. I wouldn't underestimate their imaginations. You hunt terrorists, you learn to think like a terrorist.

"THIRTY SECONDS!"

We were coming in way fast. This was going to be one fucking hairy rope ride. I'd ordered the pilot to come in just above the roof and to flare hard. That way anyone on the roof or the target balcony would be hammered by the fierce rotor wash of the powerful special ops chopper. A PJ would kick the rope over the side and the kids, Danny and I would then damn near free-fall onto the wide balcony from which our little pals had enjoyed a panoramic view of the river. It would be tight, very tight. Asshole pucker time tight. It would take about thirty seconds for all of us to make it onto the balcony, hopefully fast enough to surprise the bastards. The sliding glass door onto the balcony was reported closed and the curtains inside were drawn. I was counting on that combined with the general surrounding city noise to mask the sound of the approaching helos long enough for us to make our move. One slip, one miscalculation and it was a twenty-story free fall to the pavement. The aircrew and the PJs had to be right on the money or the team and me would be cashing in our chips with the Man Upstairs. If that happened, HRT had their orders. Get in and take 'em out. The fire department could hose what was left of me off the sidewalk afterward.

The Fitz was coming up fast. I felt a light shoulder squeeze and knew the PJ behind me was letting us know we were nearly on-target. I'd hit the rope first. Lead from the front, even when the front means going down. Trace was #2 to ride the string, then Paul. Danny would cover our six and be last man on the deck. As fucking big as he is, we'd want to be inside and kicking ass before his boots hit the cramped confines of the balcony.

To get us through the sliding glass door, I'd brought along a 37-mm Less Lethal beanbag gun. Slung around my neck the short, powerful little hand cannon was set up to fire a hardened breaching projectile recently developed for use by both DELTA and SEAL Team SIX. My plan was to slide like a raped ape down the fast rope and as soon as my go-fast boots made contact with the balcony I'd blast the glass and then launch all 240 pounds of Rogue Warrior badass into the suite. Once inside I'd transition to my Glock 26 and we'd go toe-to-toe with whoever was home. I knew I had to get off the balcony and into the suite *fast*. If I got hung up after touching down I'd get clobbered by Trace, Paul, and Danny coming down the rope hot on my heels. Plus, the jig would then be up and the BGs would most likely strafe the balcony with more firepower than I cared to think about. If that happened we'd be ground round perfection on a bun. Not my idea of a successful end to the mission.

"GO!"

The helo flared hard then flattened out and assumed a hover. As if in slow motion I watched the heavy coil of rope get kicked clear of the deck and become taut as it dropped to its full length. Reaching out with gloved hands I grabbed the string and launched my ass out of the bird. With a slight twist I cleared the lip of the cargo platform and began spinning around and down the rope. I left my feet free and used the heavy rope as a guide. There was no time or need to slow my decent. I had to get to where I was going *fast*. I figured we were about forty feet above the balcony. As soon as Danny landed, the crew would release the fast rope and it would fall to the street below. The helo would have to get away from the target *muy rapido* as the expected firefight was bound to erupt as soon as I pulled the trigger of the 37-mm. Then we'd be on our own with nowhere to go but forward, straight into the lion's den.

I grunted hard and loud as the heels of my Nike tactical boots bounced off the wrought iron railing of the balcony and my ass struck it dead center of my tailbone. Fuck! Ignoring the sharp pain that shot up the length of my spine and exploded inside the core of my brain I stepped clear of the rope and moved off to the left. Trace was hitting the deck even as I raised the 37-mm hand cannon and pressed its squat, ugly trigger. *BOOM!* I heard the round go off and felt the recoil of the weapon as it bucked rearward and up. The specially designed projectile hit the glass door and—

—Nothing happened.

Well, not exactly *nothing*. More like, *not a fucking thing!* The damn round struck the thick window glass and bounced off! I heard someone behind me—Paul, I think—yelp as the fucking beanbag ricocheted into him. At the same time I felt the exposed platform of the balcony shudder like it had been smacked with a pile driver from hell. That would be Danny, I thought. For an instant I had a vision of all of us falling to our deaths as the balcony gave way beneath our combined weights. I didn't know how much it could support, but there was some serious beef slamming into it and most such luxury options were not constructed to be landing pads.

I fired a second beanbag at the glass. This time I was rewarded with an impressive spider web as the second 37-mm round whacked the sliding glass portal hard. Still no entry point but at least I was making some mighty fucking progress. With the helo now gone I could hear the sound of muffled gunfire coming from deep inside the apartment. There was a huge explosion off to my right and then all hell broke loose to my front. As predicted, Nemesis was trying to bust out through one of the adjoining apartments and had run straight into the HRT blocking force I'd put in place for just such a contingency.

As I was pressing the fucking trigger of the 37-mm one more fucking time I watched an impressive chunk of glass disappear just above my head. The portal began to crumble as the impact of a .300 Magnum Winchester round went through the already weakened window. An HRT sniper on a neighboring roof, observing our predicament through his 10X scope, had saved our asses with one well-placed round.

"GOGOGO!" I yelled as I booted the rest of the glass and dashed into the main living room of the suite. Off to my right I could hear what sounded like a furious gun battle taking place and I motioned hard to the team to swing away from the walls and toward the left portion of the room so we could see what the fuck was happening and not shoot each other in the process.

The Nemesis breaching charge had started a small fire and smoke was rapidly filling the apartment. The damn smoke detectors started beep-beep-beeping like crazy and then with a sudden *pop* the overhead fire sprinkler system went off. The entire suite now felt like it was home to a freaking tropical rainstorm! We'd just taken cover behind a very nice (though now very wet) sofa and chairs when one of the Nemesis operators burst in from the adjoining bedroom where all the gunfire was happening. I was trying to get a good bead on him when he saw me and swung a Colt M-4 assault rifle up and began sending one long stream of 5.56 skull busters down in my direction. Time for Dickie to make himself scarce!

No one could hear shit over the roar of gunfire that was bouncing around the apartment like thunder trapped in a fifty-five-gallon oil drum. The fucking sprinkler system was working just fine, which meant it was practically drowning us and making it near impossible to get a good sight picture on anything more than three feet in front of our faces! I hoped to hell as I rolled and tucked up behind a non-bullet-stopping lounge chair that the HRT team outside the door in the hallway would hold their position. If they blew the fucking door and flooded the room we were now in, there'd be one helluva lot of friendly fire causalities to account for.

"DICK!"

Hearing Trace yell my name I chanced a peek and watched her as she heaved a flash bang grenade toward the Nemesis shooter. I clamped my eyes shut just as the damn thing went off. The resulting explosion made me even harder of hearing than I already was. I barely registered the rattle of subgun fire as the kids and Danny maneuvered their way around the fucking mess we'd made of things. This little surprise attack was going nowhere fast. And where the fuck was that other BG?

The high-pitched stutter of a squad automatic weapon erupting behind me answered that question. BG2 must have been holed up at the opposite end of the spacious suite and he was now putting in his two cents. Me and my team were now caught between BG1 and BG2. I didn't know exactly where BG1 had slithered off to, but he sure the fuck wasn't still in the hallway where I'd last seen him trying to kill my big ass. The fucking automatic weapon working its way up and down the walls and tearing the absolute shit outta anything in its way was now my primary concern. That shit had to stop!

Scrunching over on my side and changing my pistol's empty magazine I saw Paul. His face and both his hands were bleeding badly. He was lying flat on his back in front of the shot-to-shit couch and yelling like a motherfucker into his handheld ICOM. I couldn't hear a fucking word he was saying. I didn't have a clue where Danny was. Trace was hunkered down to my right, flat on her belly, sending a full magazine of 10-mm hornets into the hallway where the SAW gunner was holed up and pinning us the fuck down. Well, suppressive fire is better than no fire at all.

I did a quick battlefield assessment of our situation. First, we were fucked up beyond all repair, or FUBAR. I could live with that. Been there and done FUBAR many times before. I—we—just needed to keep our heads and fight our way out. The BGs were split up, which was good. They were holding their own, which was bad. It was pretty fucking clear HRT couldn't get into the apartment from where they were. They were still in a firefight with BG1 who was tossing lead to his front and rear with great skill. That was bad. It was also clear BG2 was in full control of his half of the homestead and with the fucking SAW he owned our asses. Of the two Nemesis players he was the greater threat. If it were me I'd be getting ready to stroll down the hallway and into our damp little patch of Hell with a 250-round drum of man-killers on full auto. Unless a lucky shot took him out we'd be chopped to bits as he worked the gun around the room. After that it wouldn't matter who won. Me, the kids, and Danny Barrett would be hunka-hunka bleeding corpses. End of story.

What to do?

Sometimes, the right answer is just handed to you. In this case, it exploded on top of me, literally, courtesy of the HRT team in the penthouse directly above us. It felt like my eyes had been blasted outta my thick Slavic skull when the concussion of an overhead breaching charge slammed into me with all the gentleness of a tidal wave. Forcing myself to respond, I got to my knees and emptied the little Glock down the hallway where BG2 was holding out. I holstered the pistol in one smooth motion and jerked my MP-5 up to my shoulder. ATTACK-ATTACK-ATTACK! To my left I saw Trace, who now looked like a drowned she-rat, throw another flash bang hard into the hallway. Closing my eyes, I pressed the MP-5's trigger and began running forward. The first magazine emptied itself on full auto as I sent its full load down range where I hoped BG2 was. The full force of the flash bang's explosion hit me square in the body, bouncing me sideways and off the fucking wall. I opened my eyes. At least I could still see. ATTACK-ATTACK-ATTACK! Thousands of hours of doing magazine changes took over as I switched out the empty mag for a full one from my left thigh cargo pak. I found my balance and kept moving forward. I couldn't hear shit over the sharp staccato of continuing gunfire. It was clear HRT had blown through the ceiling above us. We were now reinforced and could begin taking the fucking fight to Nemesis.

I cleared the short hallway with Trace backing my play. A quick glance backward showed Danny leading the charge on BG1 with HRT covering his six. BG1 was not going to have a good day. Sandwiched between HRT blocking elements and Danny on point he was pretty well fucked. I couldn't stop to think about Paul's status. He'd been breathing and talking when I last saw him so I figured he'd live. Right now I wanted BG2 alive and talking if at all possible. I turned to Trace. "Got any 'bangs left?"

She nodded and hauled two of the small black grenades out of a thigh pak and hefted them so I could see they were good to go. I nodded in the direction of the bedroom where I figured BG2 was now preparing to make his last stand. I knew I could have HRT blow the far wall and make an entry but if that happened they'd probably kill the silly fucker. I needed information. Dead guys can't talk. So it was up to Trace and me to get the job done.

"FIRE IN THE HOLE!" Trace called as she tossed both flash bangs into the room. As they bounced in, the damned SAW opened up again, this time its fire chopping through the plasterboard walls of the room where we were crouched. I hit the floor and hugged the water-soaked carpet for all I was worth. I figured Trace was doing the same. Bits of debris swirled around us as the high-velocity slugs turned the hallway into a nightmare of death-dealing fragmentation. The double *BOOMBOOM* of the flash bangs was sweet music to my ears. With a roar I leapt up and rushed into the bedroom. Kicking torn up, ruined hotel furniture out of my path, I clambered across the soaked king-size bed, the barrel of my H&K swinging in short little arcs back and forth as I searched for BG2. Trace, her H&K at the ready, covered me from the doorway. I saw the silly fucker where he lay all stove up and stupid from the combined blast of the grenades. We'd rung his bell good. "HERE!" I yelled to Trace. Jumping down off the bed I pulled the SAW away from the unconscious form at my feet. A trickle of blood was running from his nose but other than that he looked fit as a fucking fiddle.

"CLEAR!" yelled Trace back down the hallway toward HRT. "WE GOT ONE DOWN BUT ALIVE! NEED A MEDIC PRONTO!" She checked her weapon then gave me a thumbs-up. It was only then I saw she was bleeding from a flesh wound near the base of her throat. If she knew she'd been hit she didn't give any indication of it. I wondered how Danny had made out. All I could hear were the sounds of men shouting instructions back and forth and the damn BEEP-BEEP-BEEPING of the fire alarm system. The sprinklers had stopped, which was at least some improvement. *Shit*, I thought, *what a fucking cock-up!*

Two HRT operators called out to us before entering the room. I jerked a thumb toward the Nemesis geek and said, "Hook him up and get him outta here!" The two nodded and roughly checked the inert form out for any hidden weapons. They then flex-cuffed his dumb ass and dragged him away. I'd be talking with him later. Right now I needed to check on Danny and Paul, not to mention the HRT guys and BG1. Placing my H&K on "SAFE," I headed back down the hallway to the suite's living room. Trace fell in behind me. "Get your throat checked out by the medic," I growled at her. "You're bleeding like a stuck pig!"

She punched me hard in the back. "You love me and you know it!" she quipped. "You *care* about me! I think that's sweet. I think you're sweet. You can't shoot worth a shit but you *are so sweet*. I think I love you, Captain. Really, I think I do." She slipped past me before I could clobber her, her teasing causing me to smile for just a moment.

"Kossens! Where are you, you son of a bitch!" I was now standing in the middle of the shot-to-shit room where we'd made our less than dynamic entrance. The fucking fire alarm had FINALLY been turned off. Still, my ears were ringing and my eyes stung from all the cordite swirling around the suite. I still couldn't see Danny and now HRT was all over the fucking place. Looking up I saw where their breachers had blown a beautiful entry point through the floor to get to us. It had been a good thing, too. If they hadn't dropped down the chimney like Santa-Fucking-Claus, we'd have bought the farm.

"Over here, boss!"

It was Paul. He was sitting out on the balcony, an HRT operator swabbing his face with a wet towel or some such shit. I kicked my way through the trashed contents of the room to where I could see him clearly.

Fucking glass was all over the rug, mingled in with blood, spent shells, and blast debris. Remind me never to try to blow a sliding glass door with a bean-bag round again! From now on I'll simply have some-one shoot the fucker out with a heavy caliber elephant gun. "How bad you hit?"

"Minor face and hand cuts. A few good welts, bumps, and bruises. Shit was flying pretty thick in there. My bad luck. We get anyone alive?"

I nodded. "Trace and me nailed our guy with a double dose of sound and white light. Knocked him up, down, and out. HRT just hauled him up to the roof. We're pulling out and heading for the PANG. I'm gonna chat with him there. You good to go?"

Paul flipped me a bloody bird then grimaced as the HRT shooter pulled a wicked splinter of glass outta his right eyebrow. "Ouch! Fucking-A! Yeah, I'm fine, Skipper. Dry clothes, hot meal, a few beers, and a hot tub with any female but Trace in it and I'll be perfect."

I laughed. Although come to think of it seeing Trace in a hot tub wasn't all that bad a mental picture. "She'd fuck you and me to death then ring for room service. Get patched up and let's move."

Turning I brushed past a gaggle of HRT uniforms and headed toward Danny's voice. The entire suite was shot to shit at this end. I peered into the suite's second bedroom and saw where BG1 had blown his exit point. It was a nice piece of work. Too bad for him and his buddy that we'd secured the room next door and were waiting for just such a move.

"Any of your people hit?" I asked a tall, lean HRT shooter.

"Yeah, we got two down with serious gunshot wounds and one dead." The man nodded curtly to me and walked away. Fuck! I hate losing people, especially other people's people. Good men are hard to come by. HRT operators are among the best. There'd be some more sad calls to grieving parents and spouses before this was over. I could feel it in my bones.

"Dick? You okay? How's the kids?"

It was Danny. He was soaked like the rest of us and covered with grit and glass. His H&K looked like a kid's popgun hanging from its three-point sling around his massive chest. The S&W .41 was secured in its tac-holster and Danny's black knit watch cap was pushed back on his head. He didn't appear to have been scratched during the firefight. Come to think of it I'd never ever heard of Danny taking a round at any time in his career. Some guys are like that. They just live right, I guess. "Trace has a flesh wound in the throat but nothing that will shut her up. Paul's face looks like a logger tap-danced on it with those fucking spiked boots they wear. He'll be okay, though. How about you?"

"Right as rain," replied Barrett. "No hits, all misses. We nailed the cocksucker in the bathroom. I got maybe two good rounds into him when HRT fucking filled the bastard with enough lead to choke the EPA! All that's left ain't worth squat to us. I heard the Feds lost a man."

"Yeah, one dead and two down hard. They saved our asses, you know. Fucking sniper across the way took the window out when my fucking brilliant idea about using beanbag rounds went to shit. Their coming through the ceiling when they did was heaven sent. I thought we'd bought it until then."

"That was Paul's call. With all that fire raining

down, he got on the ICOM and told them to blow the ceiling and get the fuck down to us. Gutsy kid. You got a trooper in that one." Danny shook a somehow dry cigarette from a soft pack he'd fished out from a deep cargo pocket. Lighting up he drew in a long, deep drag of tobacco-rich smoke then exhaled. "You manage to keep anyone alive at your end?"

"Got one topside with HRT. We're going to hit him with a new chemical interrogator the boys and girls at Langley have come up with. After the blood-and-guts thing with Karras, Karen made sure we got the shit before the Lear lifted off."

I massaged my skull with one hand. My graying ponytail was pleated tight and soaking ass wet. The adrenalin was starting to fade and I was beginning to feel the places all over my body that hurt. The smoke in the suite was clearing out some. We needed to keep moving and I knew it. Three down, and a hatful of terrorist assholes to go unless Blanchard went nuclear now. Then all this would mean fuck.

Danny nodded. "Dick, you know it's going to be like this—just like this—from here until we get to Blanchard. When we get to the PANG, how about you give me some time alone with this fucker? I'll bet he hasn't had a lot of opportunities to get to know African Americans. I'd like to begin his reeducation personally."

I couldn't help but smile at this idea. Irony isn't completely lost on the Rogue Warrior, you know.

And I could use an hour of recovery time. I knew Danny was right—we were in for the fight of our fucking lives. If the others were willing and able to put up a battle like these two cocksuckers had, it was going to be a long, long day. "Agreed. We'd better stop talking about it and just get the fucking job done! This whole thing is beginning to piss me the fuck off! Let's go. I'm hungry anyway. You hungry? I'm hungry. I always get hungry after shit like this. Must be a defect in my personality."

I made my way down to where Paul and Trace were waiting for us. "The 'hawk's topside. Dry clothes and more ammo at the PANG. Eat when we get there. I need an intel dump so whoever has the opportunity needs to run it down for me. Danny will have a sensitivity training seminar with the prisoner. Let's hope our POW knows something worth sharing."

We trooped out of the suite and headed for the emergency stairs. I could hear the *whomp-whomp-whomp* of the helo as it awaited us on the roof of the Fitz. Sure as shit, Blanchard would hear about this little party, if he didn't know already. What he'd do I didn't have a fucking clue. All I could do was my job. If the City of Roses turned to black glass while I was on the meter, so be it. In the meantime we needed to keep moving. I wanted to find the next cell and climb another rung up the ladder. I wanted Blanchard and I wanted the stolen nuke. I wanted payback for the dead HRT and NEST shooters. I wanted Karen to be able to look me in the face again and tell me she understood. I wanted my kids safe and sound and banging steel at the Manor once again. I wanted Danny Barrett home with his wife and grandkids.

I wanted too much to slow down now.

Upon reaching the roof I ducked low and began running hard for the bird. The first act was over. No intermission in this show.

12

"You must know then, that there are two methods of fighting, the one by law, the other by force; the first method is that of men, the second of beasts; but as the first method is often insufficient, one must have recourse to the second. It is therefore necessary for a prince to know how to use both the beast and the man."

NICCOLÒ MACHIAVELLI, *The Prince*, 1513

"DICK? DICK? WAKE UP, BROTHER. TIME TO RUN AND GUN again."

When I opened my eyes all I could see was Danny Barrett's massive face not a foot from my own. The room the base commander made available to me was wrapped in soft darkness except for a single small light atop the desk in the corner. I was comfortable. I was warm. I was sore and not at all inclined to begin moving quickly just yet. "What the fuck? How long I been out?"

Barrett pulled back into the darkness. "Forty-five minutes. I got some good poop outta the asshole we hauled in. That chemical cocktail Karen sent along may work on soft cases. But it ain't worth a shit on guys with SERE training and a religious bent toward radical racism."

I gently swung my feet off the bed and sat up. Sore is not the word to describe how I was feeling. I gingerly touched my ribs on the right side of my battered carcass. Yep, that hurt. So did my head. So did my ass where I'd bounced off the railing on the ride down the fast rope. The interior of my mouth was dry and there was a bitter, ammonialike odor to my breath. I needed a hot shower, a toothbrush, some strong, strong coffee, and some good fucking news. "So, what'd you find out?"

Danny lit up a smoke. He seemed to enjoy the shit. Me, I prefer a good cigar. My old sea daddy, Ev Barrett, used a well-worked cigar to light demolition fuses. I learned from Ev how to light a fuse and how to smoke a good cigar at the same time. "I whupped him."

"You what?"

"I whupped him. Sent everyone out of the room and bounced him around like a redheaded stepchild. Kicked his ass. Played pinball with him. Beat him like a yeller dog. Southern justice. Works every time."

"He talked because you beat his ass?" I started laughing. This was too good.

Danny nodded in the shadows. "Yes. He did. I can be very persuasive. I have a way about me, or so I've been told."

Grabbing a clean, dry turtleneck from the neatly folded change of clothes next to the bed I pulled it over my head. A shower would have to wait. Next came the new jeans, socks, and a pair of Danner Arcadia tactical boots. In under three minutes I was dressed. I belted on the Glock and checked my extra magazines. I fished the big folding fighter Kelly Worden had given me before I left Tacoma out of my ditty bag and slid it into my left front pants pocket. The Emerson would stay behind from here on out. I'd undone and brushed my hair out before lying down. Now I pulled it hastily back into a loose ponytail and triple cinched it with an elastic hair band. Finished, I grabbed my Eagle daypack and checked its contents. All was in order. I was ready to roll.

"Where are the kids?" I asked Danny.

"Asleep. I made 'em get some rack time. They got spirit, I'll give 'em that. After I had my little heart-to-heart with Fuckface, I ran our two misguided youths down and sent them to their rooms. We got all sorts of Cracker Jack admin types running around this place now. Fucking post is shut down, locked down, and staffed with the cream of the crop from everywhere you can imagine. No need for Paul and Trace to do more than they have already."

I opened the small fridge in the tiny kitchen. It was stocked with fruit and power bars and bottled water. I grabbed some water. I was dry as a boneyard! Taking a long swig from the clear plastic bottle, I reveled in the feel of the liquid as it ran down my throat. Looking at Danny from across the room, I nodded. "Good call. What about you?"

"What about me?"

"Did you get some rest, you crazy motherfucker?"

Barrett smiled. "Nope."

"Silly question. Okay, then. Next. What do we know now that we didn't when we left the Fitz?"

Danny snubbed his smoke out. "Blanchard is smart," he began. "Nemesis is still broken down into cells. While the colonel has the bulk of the team with him and the nuke, our boy told me Karras only knew to link up with him and his pal at the Fitz. From there they'd get their orders from the team's control cell, which is still at least a link away from Blanchard himself."

"If not Blanchard, who?"

"Jack Laski. SF. Nemesis. His bio says he's a top dog when it comes to intelligence work and tradecraft. All the big boys wanted him on their payrolls but he hooked up with Blanchard and Nemesis. File says he's as cold as they come. Likes to use a knife. He's Blanchard's techno wizard and he's operating solo out of the Hotel Campbell in Tigard, just outside Portland."

"Does this Laski know what Blanchard intends to do, and where and when?"

"Our little bird seems to think so. He told me Brother Jack is Colonel Max's *numba two* man in the organization. Laski is the operational control for all the cells. He runs them. They report to him and receive their orders from him. They only know what they need to, when they need to. Our songbird knew Jack was setting up at the Campbell because he overheard Blanchard talking to Laski on a secure cell before the crew left some little burg in eastern Oregon called Bend."

This was good. Real good. We'd bagged three out of twelve and had a fourth in our sights. And if Danny was right, we were ready to close in on the information hub of Nemesis and therefore a direct link to Blanchard and the SADM. I finished my water and grabbed an apple. I was starving! We needed to move. Take a note: There's no wickedness for the rested in my book. "Have you confirmed that Laski is still at this hotel?"

"Yep. Local law enforcement showed his old army pic to the hotel desk clerk. He's registered under the name of Morgan. Room 910. Top floor, corner. No exterior balconies, you'll be glad to hear, but the hotel is built around a big central courtyard, a glassed-in atrium kind of thing. The guest rooms circle the courtyard. Fountains, pool, eating areas, the works are all open to guests and visitors. Safety railings run the length of each floor. You can step out of your room and from the comfort of your doorway look down and see what everyone is doing in the lobby. The entire place is very posh and very busy. And it's a very smart place to run a clandestine command and control pod from."

"Do we have eyes on target yet?"

"HRT is setting up now. Exterior perimeter. Soft clothes. No uniforms. They have scouts inside. Laski is in his room. Made a call for room service about twenty minutes ago. Maids say the room is neat and clean when they come in. No booze. Two carry-on bags and a daypack. Daypack is in the main room by the door. Laski is quiet, friendly, the perfect guest. Room is on a credit card in the name of Gregory Morgan. Using it instead of cash means no driver's license checks and copies at the front desk. Our boy probably created the identity alongside his various covers at Nemesis and masked the paperwork from the brass hats. After all, these guys were trusted."

"Get Paul and Trace up. We're going now. Snatch and Grab. He won't fight. He'll run first. The daypack probably has his techno shit in it. Close to the door, easy to shit and git. Blanchard needs Laski to coordinate the players and the hit. He'll have a safe house to run to, probably another hotel or motel within five miles of the primary. He'll have secure cell capability and an escape and evasion plan. If we miss him now, we're not gonna find him again so easily."

Danny pulled the door open for me and I rushed past him. My mind was going a million miles an hour again. A little rest, a little food . . .

"Speaking of plans, Dick. Do we have one?"

"Of course we have a plan! I'm making it up right now, Danny Boy. Fire up the helos, we're airborne in fifteen minutes!"

I actually meant that when I said it. The best laid plans . . .

I was in the communications center at base headquarters about to place a call to Karen in Washington when the news flashed across a bank of television monitors installed by the PANG's crisis management team. A local Portland station was announcing an unconfirmed report that a nuclear device had been found near the Chinatown section of the city. A ten-block radius of town was being roped off by the local police and the Oregon National Guard was reported to be en route from their airport staging area. The pretty female announcer promised she'd be back with late breaking news so we shouldn't change channels!

Fuck me to absolute tears.

"Mr. Marcinko? Your call, sir. Ms. Fairfield's on the line for you. You can take it over there if you like."

I thanked the airman and grabbed the hardline phone's receiver off its cradle. "Karen? Have you heard the news in the last two minutes?"

"Yep. That information is coming out local. No leaks here yet. We came down hard on the press in New Mexico about the NEST team story in the interests of national security. I can't guarantee how much longer before they run with it anyway. With this latest in Portland, I'd say all hell is about to break loose."

"Agreed," I replied. "You heard about our little party earlier today?"

"Yes. We got a good report from HRT. It's national news, in case you hadn't heard. The FBI is playing it off as a 'Ten Most Wanted' shoot-out. But that story will be in the toilet once this nuclear bomb in Chinatown bullshit starts rolling downhill. Are you okay, Dick?"

The tone of concern in Karen's voice was real. "Yeah, I'm okay. A few bruises, that's it. Trace and Paul got the worst of it but they're okay. Danny's fine. Didn't even muss his hair. How about you?"

I smiled as she laughed softly into my ear from clear across the country.

"Tired. The president is going day and night. I don't know how he does it. I'm okay, though. Thinking about you."

Well fuck me to tears again! "Does this mean I'm forgiven?" I asked.

"It means I understand more now than I did then. Clay sat me down and gave me a lecture on the real world. Your world. We intellectuals forget there are lions and tigers and bears out there, you know. I couldn't do what Trace did in a thousand years. But I understand why she did it and why you approved. You get this mission done and come back to D.C., understood Captain?"

"Understood," I growled. "We're going after Blanchard's 2IC in a few minutes. If we're lucky and get him alive it could be the break we need. We're hunting a needle in a haystack but the haystack is getting smaller. This nuke thing downtown is a surprise, though. It doesn't make sense. Blanchard wouldn't just set the fucking thing down in a bus terminal and walk away. I'm not liking this."

"I can't say, Dick. You're there. You deal with it as you see fit. If you need anything just call Clay. I've got to brief the president in ten minutes. Bye for now."

The line went dead. As I hung up, Paul and Trace made their way toward me from the far end of the busy command center. I could see Danny talking with the pilots outside by the two helos. Two teams of black-suited HRT shooters were loading into the birds. They would be our security teams on this hit. There was no time to run down the source of the breaking story downtown. I'd have some hotshot civil affairs geek here at the PANG monitor that shit for me. Right now we needed to get airborne.

"Who's next on the hit parade, Skipper?"

"How's your face, kid" I asked.

Paul gently touched the row of stitches running along his lower left jaw. "Hurts."

"Only fair—your face has been hurting me for a long time. Ready to go hunting again?"

"Who's the target," asked Trace. She was likewise stitched up. A bullet had zinged her alongside her carotid artery on the right side of her throat. Another millimeter and she'd have faced a little problem of bleeding to death.

"Let's get out to the birds. I'll fill you in as we walk. One thing I can promise you is that we won't be fast-roping onto a postage stamp balcony on this trip!"

As we walked and I explained the situation to them, the pilots climbed into their cockpits and Danny issued last minute instructions to the HRT security teams. The sun was starting to set out over the western hills ringing Portland's very pretty skyline. Beyond them, I knew there were some of the prettiest beaches to be found anywhere in the world, created over centuries by the constant ebb and flow of the Pacific Ocean. Why anybody would genuinely think it was a good idea to detonate a nuclear bomb in the middle of all this God-given perfection was beyond me.

I belted Trace and Paul in, then climbed aboard our helo and sat next to Danny on the deck. The crew chief checked us out and then closed the doors so we'd be a little warmer during the short flight over to Tigard. I began digging through my daypack and hauling out the shit I wanted to take in with me this time around. Danny and the kids were busy doing the same. My brain was working overtime turning the general plan I'd come up with into a more precise and detailed map of attack. I wanted Jack Laski alive and well. At the same time, if the news reports were accurate about the threat now being handled by Portland's finest, I was half-afraid I'd be seeing the city evaporate before we got close to Laski. Shit was moving too fast for my liking. I could imagine the local and national media igniting a general panic. If that happened we'd have chaos on the streets. All of Portland and the surrounding area would go into gridlock. Emergency response systems would be overloaded. Law and order would go out the window since the cops would be incapable of getting where they needed to, when they needed to, and in any sizable numbers.

I felt the bird lift from the landing pad and slowly begin a gentle rotation into the wind. There was no turning back now. And there was no place to hide if we wanted to. The stakes had just been jacked up a thousandfold and the hand I was holding couldn't beat Blanchard's. At least not yet. As the hawk lifted us higher and higher into the setting sun I ran my hand over the well-oiled receiver of the 12-gauge cut-down I'd dog-robbed off a DEA agent in Colombia years ago. At just fifteen inches from stem to stern, the little equalizer was the best close-in manhandler I'd come across in a long time. Although it held only three shells in the tube and one up the pipe, the devastation it could wreak more than compensated for the little gun's small combat load.

With any luck at all, I'd be jamming its barrel down Jack's throat in just a few minutes. Anyone on-site and in my way would get cut in half, courtesy of Dr. Remington and his four little friends from Federal. This *had* to be an easy do compared to what we'd been through earlier in the day. After all, it was just one guy and I had the best three shooters I knew on my team plus the good lads from HRT as backup.

What could possibly go wrong?

13

"It is fatal to enter into any war without the will to win it."

GENERAL OF THE ARMY, DOUGLAS MACARTHUR,
7 July 1952, " Address to the Republican National
Convention"

THERE IS NEVER A RIGHT WAY TO DO A WRONG THING. AT least that's what was pounded into my head from the moment I showed up at UDTR Class 26 at the U.S. Naval Amphibious Base in Little Creek, Virginia, looking to become a Navy frogman. On the other hand, I've learned over the years that there's a hundred ways to do a wrong thing with the results always coming out, well, wrong. Mistakes are more often remembered than successes. Mistakes are embarrassing and sometimes lethal; successes grow in magnitude and often become legendary war stories as more time elapses from the actual event. Mistakes, on the other hand, can *kill*. In the run and gun world of special warfare doing something wrong will get you or someone close to you zapped. That's why throughout my career as both a frogman and a SEAL I've always,

always made realistic, balls-to-the-wall training the number one priority for those under my command. Training, good training, is the time when you are allowed to fuck up. It's from our fuckups that we learn how to do it better, and therefore eventually to do it right. The battlefield is not the place to experiment. The battlefield is unforgiving. This is true in both warfare and business. Training is where you hone and perfect your skills. The field of battle is where you find out if your training was worth a shit. Anyone who thinks otherwise is one dumb motherfucker.

At least in my book.

Which is why I wanted the hit on Jack Laski to be done right. We'd lost an operator earlier today, with another two wounded and in serious condition. This, to me, was unacceptable. Only our training, the blood and sweat we and the shooters from HRT had paid with hour upon hour of hard fucking work, had allowed us to adapt, improvise, and overcome. This time the plan would be simple. Straightforward. And I would lead from the front, as always. Of course I've learned to expect the unexpected, and that's the x-factor managed by the infamous Mr. Murphy, of Murphy's Law fame. What is Murphy's Law, you ask? Allow the older and wiser Rogue to refresh your short-term memory, true and faithful reader.

Murphy's Law says anything that can go wrong will go wrong and will go wrong at the worst possible moment. Murphy's Law cannot be gotten around. It is the one obstacle I have never, ever been able to escape or evade during my career and throughout my many adventures in the Land of the Rogue Warrior. In the process of becoming older, wiser, and just a tad bit grayer around the temples, I've learned life is far less stressful if I relent and make Murphy my friend. Especially at times like this when I'm trying to figure out the best way to snatch and grab an asshole like Jack Laski, on the spur of the fucking moment with about as much hard intelligence as I can fit into a thimble. Having Ole Man Murphy nearby to chat with is strangely comforting. I ask him what he thinks of my plan and he tells me it's damn good. I tell him that's what worries me because I know it's Murf's mission in life to fuck my good plans up. He snorts and says I'm just not trusting enough. I laugh back and tell him I'd rather be a virgin whore in New Orleans during Super Bowl week than trust him. We shake hands and go our separate ways. He's got his job to do and I've got mine. Old Murphy keeps me on my toes. And in my business, being on one's toes can make the difference between life and death.

I was sitting at a table in a tiny coffee bar across the street from the Hotel Campbell, the hotel where we'd pegged Laski to be holed up. It was a nine-story, glass and stone box. The ground floor was given over to the usual blend of chain clothing stores and other retailers. From here, the whole complex looked like the kind of service-oriented hotel that catered mostly to anonymous visiting businessmen who wanted their messages and their cocktails delivered on time. Since we were right on the edge of Portland's so-called Silicon Forest, that made sense. The L.L.Bean down vest I was wearing concealed my Glock and two spare magazines from view. The daypack at my feet added to the impression that I was just a hardworking Hells-Angel kinda guy getting a hot cup of java at the end of the day. Nothing terribly unusual in this part of the world. A chilly evening breeze blew over me every time someone new came in.

When the 'hawk had dropped us on a soccer field a few blocks from the hotel, I'd told HRT to sit tight and await my instructions. Right now Trace and Paul were conducting a soft recon of the hotel's interior. Posing as man and wife, they'd wandered across the street and disappeared into the building ten minutes ago. I stayed put and out of sight. Laski was an intel monster. He'd been around the community as long as I had. There was a fucking good chance he'd know me by sight. I didn't want to lose him just because he saw me before I saw him.

A tiny television behind the counter was burping out updates on the alleged nuke found downtown. News crews were already crawling high and low to get a glimpse of what the police and HAZMAT people were dealing with. Side stories were starting to erupt about how the 911 system was getting jammed up with calls from frightened citizens. "Please don't call 911 unless you have a real emergency," begged some poor overworked city employee on the screen. Story of my fucking life, I thought. When they needed Dickie and his war-makers it usually meant the world had gone to hell in a handbasket. Nine-one-one had been my home phone number for as many years as I could recall.

As worrisome as the nuke report was, I couldn't let it distract me from my mission at the moment. Laski was here and so was I. Sipping at my steaming coffee, I watched Paul and Trace make their way over to the café. A long wool scarf wrapped around her neck concealed Trace's recent wound, and thanks to his athletic frame and well-worn Nike baseball cap, the scratches on Paul's face looked more like the result of a rock-climbing incident than a gun battle. They looked every inch the young married couple. Whoever had trained them had done a fine job of it. The kids could take on almost any role at the drop of a hat.

Role-playing was mandatory training at both SIX and Red Cell when I ran those outfits. A counterterrorist must be able to shed the unmistakable gloss of his or her military background in order to operate safely and effectively in the terrorist underworld. And that underworld coexists alongside your daily life, dear reader. Yes, there are guerrillas in our midst. And terrorists. More so today than ever before. I've made my living being smarter, quicker, and more deadly than those I hunt. Being able to look like John and Jane Q. Public helps accomplish the mission. The brass hats and their butt puppets don't like it one bit. They never will. After they've spent years minting the shiniest toy soldiers they can, I turn their pride and joy back into something that looks like just another college student, or yuppie, or street-corner bum. But looks can be deceiving. And besides, the brass hats don't like to get their hands dirty. That's my job.

"Coffee any good?" Trace slipped into a chair beside me. The cool air had brought the blush out in her cheeks. She pulled a knit cap off her head and shook out her long, thick hair. I wondered for a moment if there was anyone special she cared for, or who cared for her. I'd never asked and she'd never offered. I hoped there was someone in her life. Loneliness is something this old Rogue understands all too well.

"Yeah. Hits the spot. Whadda we got?"

Paul joined us. He slid a big mug of Colombia's

finest blend over to Trace and sat. "Danny's still inside. He's at a table in the lobby having coffee and reading the paper. From where he's sitting, Laski's room is visible, but just barely. HRT has six teams of two positioned inside as best they can on such short notice. The exterior perimeter is set. It looks good. Laski's bedroom window faces the mall area northeast of us. Sniper team says his curtains are drawn but the front desk gal says he's home. She said he always checks at the desk for messages when he leaves and when he comes back. Doesn't trust the security of his voicemail, I guess."

I looked my two shooters over closely. They appeared tired but alert. It had been a long day for everyone. "Trace?"

"Hotel's at three-quarters capacity. People all over the place. If any shooting starts, the collateral-damage factor could be very negative. I overheard a lot of talk about the shit happening downtown. People are getting worried, talking about early flights home and such. I did a scan on Laski's door and the walkway left and right. Used my mini-binocs from across the way and one floor down."

"Anything of interest to us?"

"Yeah, I think so. There's one of those expensive French-made miniature snap links hooked around the bottom support of the railing right in front of his door. It's been painted the same color as the railing. You'd never notice it unless you're looking for it or know it's there."

Now *that* was interesting. I'd seen and used the same snap link for high-speed, low-drag rappelling and as a safety link while hanging my wild and crazy ass out of Little Birds from the 160 SOAR. Each tiny link cost us a cool $50 per unit. The French firm that makes 'em guarantees their product to be defect free. They x-ray each and every damn link to make sure there's no hidden flaw in the workmanship. The Army's ranger battalions bought boatloads of these things to use for individual safety harnesses. This after they lost a few good men in a helo accident some time back. The best part about the link is its patented quick-release lever. Once down you can get away from your harness with one quick tug of the lever. That's what killed the rangers using their old system. They couldn't clear the wreckage before the chopper blew. This due to the shitty 'beaners they were using to attach themselves to their safety lines.

"Can he BASE jump the walkway?" I asked.

"Fuck no!" replied Kossens. "Way too low, boss. It's only nine stories. A 'chute would never open in time."

"He *could* rappel, however, using the railing support as an anchor point and the link for his descent line. All he needs is 120 feet of half-inch tubular nylon sling and a brake bar system. He could be out the door and on the floor in nothing flat," mused Trace as she sipped at her coffee.

"That's how I'd do it," I said. "Keep my shit-and-git bag near the door and have my lowering line rigged to hop-and-pop on a moment's notice. Where's the nearest exit outta the hotel from where he'd land on the ground floor?"

Paul glanced at Trace before answering me. The look on their faces told me they'd had the same thought. "About fifteen feet away if he dropped straight down. It opens out into a small parking lot. He'd only have to bust the exterior perimeter to escape."

"Bingo!" I said. "Now's here what we're gonna do . . ."

* * *

It was a good plan. However, Papa Murphy was nowhere to be found so I couldn't run it past him for his expert opinion of my work. No matter. Murf is a motherfucker anyway. I've yet to get an honest answer out of him. He enjoys a good laugh at my expense too much.

I sent Paul and Trace back to the lobby. They'd be my backup team. I briefed Danny over a (I hoped) secure cell phone and then he casually drifted over toward the predicted exit point at ground zero. Using the German-made monocular I carry in my daypack for just such occasions, I double-checked Trace's observation about the frog snap link. She was right. Dahlgren was also right about the people in the hotel. There were so many assholes moving in and out and wandering around the big lobby that even I was able to lose myself in the crush. I worked my way over to where I could clearly see Danny and took up a position beneath the first floor balcony that ran around the perimeter of the atrium. I couldn't be seen by anyone looking straight down from any of the floors above me. Danny gave a discreet thumbs-up sign, telling me I was directly in line with the speedy little snap link nine floors above my head. When Laski left his room to do his rappel thing down to the lobby—which my plan was sure gonna encourage him to do—I'd be waiting for him right when he hit the ground. Once I had him under physical control, Danny and I would hustle his ass out the side door and into a waiting HRT mobile unit. From there we'd hit the makeshift helipad at the sports field, and then wing like a bat outta hell for the PANG.

Then I'd have a chat with Jackie-Boy in private.

Like I said, it was a pretty good plan for the spur of the moment.

I gave Danny the high sign and watched him make the call from his cell. Seconds later the distant, high-pitched wail of a half-dozen police sirens could be heard in the hotel's lobby. I'd made it clear with the captain in charge of my little diversion that I wanted his officers to drive around the hotel at least twice. I needed Jack to hear "The Man" coming and decide to grab his shit and boogie. For good measure I'd requested a flyover by one of the two hawks we'd left on station at the sports field. The *thumpa-thumpa-thumpa* of the ANG bird added a nice counterpoint to the police sirens as the hawk flew at speed directly past Jack's ninth floor window.

Yeah, that should get things moving upstairs.

I'd moved an HRT team up to Laski's floor and stationed them directly in front of the twin elevators where Jack couldn't help but see them the second he left his room. Another two operators were manning the walkway directly across the atrium on the other side of the hotel. Again, Jack wouldn't be able to miss them. With those avenues of escape sealed off, there'd be no way out but down. And down is where I like to be.

All around me people in the courtyard were registering the fact that the noisy commotion outside was starting to converge on this very hotel. Dads started hustling their families out of the pool, and the lobby began to empty as guests and visitors went outside to see what was happening. I wondered if they expected to see a mushroom cloud rising over the downtown area. Numerous doors opened on the floors opposite me. Guests, some scantily dressed, came to the railing, leaned over and began scanning the area below.

People are nuts, I reminded myself. The last place anyone should want to be is where police sirens are. It's the curious who end up dead. People who mind their own business and use good common sense seldom get the shit kicked outta them.

Mutherfucking showtime!

I saw Danny look up and then gaze right at me. He gave a curt nod. Jack had taken the bait and was making the leap. I readied myself. The cut-down shotgun was slung on a simple black nylon sling beneath my vest. I had jacked a federal tactical load into its chamber at the sports field when we'd landed. If Jack went ape-shit on me I'd blow his legs out from under him, then kick him in the pumpkin to put his lights out for a few minutes. Between Danny and me it would be no problem to manhandle Laski, conscious or not, out the exit and into HRT's getaway rig. I didn't want to kill the bastard unless there was no other option. I figured Laski would have programmed all his electronic gizmos with eleborate security codes. We didn't have the luxury of time to let NSA crack his fucking firewalls, nor superhero decoder rings to do the job ourselves on-site. I needed Jack alive and able to talk. We'd take care of the "willing" part later.

Even though I was waiting for it, I was startled when the rappel line suddenly snapped into view from nowhere. Jack was using half-inch nylon sling, which is both compact and extremely strong. It easily held his weight as he dropped from Point A to Point B in less than three seconds. I figured he'd have to use a lightweight, probably aluminum, brake bar and snap link to control his rapid decent. Once on the ground he'd have to pull the remaining length of the nylon sling through the snap link and over the brake bar in order to get clear of the line. He could also simply begin running for the exit point and let the line play itself out as he disappeared. But I wasn't planning on letting him take a fucking step once he touched down.

By now people were pointing upward and yelling about the man climbing over the railing. The cop cars were outside the main lobby, some of them with their sirens still blaring and light bars spinning. Pandefuckingmonium was about to break loose. I saw Danny trying to make his way over to me. He was having trouble getting through the crowd despite his size. I was beginning to wonder what was taking Jack so long when he materialized in front of me. His daypack was tightly molded to his back and he was wearing black Nomex work gloves to protect his hands from the burn a high speed, balls-to-the-wall, ninety-foot rappel will give you. Even before his booted feet touched down we had locked eyeballs. I recognized him from the photo bios Karen had made for us back in D.C. It was clear Jack recognized me from some-fuckingplace as the pupils of his eyes widened for half a second and then a not-so-nice smile erupted across his Eastern European face.

"MARCINKO!"

I jerked the pump gun upward and took a half-step toward Jack's smiling face. That's when that asshole Murphy came back from wherever it was he'd been when I'd so badly wanted to consult with him about my plan. Instead of stopping to disengage himself from the line, Jack simply whipped out a vicious little switchblade from where he'd clipped it to a loop on his daypack and cut himself free in a single stroke. Hmmm, I thought to myself, I hadn't considered *that* solution. But Jack didn't stop there. In one fluid motion he sidestepped toward me while dropping into a tight crouch. His fucking knife never stopped moving. It buried itself into my forearm between the elbow and the wrist. My right forearm. Which is connected to my right hand. Which is connected to my *fucking trigger finger!*

I didn't know Laski was left-handed. It was not a good time to learn this little personal detail.

I let out a howl as I felt my index finger pop off the trigger's smooth metal face on its own accord. Laski pumped his embedded blade once into my arm and the jumble of nerves he hit went stark raving mad. I lost all feeling from my elbow down. Jack then executed a very pretty little snap kick that damn near busted my hand holding the 12-gauge's wooden pump, which at this point was the only hand holding onto the gun at all. Murphy was working overtime and I was paying the price. Now Jack came directly at me. I threw myself backward and in doing so saved my right eye. But he wasn't backing off. I stood between him and a chance at freedom. If I went down, he had a clear shot out the door. And if I gave him half a second he could grab one of the civilian fuckers now going crazy around us and it would become a hostage situation. That I did not need.

Laski lunged. I hollowed out as I'd been taught to do by Mr. Worden. Jack's blade missed my belly by less than half an inch. It tore the shit out of my new L.L. Bean vest, however, and *that* pissed me the fuck off! I drew the Wor-Tech from my left pocket with my left hand. Snapping the big blade open I heard it lock into place even as I executed a quick snap cut at Jack's right cheek. Surprise, surprise *cocksucker!* The razor-sharp point of my blade sliced him open like a piece of

soft fruit. Blood rushed from the wound like dirty
water from an open sewer. Laski danced back, bump-
ing into a fat, elderly woman wearing a parrot-pink
muumuu. It was almost comical . . . until he spun
around and knifed the poor old lady in the throat.

I heard Danny calling to me from somewhere
nearby. The crowd was wild at this point with a stam-
pede of crazed jerk-offs trying to get out the very exit
Jack had been making for. I prayed the HRT guys outside wouldn't fuck up and open fire on the first person
who came through the door, and I prayed the HRT
guys *inside* on the upper floors could get a shot at Jack
before he whacked anyone else, especially *moi*. Where
Trace and Paul were I had not a fucking clue. Just
when I thought it couldn't possibly get any worse, it
did.

I rotated my knife from the forward to the reverse
grip as Jack unholstered a full-size Glock 17. Fucker
was apparently as good with his right hand as he was
with his left. I stopped advancing and swiftly stepped
to the left to get clear of his line of fire. But it wasn't
me he was concerned with. Raising the high capacity
automatic pistol Laski began squeezing off round
after round into the guests now clogging the upper
floor walkways. I knew he had eighteen rounds of
high-power ammunition in the gun. With each shot I
saw a man, a woman, or child stagger and fall. With a
furious bellow I began bulling my way toward the
fucking asshole, pushing and shoving and kicking out
of the way anyone in my path. I had to get to Laski
before he killed anyone else. I still couldn't feel my
lower right arm and hand, so going for my own Glock
was pointless. Besides, the thought of both of us blasting away at each other at close range with all the inno-

cent bystanders now running helter-skelter through the hotel lobby was unacceptable.

I suddenly saw Danny emerge out of the chaos of the melee. In his hand was the massive .41 Magnum. He yelled something incomprehensible and then leveled the stainless steel revolver at Jack's back. Like a freaking wraith the Nemesis operator dropped to the floor, spun around on his side, and fired a string of rounds at Danny's fully exposed figure. I saw each round slam into the big man's chest, their combined force shoving him backward into the crowd. I heard the Magnum go off and the resulting screams as those around Danny's fallen body went even crazier than they had been before. Laski began scuttling across the floor like a crab in heat and I chased after the bastard as best I could. Every time he evaded someone I ended up pushing them down and out of my way. I still had the knife in my left hand and it was my very best intention to ram it up Jack's ass when I caught up with him. The world as I knew it had turned to shit. Where the *fuck* were Trace and Paul?

Laski gained his feet and executed a near perfect combat magazine change just as I reached him. Jacking the Glock's slide back he chambered a round and immediately shot a man off to my right and half a step behind me. He then shot a woman who'd made the mistake of cutting in between us. Pieces of her brain and jagged shards of skull bone splattered over my face. I dropped to one knee to make a smaller target of myself. Dropping the fucking knife I reached around with my left hand and managed to jerk my G-26 free of its holster. I was in a gunfight whether I wanted to be or not. When in Rome . . .

I brought the little pistol to bear even while expecting to take a round between the eyes as I was doing so. My chest was heaving and it was hard for me to see with the chunks of gooey-sticky brain matter now clinging to my face. I heard the unmistakable sound of a high-power rifle being fired in my direction. Rolling, I knocked over two little kids screaming and crying for their mother. I heard the rifle's report again. This time I threw myself forward and rolled to a standing crouch, the Glock outstretched and sweeping the area in front of me.

I saw Jack just as he shot Trace in the chest. *GOD-DAMN!* She rocked back, her Kimber still coming up as she tried to get a bead on the miserable bastard. I was screaming now, howling like a wounded dog, frothing at the fucking mouth like a lunatic who's just cut his own dick off. Tunnel vision set in. I only saw Jack Laski smiling like the evil SOB he was, preparing to pump another round into Trace's upper body. Anyone in my path was being thrown aside as I plowed my way through the mass of idiots and moth-erfuckers separating me from my teammate. I lost it completely when I heard the Glock's report and saw the all-black handgun buck in Laski's hand. Trace jerked hard as a second round hit her. She then half-turned and slumped to the ground, her pistol falling free and clattering away as someone kicked it in a mad dash to escape the insanity.

"JAAAAAAAACK!"

He heard me. Then he saw me. What he saw must have been *velly velly* bad because his eyes opened wide and for a moment I smelled the stink of fear coming off him like smoke off a burning tire. I fired with my left arm extended and kept moving forward. Every time my left foot hit the deck I pressed the little gun's trigger. I didn't feel its recoil, I didn't see its front sight, and I didn't hear its roar. I just kept pressing the trigger and keeping my eyes locked onto Laski's as the gap closed between us.

I saw the first round clip his right ear lobe. If he felt the wound he didn't show it. My second and third rounds hit him low in the belly. He raised his pistol at me and squeezed off a round. I felt a sharp tug at my hip but that didn't stop me. Danny was down. Trace was down. Jack was going down and I was putting him there. I felt nothing but rage. My fourth, fifth and sixth rounds took him squarely in the chest. He jerked back under their combined impacts, the open snout of his barrel now pointing upward and away from me. A huge explosion blew past me from behind my right flank. Dahlgren! The little bitch was up on one elbow, her backup gun in her hand. Where the FUCK she carries that little shit I don't know! Jack's mouth dropped open as the .380 JHP hit him square in the groin. He dropped his pistol and fell to his knees. When I reached him he was doubled over holding whatever was left of his dick with both hands.

He was still breathing.

"Game's over, Jack!" I wheezed as I pointed my gun at the back of his head. "Give it up."

"DICK!"

I was already pressing my trigger when Trace's hoarse warning reached my ears. I saw the fucking switchblade's gleam as Laski tried to right himself and shove the damn thing into my gut. My round entered his skull at the crown and skittered along his scalp. Trace's bullet did much better. It punctured his left temple and blew out the right side of his head in a spray of oxygenated blood and splintered bone. Laski dropped dead at my feet. Yeah, I'd wanted him alive.

Shit happens.

I holstered up and knelt beside Trace. "Where you hit?" I asked her. The lobby was suddenly empty except for a blur of black HRT uniforms coming at us from every direction. Trace tried to sit up and I gently pushed her back down. Thanks to her all-black outfit, I couldn't see where she was bleeding, or how much. "Easy, easy there. Help's on the way. How bad is it, can you tell?"

Trace nodded. "He shot me in my tits, damn it! Oh, this hurts! This hurts bad, Dick!" Pushing my hand away she sat up and leaned over so her head was resting on her knees. She wrapped both arms around her self and began slowly rocking back and forth.

A lightbulb went off over my head.

"You're wearing your vest, aren't you?" I roared in relief.

"Uh-huh," she moaned. "I always do, unlike some dumb Slavic motherfuckers I know!"

"Point made! I'll never leave home without it again."

I looked up and saw Barrett standing half a mountain tall. He was smiling, the massive hand cannon he carries hanging lazily by his side in one huge hand. "Fucking 9-mm bullshit! Hits like a sissy! If it ain't a .40-plus it's worthless as tits on a boar!"

"Hey, watch the tits jokes, okay? The girls are hurtin' here. We got some serious pain!" Trace looked up at Danny and smiled weakly. "I got him, Danny. I blew his fucking brains out for this."

"Help me get her up!" I ordered. Danny holstered his revolver and together we carefully lifted Trace to her feet. "Can you walk?"

"Yeah, in a minute maybe. Just give me some room, a little air. I'll be fine."

"Danny? Strip the daypack off this dead fuck's back. All the shit we need is in it. I wanna find Kossens and get the fuck outta here." As Barrett cut the bloody pack from Laski's body, I saw Paul waving from the third floor, a big-ass black HRT rifle slung across his back.

"GET YOUR FUCKING SELF DOWN HERE, SAILOR! WE GOT SHIT TO DO!"

Paul nodded his understanding and began running for the elevator. Fuck, I sure was happy to see him all in one piece. It was then the pain hit me. Reaching down I felt around my upper left hip. Sure as shit, I was bleeding! "Ah, fuck me to tears, Danny! I took a round. Upper hip. Feels like it nailed me good!"

Tossing the dead man's daypack to Kossens who'd just reached us Danny knelt beside me and began feeling around the wound. I grimaced but kept my fucking mouth shut. There were people lying all around me in much worse shape. "Yeah, he took a hunk of blubber outta your SEAL hide but you'll live."

"Fuck you very much," I countered. "Let's go. I'm starting to get depressed." I started for the wide glass doors leading from the lobby to the great outdoors. Paul, after recovering the Kimber, slipped an arm around Trace and stayed with her as we left the now shattered Hotel Campbell. Danny covered our six, telling the HRT commander who'd appeared out of nowhere that we were headed back to the PANG.

"Before you leave you might want to hear this, sir."

I stopped. "Hear what, brother?"

The federal counterterrorist officer looked each of us over. We were a fucking mess. But we were alive. It had been one hell of a firefight. At least this time it had been us and not HRT who'd taken the hard hits.

"That device they had downtown was command detonated about five minutes ago. Blast killed a shit-load of people in the area. There are bodies all over the place, mostly cops and firefighters. We can't get to the wounded . . ."

"Why the fuck not?" I asked.

"HAZMAT is registering radioactive contamination at the blast zone. They're pulling back another ten blocks and suiting the Guard up to go in with protective gear. The bastards set off a dirty nuke! The whole city is freaking out and the mayor is one of the dead at the scene. It's a fucking mess."

"And it ain't over yet," I said quietly. "I'm afraid we've only just seen the beginning." I didn't know exactly what Blanchard was up to, blowing a fucking dirty nuke instead of the SADM he'd gone to such trouble to steal. I started walking toward the soccer field where my helos were warming up for the flight back to the PANG. My team fell in beside me, each of us silent and alone in our private thoughts. Night had fallen and with it my spirits. Despite my best efforts, Blanchard still controlled the agenda. I promised myself that would change soon. I was coming for Max Blanchard. It was just a matter of time. It was just a matter of will.

14

"The vital point in actual warfare is to apply to the enemy what we do not wish to be applied ourselves and at the same time not to let the enemy apply it to us. Therefore, it is most important that what we consider would embarrass the enemy we should apply to them before they can do the same to us; we must always forestall them."

ADMIRAL MARQUIS TOGO HEILHACHIRO
to the Officers of the Japanese Fleet, February 1905

IT HAD BEGUN AND I WASN'T IN ANY POSITION TO STOP IT. Before now I'd always played out scenarios of this magnitude in a war room somewhere, or around the bar with my shooters. What if this . . . ? What if that . . . ? "The sky is falling," warned Chicken Little. No one listened to the little feathered fucker. I can relate. When Red Cell began its operations I began warning my superiors about the clear and present danger terrorists posed to our poorly protected nuclear weapons sites. Forget the nuclear power plants scattered around the country. Security at those sites was and is still absurd; they're wide open to assault and attack. I didn't waste time analyzing *that* vulnerability. Why bother to fuck with a clumsy old power plant when you could so easily walk off with a convenient, handheld world buster?

Like poor old Chicken Little, I learned how easily the powers-that-be can turn a deaf ear. How much they *want* to turn a deaf ear. Even when we were tromping around setting demolition charges in nuclear submarines' torpedo rooms, the brass deemed it politically correct to turn a blind eye to the truth. Terrorism and terrorists were a joke to the senior Pentagon statesmen. They were working on fighting the real wars. Wars with ships and tanks and airplanes and divisions of hairy-assed men all loaded down with 200 heavy pounds of lightweight equipment on their backs. The problem was the wars they wanted to fight had already been fought decades earlier. Our new enemies were renegade nation-states with miniature armies and limited resources. Their leaders knew a face-to-face with the United States military machine was a no-win situation. So they had begun conducting their wars against us using small bands of highly organized, motivated, and trained terrorists. State-sponsored terrorism was the Black Plague of the new millennium. I'd seen it coming a long, long time ago. I'd seen the sky crashing in on us and had raised the alert. I'd been ignored, banished, and then disgraced for failing to toe the party line. Yep, Chicken Little was a fella I could identify with. Especially now at 3000 feet above the earth in a helo filled with my wounded shooters.

A disaster of fucking huge proportions was unfolding below us, and I knew even more bad things were just waiting in the wings for their cue.

"My God, Dick! What the fuck . . . ?" Danny Barrett's voice crackled in my headset as we stared out the port side of the 'hawk as it hauled ass for the PANG base. On the streets below, major gridlock was building as thousands of cars sat on Portland's freeways and highways, stalled bumper to bumper in their owners' efforts to flee the city. As we reached the Columbia River I asked the pilot to take her down to 1000 feet and fly the river. We dropped hard and fast, leveling out in the darkness and assuming a course that put the well-lit city on Danny's and my side of the 'hawk.

"Big smoke over there," I pointed out to Barrett. "I take it that's where Chinatown is?"

"Roger that, Captain," interjected our pilot. "But 'was' might be a better word. That's where the device went off. I understand the explosion was pretty nasty. Natural gas lines got busted open and at least one gas station went up. The firefighters can't go in because of radioactive contamination. They haven't got the gear or the training to deal with a major fire *and* radiation poisoning. The perimeter was pulled back from ten to twenty blocks in all directions. An evacuation of Ground Zero was ordered and the entire police bureau is handling that, even reserve officers and cadets have been called up to help."

"What about the fires?" Barrett asked.

"They're gonna burn, sir. Until someone down there with some authority sorts things out and makes some good decisions, all you see going up in smoke will be allowed to do just that. The mayor's dead, the city council is on tranquilizers, and the uniformed brass is arm wrestling to see who gets to call the shots. They're all fucked up down there. My guess is the Feds will step in any minute now and take control."

Even from a thousand feet in the air, the devastation below was unmistakable. The fire department had already trucked in a half-dozen powerful klieg lights that gave the whole scene the surreal look of a movie set, or a scene out of an old black-and-white war movie. But this was no Hollywood make-believe. Through the dense veil of smoke and airborne debris, I could see that almost a full block of Portland had been leveled to nothing more than a steaming mass of twisted iron and rubble. Pockets of bright orange flame punctuated the entire area like a parody of streetlamps. At one side of the blast zone I saw that part of an elaborate Chinese-style gate still stood. Adorned with the figure of a massive stone lion and dozens of dragons, it struck me as an oddly appropriate entranceway to this small piece of Hell that had materialized beneath me.

And this, I reminded myself, was just an appetizer. A so-called dirty nuke is a poor cousin to a real nuclear weapon. It's just some civilian radioactive waste strapped around a high explosive charge. And radioactive waste is surprisingly easy to come by. Visit a few big city hospital dumpsters and you'll likely be able to recover medical grade radioactive "garbage" that's been improperly disposed of. Scrape the insides of some old glow-in-the-dark watches and you'll probably get a nice bit more. Put that crud with some C-4 plastic explosives and run like hell. You've built yourself an oversized pipe bomb with some added radioactive fallout as a special bonus. As bad as this looked, it was a far cry from what would happen if Blanchard detonated the SADM. What the fuck was his game? Why bother firing a warning shot like this, allowing us more time to organize against him?

As I gazed down at the panic-stricken city, I thought about what the pilot had told me. Every son of a bitch who had anything resembling a uniform, even reservists and cadets, was being brought to the blast site. There wasn't going to be anybody left to keep the rest of the city under guard. Unlike New York City, which had enough cops and firemen to handle a catastrophe like 9/11 and still keep men on patrol, Portland would have to use every last man they had to handle tonight's ratfuck. Blanchard would have free reign to plant the SADM anywhere he fucking wanted without interference. Hell, he could probably stroll into City Hall with the goddamn thing under his arm and leave it on the mayor's desk. (Former mayor, I mean. R.I.P.)

Then I remembered Karen's comment that they wouldn't be able to keep the missing SADM out of the news much longer, given what was going down in Portland. Of course, Marcinko, that's the other reason for this first bomb. Blanchard was just clearing his throat, making sure he had everybody's attention. Testing the microphone, as it were. The whole point of this fucking bullshit wasn't to blow up Portland, it was to spread his sick message to the masses. And the best way to do that was to make sure all cameras were rolling when he pulled out the big bomb. Better TV that way. He was going for ratings, the dirty cocksucker. I didn't like it, but at least I felt I was starting to get some sort of understanding of the way Blanchard's brain worked.

Sitting back, I looked over at Trace. A PJ was using a penlight to check her out. She'd pulled off her turtleneck and peeled off the damaged ballistic vest. I could see a baseball-sized crater that had already turned black and blue—almost green, really—due to massive internal hemorrhaging. I knew she'd been hit twice like that by two high-velocity rounds. Even now the pain must have been excruciating but Dahlgren just sat there with her eyes closed as the trauma medic worked on her.

"She'll be fine," Danny said reassuringly. "One tough soldier."

"PANG coming up, sir," the pilot announced. We'll be on the ground in five mikes. I've asked for an ambulance to stand by so your people won't have to walk. Our clinic staff is on call and ready to receive patients. They're shit-hot docs. You're in good hands."

I thanked the aircrew, then turned my attention back to my next order of business: Laski's little black bag. Eyes closed and chin down, Paul was holding onto it with a death grip. We'd quickly rifled through it before taking off from the soccer field and found an impressive little collection of cell phones, a laptop, a Palm Pilot, and two beaten-up notebook computers. These two laptops were my main interest and I wanted to crack them wide open as soon as possible. I'd already called Karen using Danny's cell and briefed her on how the hit on Laski had gone down. I told her we'd grabbed the command and control gear for Nemesis and that I needed an egghead on the ground ASAP who could bust through the security firewalls keeping me from what I needed to know in order to locate and recover the nuke. She promised me OISA would fly an asset who lived in Seattle to the PANG immediately. "He's one of Bill Gates's golden boys," she said. "Inner-circle type. As smart and capable as they come."

Which was exactly what I needed.

"When we're on the ground get yourself and these two squared away with the docs," I told Danny. "I'm gonna have the PJ here slap a Band-Aid on my hip so I can get Laski's shit over to the Op-Center, ready for Karen's hotshot to crack when he arrives. I want Trace and Paul to get some sleep. We need ammo, full tac-harnesses, new vests, and the most up-to-date intel dump Mulcahy can provide from D.C. Let's link back up in thirty mikes at the Op-Center. Got it?"

"Loud and clear."

The 'hawk lined up on the PANG runway it had been assigned and began its descent. Off to my right I could see Portland International Airport. It was totally locked down, no flights coming in or going out. All air space for a hundred miles round Portland was off limits to anyone but the military. The PANG F-16 pilots were flying fully loaded fighters and had orders to shoot down anything that didn't do *exactly* as the pilots ordered. Additional fighter and refueling support had been tasked out of McChord Air Force Base outside Tacoma, Washington. Three platoons of SEALs from ST-1 at Coronado were en route to start checking hulls and doing ship searches in the Port of Portland and on the Columbia River. A combat control team from McChord was also inbound to assist in handling the growing military air traffic at both the PANG and the civilian airport, which would soon fall under the military's control. Out in civilian land, no such direction or order was possible.

We were seconds from touching down. I nudged Paul and woke him up. Shit, I wish I could still fall asleep anywhere and anytime!

"You think the colonel knows his cells are being taken down by now?" Danny asked me.

I turned toward him. We were near nose to nose, the hot air of the turbine engine washing over us and the familiar smell of JP-4 reminding me of a thousand other launch sites. "Yeah, he's got to know we're on his ass. But it doesn't matter to him. He's still in control of the device. He's still in control of the mission. He's still got half a dozen badass gunslingers at his side, and he's the only girl in town who knows where and when the hammer's going to drop. He'll be more cautious now, but that's about it. All we got is bodies, bullet wounds, and a ticking clock. Blanchard is still the target, and we still got a job to do."

As the bird flared and settled I leaned over and slid the armored port side door open. I wanted out of the fucking helo in the worst of ways. I wanted to walk on the runway and for one fucking moment be alone with my own thoughts. I needed space.

I tossed the headset to the chief and headed out onto the dark tarmac of the runway. Shoving my swollen hands into my fucking *DEE*stroyed down vest I headed for the most remote corner of the field I could find. No one challenged me. No one dared. I needed some time to think about my next, and possibly my last move.

15

"Go into emptiness, strike voids, bypass what he
defends, hit him where he does not expect you."

THE "MARTIAL" EMPEROR TS'AO TS'AO (A.D. 155–220)

"YOU'RE SHITTING ME? WHEN? YOU'RE BRINGING HIM
here? Yes, yes. Perfect! Great. Let's do it!" I punched
off the cell and tossed it back to Danny. At last we'd
gotten a fucking break!

"What's up?" After getting Trace over to the clinic,
Barrett ran me down at the Op-Center. Unlike Dahlgren, he favored a Level III ballistic vest with both
front and rear ceramic plates. Because of this extra protection, the rounds Laski threw at him had done no
more than raise a few welts on his chest under the vest.

"That was one of the local FBI guys. Two street cops
stopped a guy carrying a black daypack hotfooting it
away from the blast site downtown. He didn't have
any I.D. and tried to run. With all the commotion going
on, they just threw him in a holding cell and hauled ass
back out on the street. Well, they finally got around to
booking the guy and guess what? His fingerprints are
in the system. His name is Richard Lassiter, recently

retired Chief Richard Lassiter of the U.S. Army. Warrant officer type. Special-fucking-Forces."

Barrett smiled up at me. "Let me guess—a close personal friend and associate of Colonel Max Blanchard?"

"You got it. Lassiter's specialty is communications and computers. He designed Nemesis's hi-tech load package for Blanchard. When his name popped up on the NCIC hotlist, the local cops called the Bureau's Domestic Terrorism squad in Portland. They picked up Mr. Lassiter and the bag he was carrying while we were in Tigard doing the bad thing. Lassiter is en route here under heavy guard."

Barrett grunted. "Figure he's the one who detonated the dirty nuke?"

"Probably. I'm starting to see where Blanchard is going with all this. Not only has he got national attention focused on Portland right now, he's got the whole fucking world watching! If he'd just detonated the SADM without warning, there'd be no way he could be sure his message would get out after the fact, no way to claim responsibility. This way he ups the ante a step at a time. Plus, he's got thousands of people trapped out on the streets and in the open. He's got panic building big-time. This is a world-class media event right now and he's using it to his best advantage. The longer the threat hangs in the air, the more his power increases. He figures that when he finally does detonate the real deal, the entire planet will know who he is, why he's done it, and the civilian body count will be maxed out to boot because half the city will probably be sitting in their cars on the freeway. Let's face it, it's never been fucking politically expedient to prepare Americans for the reality of evacuation."

Barrett shook a cigarette out of a crumpled pack and lit it up. "So we should be hearing from him pretty soon, yes? I mean, there's been no communication about *Yahweh* or any of the other silly shit we heard on the tape in Washington after Beckstein was hit. The president sure as shit isn't going to release the tape to the media. Blanchard needs to announce his agenda, and he needs to do it pretty damn quick because he doesn't know how much time he's got before we might get to his cell."

Danny was right. I'd been so close to the action I'd failed to see the obvious second part to Blanchard's plan. There *had* to be a public communiqué coming from Blanchard that would announce his agenda and intentions. He was a terrorist. Terrorists have grievances and demands. I'd bet my last bottle of gin that Blanchard was enough of an egomaniac that he'd be sure the nation heard his, and directly *from* him.

A senior airman approached with a secure cell phone in hand. "Mr. Marcinko? Phone, sir. Ms. Fairfield in Washington." He handed me the phone and promptly disappeared.

"Whaddya got for me, Karen?"

It was a flawless connection. The best American taxpayer money can buy. "Dick, I've got two teams of investigators combing Colonel Blanchard's two personal properties in Gibsonville, North Carolina, and Bend, Oregon. Nothing interesting out of North Carolina yet, but the Bend site shows signs of recent occupation. A lot of sterilizing of the area appears to have occurred. My people on the ground believe that's where his crew took the device after the hit on NEST."

"Good news, Karen," I told her. Actually the information was worth fuck-all to me. We were *behind* Blanchard. I needed to get out in front of the bastard. I didn't care if he'd taken the nuke home to meet his mama over a meatloaf dinner. Where the fuck was it right now? "I assume you've heard the local cops have a guy named Lassiter in custody? He's one of the Colonel's men and I'm betting he's responsible for setting off the dirty nuke downtown. The feds are flying him here right now. We're gonna chat with Mr. Lassiter in a short-short. Where's the egghead you promised me?"

"He's in the air now. Should be at your location anytime now. Who's going to interview this Lassiter character?"

I heard the concern in Karen's voice. I had to admit my record to date wasn't too reassuring when it came to this shit; we were a paltry one for five now in the Blanchard survivor series. "The Feds," I told her. "He's their prisoner. We'll sit this one out and see what they come up with."

I thought I heard an audible sigh of relief on the other end of the phone. "Dick, that's the best way to go right now. Let the FBI do their job. As hard as it may be for you to believe, they're actually better trained than you are in this one particular area. Did they get any gear off him?"

"Yeah, a backpack like the one Laski was carrying. Matching cell phones, laptop, the works. He had a key to a room in a downtown hotel not too far from Chinatown. These guys are all spread out and running their operations from some pretty high-class digs. There's even more of a pattern to all this but I'm not seeing it yet. Gimme some time, though, and I'll figure it out."

"How's your team holding up? I understand everyone's taken some pretty hard hits."

I turned and looked out the window. A light plane was landing—my computer geek from Seattle had probably arrived. Running my hand through my hair, I considered the proper response to Karen's question. I didn't want Karen even to think about pulling us out because of the semi-battered condition we were in. I finish what I start and Blanchard had made this feel very, very personal to me.

I looked over at Danny Barrett. He'd told me Paul was fine, no further bumps or bruises. Trace was sore as shit and bruised to beat the band, but absolutely mobile. My hip ached but the PJ had sewed me closed with a few stitches, given me some pills for the pain and a shot of something or other to ward off infection. If Danny was feeling poorly I sure couldn't see any sign of it. The big bastard was busily cleaning his .41 and drinking black coffee by the gallon. "Karen, at the rate the team is getting dinged, I could use a wheelbarrow full of Mix and Match pig parts and Doc Frankenstein to attach them! We're hurtin', but we're good to go."

"Then I'll get off this line and let you get on with it. The president sends his regards. He's weathering a pretty nasty political storm right now. But he says he'll hang in there if you will."

"Tell him we're gonna pull through. I'll get this fucker, Karen. Believe me, I'll get him."

"I know you will. And rest assured, if I find those pig parts, you've got first dibs on them. Not that you need any more pig in you, sweetheart."

She hung up while I was still laughing.

The door to the Op-Center opened and a tall black

man in khaki pants and a navy blue button-down shirt entered, escorted by a heavily armed Air Force security guard. The stranger walked over with his hand out and a friendly smile on his face. "Mr. Marcinko? I'm George Moore. I work for our mutual friend in Washington. I believe you have need of my services?"

I shook hands with George and invited him to sit down. "Danny, will you get the fucking bag of toys we got off Laski?" As Barrett headed out the door for the secure lockup where we'd stashed Jack's boogie bag, I looked over Mr. Moore. Karen had said he was one of Wild Bill Gates's inner circle. I wanted to know what the fuck that meant exactly.

"Karen says you work pretty closely with Bill Gates. That so?"

Moore laughed. "Yes, in a manner of speaking. I started out with Mr. Gates but later, after I made me a few bucks in software development for his company, I decided to go independent. Now I'm a consultant to the technology business specializing in software. Many of the programs the military relies upon I've had a hand in creating. In fact, I'd be surprised if you hadn't encountered some of my work yourself somewhere along the way."

"Very likely. But what I'm looking for today is somebody who can bust the firewalls I'm thinking are in place on these laptops we picked up today. Sound like something you might be able to handle for me?"

"Most certainly." There was a quiet strength and confidence to Moore I liked. He was no namby-pamby cyber-cowboy. He'd been around and he knew the score. Moore was a player in a world I wasn't privy to. It wasn't my world, but he deserved my respect and I gave it to him. Unlike some of his less evolved warrior brothers, the Rogue always appreciates people who genuinely excel at whatever their chosen field might be. I don't give a fuck if you can shoot a gun or hold your own in a fight, as long as you know your own shit better than anybody else. If you know what you know, you're probably gonna be okay in my book.

"What are you hoping to find on this man's hardware, Mr. Marcinko?"

"The location of a man named Colonel Max Blanchard. And with him I expect to find a stolen nuclear device that's due to be detonated here in the city of Portland at any fucking moment."

Moore's eyes widened. "Well, sir, at least you're direct. I'll do my best for you."

"That's all I can ask for, friend."

We shook hands on it.

When Barrett returned with the bag, Moore laid out its contents in an orderly row. "I'll need a few minutes with this. Pretty standard hardware. We designed this operating system and the security firewalls for the special operations people. The owner has most likely thrown a few curves into the system but I should be able to get around those fairly easily. I'd say no more than thirty minutes and you'll have anything of value that's on the hard drive."

I grabbed Jack's two handwritten notebooks and Danny and I headed for the officers' lounge at the rear of the building. Laski may have jotted down something of interest to us, or perhaps he just liked keeping a poetry journal. White supremacist haikus. In any event I'm computer illiterate and proud of it! I only care about results and George was here to give me those, and probably for a pretty penny once he billed

Karen. Take a note: When the job is truly important, hire the best experts you can find no matter the cost. At least you'll make that bastard Murphy do some real work when he fucks you over.

"You take one of these notebooks, I'll take the other," I told Danny as we reached the lounge.

But before we could even find seats and read the first word, we were stunned by the sound and almost instantaneous shock wave of a massive blast that clearly originated somewhere quite nearby. A rush of hot rippled over us and we hit the floor out of an instinct that dated back to our training decades earlier in Vietnam. The lights throughout the building flickered off, then on, then off again. Seconds later the emergency generator system kicked in. Thanks to the emergency lights, I could see well enough to get around—and to notice that both Danny and I had drawn our guns. "What the *fuck* was that?" I asked him.

Barrett raged, "Fucking bomb, Dick. Somebody just hit the Op-Center!"

The bottom fell outta my guts. Dammit to hell, with all that was going on, something that now seemed obvious had never occurred to me. I was instantly up and running back the way we'd just come. I tripped over an unmoving body in the dim hallway but managed to keep my balance and forward momentum. Back in the Op-Center, people all around me were calling out for help and moaning in pain. The table where Moore had laid out the electronic equipment was an absolute bonfire and that entire portion of the room seemed to be in ruins. The air was full of the hard, pungent odor of C-4 plastic explosive. Sirens were approaching from every direction. The airman who'd patched Karen's call through to me was on his hands and knees puking. Then, in an instant I saw that he wasn't in fact kneeling; rather, his legs were simply gone from the knee down.

"We've got to find Moore!" I called to Danny.

I found George Moore almost exactly where I'd left him. Or more accurately what was left of George Moore. His lower trunk and legs were still seated in a chair, but the blast had blown the upper portion of his body clean away. There was no sign of the laptop or anything else we'd left him with. While someone was working valiantly to put out the fire with a woefully small emergency extinguisher, I could see powerful flashlight beams cutting through the smoke and gloom in the Op-Center looking for survivors. Confusion whirled around us like a sandstorm.

"C'mon Danny, we need to keep moving, let the medics do their work here. Moore is dead . . . poor bastard. Lassiter will be here any minute. And no matter what I told Karen, I'm in no mood to go easy on him after this fuckup. Someone should have to pay in kind for what happened to George Moore, and I think Lassiter is a damn fine candidate."

I turned and Danny followed me through the acrid gloom of the bombed-out Op-Center. In retrospect, it was obvious what had happened. Laski had booby-trapped his laptop and in my frantic state I'd failed even to consider the possibility. Jack Laski had gotten the last word after all, and George Moore had paid the price for my oversight. And obviously I'd just lost everything George might have retrieved off the computer hard drive and the Palm Pilot. Goddamn it! Every fucking time we'd seen a hint of light at the end of the tunnel, it turned out to be a train headed in our direction. I was getting seriously sick of this shit. Kicking a door that was half blown down outta my way, I marched out into the cold crisp night. Danny was coughing his lungs out from the bullshit we'd been breathing ever since the bomb went off. I was so fucking mad I didn't care what I'd been inhaling! At least I still had the two notebooks. And Lassiter's shit from his daypack would be in our hands soon. That thought made me stop in my tracks.

"Goddamn it, Danny!" I hollered. "We gotta get to a radio right now and tell the Feds not to fuck with Lassiter's laptop! Damn thing is probably rigged like Jack's was. We need EO-fucking-D on-site now. I want that fucking hard drive pulled the very instant *after* they disarm the cocksucker. You handle that. I'm calling Karen and getting another egghead sent down. I hope Gates pays his people combat wages 'cause this next fucker is going to earn 'em!" I gave Danny's massive shoulder a friendly punch and began trotting for the control tower. From there I could reach Karen on a secure line. Danny would alert the FBI about the IED Lassiter most likely had in his kit. That would make their fucking day, I thought.

As I dogtrotted across the tarmac for the tower, I replayed in my head everything we'd faced in the last two days and, grudgingly, I realized I had to give Blanchard a certain kind of credit. I've taken on some serious international players in my career and been nearly done in by one or two of the best. But this homegrown son of a bitch was giving me a run for my money like no one else had. It didn't help that he was an operator, and had a team of operators riding shotgun for him. I'd run out of options and Lassiter was my only card left to play. I knew Blanchard hadn't already detonated the SADM only because he didn't think he was in any danger of getting caught. I knew he wasn't bluffing, he wasn't going to get an attack of conscience and decide that he couldn't do such a bad, bad thing. Nope, he was just biding his time. We—I— was nowhere close to him. I was getting the shit shot outta myself and my team and the fucking HRT. We were just nibbling at the edges of Nemesis and its self-proclaimed mission from *Yahweh*. I gave us a few more hours at best before the shit would really melt the fan. Lassiter's capture would not go unnoticed by Blanchard. If Jack was *Numba Two* in the organization it stood to figure Lassiter was the man behind the scenes when it came to having the whole fucking plan either on his laptop or in his head. That meant he knew where Blanchard and the rest of Nemesis would be found and where the nuke was to be detonated. He'd also know Blanchard's E&E plan. If nothing else, I planned to be waiting for him somewhere along that route with Trace, Paul, and Danny.

If my hunch was right we'd be hearing from Blanchard on the news very soon. He'd make his media appearance and scare the fucking shit outta anyone not already pissing in their drawers. Such an announce-ment would put even more unshielded targets on the streets and add to what was promising to be the largest mass murder in world fucking history carried out by a single terrorist organization. If it was a race war Blanchard wanted, he'd sure the hell have done his best to get one started. At the very least, the current admin-istration would crumble under the political repercus-sions of its failure—*my* failure—to prevent Portland from becoming a nuclear waste dump. The country would skew sideways under unimaginable pressures, with the already struggling economy going full tilt boogie into the shitter and our foreign policy collapsing as all efforts were turned inside our borders to save the Republic from self-immolation. Fuck! Deep breath. Okay, I needed to put this big-picture crap out of my head and focus only the task at hand, only deal with things I had a shot at controlling. If I started dwelling on the global implications of this situation, I wouldn't be able to keep my eyes on the prize. In this case, a titanium suitcase with enough firepower to take out a million or so of my fellow citizens. Not to mention yours truly!

Taking the tower's steps two at a time I burst into the controllers' bullpen and promptly found myself staring down the barrels of two M-9 Berettas and a 12-gauge riot gun. "Hi, fellas," I smiled while putting both hands up, "I'm Captain Richard Marcinko. How do you like me so far?"

It took five fucking precious minutes for the air police to sort things out. While they fiddle-fucked around I lay on my belly on the floor spread-eagled like a new bride after a hard ride in the sack. I'd have to check with the accountant and see what I was charging OISA for all this fun. Whatever it was we were going to triple it!

With brusque apologies I was finally hauled up off the floor, dusted off, given back my Glock and my knife, then handed a secure cell and told to go stand in the corner. Aye-aye, motherfucker! I got hold of Karen on the third ring and ran down the most recent disaster for her. I placed my request for Egghead #2 and told her I wanted a team of shooters from SIX sent my way ASAP.

"Why SIX, Dick?" she asked. "HRT is on-site and seem to be holding their own."

"They are," I answered, "but we've taken a beating and, for the final push, I want operators who I fucking know and who fucking know me. Blanchard has *his* shooters with him and it's making all the difference in the world right now. They are thinking and moving and fighting as a unit. It's an edge I don't have. HRT is shit-hot and I love the bastards to death, but if I'm gonna get a shot at Blanchard it's going to be up close and very personal. I need SEALs to back our play and I need the best fucking SEALs in the Teams and that's SIX. Can you make it happen?"

There was a pause at the other end. I heard a muffled whisper, then someone in the background talking. Suddenly Karen was back. "Dick, Clay just called his contact at the Navy. They don't like it but he used the president's authority and explained to them that anything less than immediate and total cooperation would see court martial proceedings initiated regardless of rank. You'll have your shooters. There's a couple of boat crews up in Bremerton that have been doing some training at the base there. I'll have the Air Force chop the fastest plane or chopper they've got at McChord over to Bremerton and then down to you. Will that do it?"

What a fucking gal! "Yeah, and tell Mulcahy I owe him one."

I heard Karen pass along my kudos. "He says you just need to do your fucking job, Dick. He's doing his."

"That's a hard-ass motherfucker you've got working for you, lady. I'm on it."

"I'm so sorry to hear about George. He was such a

brilliant man. And a kind one. Gates will be furious
when he hears this."

"All I can tell you is that it was quick," I said.
"Wasn't pretty, but at least he never knew what hit
him. Karen, I gotta go. Lassiter's chopper is coming in
and we've still got to disarm the fucking computer
and get a secure spot for the Feds to interrogate the
miserable bastard. Will you call Danny and tell him
when the egghead is going to arrive? And let him
know we've got shooters coming in. He'll handle the
arrangements. Out here!"

I tossed the cell to the nearest air cop and jogged
down the steps and out onto the tarmac. No tearful
farewells with my new buddies who almost blew my
fucking head off. Fire and medical crews were cleaning up the wrecked Op-Center. I could see the out-
line of several full body bags under the harsh glare of
the banks of emergency lights that had been set up
all around the building. Despite all this, I was once
again feeling confident. Like Clay said, all I had to do
was my job. If Blanchard punched our tickets right
now it wouldn't matter, just as long as I went out trying my very goddamned best. And for me to be able
to do my best, I needed to know I was surrounded by
the best.

When Karen asked why I had to have SEAL Team
SIX join this party, I told her the truth—but only part
of it. Full disclosure, it was a lot more personal than
I'd wanted her to know. If this was the most important
mission of my career, then I damn well wanted to
carry it out with the support of the team I'd created
out of my own sweat and blood. HRT might have
been just as skilled in the mechanics of waging war,
but I couldn't know with absolute certainty how

they'd respond in any and all situations. I knew SIX—because, in a lot of ways, I *am* SIX and SIX is me.

When the green light was given for me to commission a naval counterterrorist SEAL team, the word came down from the chief of Naval Operations that I had carte blanche to get the job done. And to accomplish my mission I had to think—and act—outside the standard issue Navy box I'd been brought up in. The creation, training, and fielding of such a force had never been done before, so there were no standards to adhere to and no previous efforts to guide me. It was like walking off the ramp of a C-130 at 25,000 feet above the earth at midnight. You just take a deep breath and do it, and hope the landing is a good one.

I had Chargin' Charlie Beckwith, founder and first commanding officer of the Army's elite DELTA team, to bounce ideas and experiences off. As a young Green Beret officer, Beckwith enjoyed the advantage of having been an exchange officer with the British Special Air Service, or SAS, England's top-notch counterterrorist force. He'd participated in their rigorous selection course and been tabbed after successfully completing it. He built DELTA along the same lines as SAS. Beckwith was also able to draft off the already existing fifth Special Forces Group's in-house CT unit. Called Blue Light, it was an organic, in-house Special Forces response to terrorism made up of a number of highly qualified and blooded Green Berets with Vietnam special projects experience and know-how. But for your old friend Demo Dick Marcinko, the waters were less well charted.

When it began, SEAL Team SIX had no formal program of instruction, so we made one up. There was no existing CT operator course, so we taught ourselves. If

we wanted to learn the best way of scaling the outside
of a ninety-story building, I'd assign an operator to
become the subject-matter expert for that block of
instruction. That's why I required creative, independent, intelligent SEALs on SIX. They had to be both
instructors and students to get the Team off the ground.

The first thing I needed was someone I could count
on one hundred percent to handle details and watch
my six as the new Team was launched. I pulled in
Norm Carley, an Academy graduate, who'd trained
with Britain's elite Special Boat Service. Norm had
stood up MOB 6 at SEAL Team 2 and his shooters
came closest at the time to a naval CT asset. Carley
had participated in a number of maritime ship take-
downs with the SBS and I knew he was a rock-solid,
smart, loyal teammate. He was the right man for the
job.

Command Master Chief Ken MacDonald came
next. Ken had been my swim buddy in UDTR
Training Class 26 and had done a two-year exchange
tour with the SBS. MacDonald was a no-nonsense,
hard-chargin' senior enlisted SEAL who knew all the
ropes and many of the men we'd need to make SIX go.
Between me, Carley, and MacDonald, the foundation
was laid and the seriously hard work began.

In the Navy, the captain's ultimate responsibility is
to prepare his people for war and to take them there
when they are needed. As the founder and commander of SIX, this was my primary objective. We were
setting the standards and there was no one qualified
or knowledgeable enough in the Navy to give us a
blessing—or withhold one. I was on my own.
Brigadier General Dick Scholtes, then the commanding general of the Joint Special Operations Command,

was aware of my unique spot. When he heard the Navy was going along with my approach—as had been made loud and clear by the CNO—he gave me my lead and helped guide me whenever he could with such thorny issues as unit interoperability. More than anyone, Scholtes got that I was one helluva brain surgeon but that my bedside manner sucked! (Okay, maybe it's still not perfect.) But I wasn't the lead dog for SIX because I was good at shining brass and kissing ass. I was there because I had the vision and the will to make things happen, and to do so with immediate, verifiable results.

I was also there because I wasn't interested in punching my ticket to make admiral. SIX required—*demanded*—a commander who would fully commit to the mission, operators, and the unit. A commander who would seek first and foremost the welfare of his men as opposed to the welfare of his career. I was willing to go into the trenches with my teammates, as opposed to the hallowed halls of command. The shooters building SIX needed to know they could depend on me at all times. If we were to succeed, they needed to see me shoulder to shoulder with them every day.

Take a fucking note! Too much bullshit has been spewed over the years about how and where my operators and I spent the little downtime we had, doing what we wanted to. The short version is this. I recognized early on that the rigorous demands I made on SIX's operators would soon burn them out. Every second they were on duty, they had to maintain a state of extraordinarily high operational readiness in case a mission came down without notice. There has to be time to relax, to decompress, to come down from hour after hour of adrenalin pumping through your body like water through a high-pressure hose. When we partied, we partied hard. Period. When we worked, we worked harder, longer, and at levels more demanding than *anyone* else in either the Navy or existing SEAL teams could conceive of, much less match. Period. In my mind those who bitch about SEAL Team SIX outfighting, outdrinking, and out-fucking all the other kids on the block are really say-ing they didn't have what it took to earn the right to run with the best in the business to begin with. I make no apologies and I make no excuses. Like Clint Eastwood says, a man needs to know his limitations.

Following the example set by the legendary Admiral Rickover, father of the Navy's modern nuclear submarine service, I made the first selection of SIX shooters personally. My criteria were simple. First, I was looking for a specific personality type. For the assaulters, the SEALs who would actually kick the doors down to get at the Tangos, I wanted super-charged, type-A personalities. These were primarily younger guys, the kind who would spend hours in the gym pumping iron and then run countless miles to attain an extreme state of physical conditioning. They were *super*-aggressive types and they had to be since they had the job of actually taking it to the terrorists at any time, from any place, using any means possible. Then I looked for some more standard type-A person-alities to provide a balance to the Super-A operators and form the main body of the Team. Finally, I looked for the borderline-A personality, or the Super-B. These were often the older, more mature SEALs who made excellent snipers and senior technicians. They had all been combat tested; they had all felt a bullet with their name on it go right past their ear. These were the "War Dogs!"

Everyone on SIX had to be trainable, and that meant they needed to possess the ability to adapt, to change their way of thinking and doing things. Everyone on SIX also needed to be fully capable of "going over the railing" as operators regardless of their positions within the Team. No purely backroom talent here. I wanted and needed exceptional dedication to the mission and a level of loyalty to the Team from my operators that was unheard of in the regular Navy. If SIX was going to be writing the book on naval counterterrorism, then each operator, regardless of rank, needed to share the responsibility of making the program work.

I personally interviewed all SEAL candidates for selection to the Team. Had the operator deployed at least once with a SEAL platoon? Had he seen combat? How had he performed under fire? Did he have any apprentice union trade skills? Foreign language capability? Was he married? Shacked up? A single guy on the prowl? What were his career goals? Was he flexible in his thinking? I ran the ratline to all those hairy-assed UDT and SEAL chiefs and put the names to them. Who was this guy? Did he have what it would take to be a shooter and looter on the hardest, meanest SEAL Team ever stood up? Would you go to war with him? After I'd checked each hopeful operator or officer out as completely I could, it was decision time. Some made it, some didn't. I pissed off the overall SEAL community big-time. They saw me as having a blank check and the heretofore unheard of opportunity to skim off the pick of the litter when it came to standing up and staffing a brand new shiny SEAL

Team. They were right. I did. Those were my orders and that was my mission. Straight from the CNO himself. Seemed pretty clear to me. They didn't have to like it, the new Team, or me.

They just had to do it.

And they paid it all back to me in spades when they finally succeeded in taking my command of SIX away from me. Of all the bullshit the Navy and my detractors in the SEAL community could have pulled, this was the worst. I loved each of my operators like a son. I loved commanding the roughest, toughest, baddest, and most capable SEALs ever to walk the face of the earth. I loved leading from the front rather than from behind a desk. I loved knowing that if the call came we would whip our enemies like they'd never been whipped before. SIX was my vision. It did not exist until I created it in my mind and then birthed it with as much pain and love as a mother does a newborn child. When it was taken from me for no other reason than petty jealousy and stupidity, it was as if they'd driven a steel rod through my roguish heart. Think outside the box? We did it better than anyone. Operate faster, farther, deeper, and meaner than anyone had ever gone before? Call on SIX. However, the Navy in all its vindictive pettiness and mindless worship of the conventional saw fit to separate me from what I so carefully and skillfully had built up.

But in the end it did them no good. Men—*real men*—will only go past the Gates of Hell and into the lair of Satan himself with a leader who has trained beside them and who they know is willing to shed his blood alongside theirs in battle.

Yes, I rewrote the rule book by declaring there were no rules—just *my rules*—in the business of identifying, hunting down, and bringing to justice the jackals who too often called themselves "freedom fighters" and "holy warriors." And now I was back in the saddle and hunting a renegade Special Forces colonel and the ball-busting weapons-grade atomic suitcase he'd bagged from our own tactical nuclear weapons arsenal.

Now you know why I'd insisted that SIX join in for the final run at Blanchard. It was sweet fucking satisfaction to get back what I thought of as my own team. Murphy, that rat-bastard, must have decided to fuck with the Navy more than me for once. I liked his style. Someone wearing whites back on the East Coast had to be spinning like a fucking top over this turn of events. There is justice, and when it comes my way I drink it in with as much pleasure as a tall glass of Dr. Bombay's finest Sapphire on the rocks, no salad, no perfume. Ahhhh!

In my gut, I had the feeling that the tide of this battle might just be turning a little bit in my favor. I had a live prisoner and his commo gear intact. I had another egghead inbound—and I'd ensured this one didn't get blown up while doing his job. I had a platoon of fucking hairy-assed, name-taking, skull-crushing shooters from the finest counterterrorist team in the world now under my command again. And I had Karen talking to me like the shit with Karras had never fucking happened.

It occurred to me that maybe I could get laid after all this was over. That idea alone was enough to put a new bounce in my roguish step as I went looking for my team.

16

"They were allowed a degree of personal freedom and initiative unheard of in the military, particularly in battle. The price they paid for this, of course, was that they lived with danger and were expected to do what normal soldiers could not."

MARK BOWDEN, *Black Hawk Down*

"We're expected to think outside the box . . . to make things work even when they're not supposed to work."

Unidentified SEAL petty officer in Afghanistan,
"Commandos' Fight Abroad Also a Hit at Home,"
Gregg Zoryoa, *USA Today*

"THE FBI JUST FINISHED WITH LASSITER," PAUL TOLD ME. "All they got was *Yahweh* this and *Yahweh* that from him. A bomb tech from the Portland Police Bureau deactivated the laptop's IED and the computer geek is cracking the firewalls now. If there's anything useful on the hard drive we'll have it any minute. Whaddaya want to do with this asshole?"

Like me, Paul was dressed in new camouflage fatigues. His combat harness was heavy laden with full thirty-round magazines and forty-mike high-explosive grenades for his Colt M4A1 modular assault rifle system, complete with visible and infrared laser aiming devices, sound suppressor, day and night optics, and even a handy-dandy little flashlight. Hanging off me by its Tactical Tailor three-point combat sling was a new Modular Weapon System assault rifle with the recently introduced Rail Adapter System. The compact 5.56 Colt rifle featured an improved butt stock and M203 grenade launcher capability. The rail adapter system, or RAS, allowed me to quickly enhance the rifle's capabilities to include state-of-the-art day and night optics as well as thermal imaging and laser aiming devices. I'd ordered all assaulters to leave the MP-5s and any other sub-guns they'd brought behind. Pistol ammunition does not penetrate SOF body armor and SOF body armor was what Blanchard and Nemesis were no doubt living in at this moment. I knew from firing thousands of rounds of 5.56 ball ammo *through* every available model of lightweight ballistic vest that assault rifles were what we'd want on deck once we made contact with Nemesis. We'd use our handguns for head and lower body shots, if offered or necessary. The grenade launchers would come in handy if we needed to blast our way into or through anything. I wasn't worried about accidentally setting off the SADM during the course of a firefight. Small arms fire wouldn't affect the device one way or another given its construction. High velocity, high rate of firepower weapons systems were the order of the day when it came to taking out its hijackers.

"Where are Trace and Danny?" I asked.

Kossens adjusted his rifle's harness so the weapon now hung straight up and down from his chest. His right hand was wrapped lightly around the weapon's hard plastic pistol grip. His trigger finger lay along the M4's lower receiver just above the trigger guard. His every movement proved he'd been well trained in weapons handling. "They're hanging out at the new operations center, which is co-located with the PJs now. The bomb that killed Mr. Moore blew the shit outta the old Op-Center. Pretty intense structure damage. Base commander sealed it off and moved his staff and everybody else involved across base into the PJs' building."

"Lassiter?"

"Feds got him over at the aviation shack. They used the pilots' lounge to interrogate him. Danny told the agents to stand by until we found out if you wanted to see the little prick before they haul his ass outta here and back to D.C. for further questioning."

Fuck! I needed whatever the techno-geek could get off the laptop and I needed a face-to-face with Lassiter before the Feds scooted him off to an isolated cell for the duration. "Find Trace and Danny. They're riding shotgun on the 'hawks when we launch. Dahlgren is too shot up to move as fast as we'll need to once we're on the ground, and I need Danny as Command & Control of the helos once this party gets going.

"Get with the platoon commander and have him break his people down into two groups. I want his best assaulters going in. I want a six-man team standing by on the CH-47 to either come in hot to bail us out, or to recover the device and us once we've made the hit. Load a Zodiac, too. No snipers this time around. We'll be moving too fucking fast to use them properly and I want *everyone* on the assault team, including your young ass! Clear?"

Paul smiled. "Aye, aye, Skipper! Where will you be?"

"Lead bird, first chalk. Right the fuck where I'm supposed to be, asshole! Now get the fuck moving. I gotta do a sit-down with Blanchard's S2 and I'm in no mood for being preached or lied to!"

After Paul left I headed for the pilots' lounge. I needed to know what was on the laptop so I figured to stop by the Op-Center first and see what Egghead #2 might have pulled off its hard drive. I was also wondering when the fuck we'd be hearing from Blanchard. I felt isolated from the rest of the world at the PANG. The only way in or out was by helo or fixed wing, since the roadways were now totally clogged with throngs of fearful civilians trying to flee the area as rumors of a nuclear weapon being detonated in downtown Portland were reaching the airwaves. Things were mighty fucked up in Portland. If Blanchard's plan was to set up as many open-air targets as possible, it was working exactly as he'd envisioned. The dirty nuke's detonation had generated enormous fear and panic, driving people out into the open so that the real device's blast would do the greatest degree of killing possible. Added to this was the grim fact that there was no standard emergency response or law enforcement asset to search for Blanchard and his team. All conventional communications were by now overloaded and useless. The cops and National Guard were likewise hemmed in and unable to effectively mount any form of offensive, proactive action against Nemesis.

Portland was fucked.

There was a lot I didn't fucking know right now but what I did was key. I *knew* Blanchard was not going to kill himself in the process of taking out Portland. He and what was left of his crew wanted to survive as much as me and mine did. The colonel saw himself staying alive to lead a race war within the United States. To do so he needed to get away clean *before* the SADM detonated. Given how fucked up moving around in the city was right now, that meant he planned to travel by either air or water. Fixed wing was out as we controlled all the possible short landing strips in immediate proximity to the city. Infiltration and extraction by helo was a strong possibility and I reminded myself to have the air traffic control people start watching their screens for any unidentified or unknown choppers entering or leaving the Portland area. Shit, I thought to myself, these bastards could score a chopper easy as pie if they considered hijacking one of the half-dozen television news birds scooting around the skies over Portland with their mini-cams and eye-in-the-sky reporters! I needed those fuckers grounded ASAP, free press or no free press. Of course, Blanchard would consider this as well and opt for something far less obvious to figure out and counteract. I was up against one *velly velly* smart snake. We were playing a deadly game of nuclear chess and for every move I made, I felt like he was somehow instantly countering me on the board.

I was really going to enjoy killing the bastard when I found him.

The secure cell I'd been given by Danny began ringing its fucking little ass off. I pulled the phone from a pouch on my combat harness and hit the TALK button. "Go!"

It was Barrett. "Dick? Where are you?"

"About halfway to the new Op-Center. What's up?"

"I'll link up with you at the Op-Center. We didn't get much off the laptop. Moore's replacement says the system was scrubbed. The hard drive needs to be sent to a facility where they can recover information that's been deleted so the casual user can't see or find it. That takes time and time is what we are out of."

"Fuck me to tears, Danny!"

Barrett managed a dry laugh. "Hold on, Marcinko. The geek did find something interesting. From what I understand these freaking scrubbing programs aren't perfect. He located a partial file that Lassiter missed deleting. We may be able to use some of the information against Lassiter when we interview him. I'll wait for you here."

"Roger that!" I snapped the phone closed and began jogging toward the lights of the Op-Center. Danny was right. We were out of time. Any moment now the sky could light up as the SADM detonated and it would all be over for anyone within the blast radius of the device, including Dick Marcinko and Company. Whatever had been found on the laptop was perhaps the key to averting the ultimate terrorist act. And if Lassiter wouldn't talk with the Feds I promised myself he'd talk with *me*. I owed him that little funfest.

I burst through the door to the Op-Center and found nearly everyone there watching a bank of hastily arranged television monitors. I recognized Colonel Max Blanchard's face on the multiple screens immediately. Fuck and double fuck! My gut went sour as I heard his voice. This was the long-awaited final message from the Doomsayer himself. I shut the door behind me and stood rock still, my arms folded across my chest. If the jig was up, it would happen now and there wasn't a damn thing that I or anyone else could do about it. Son of a bitch, I whispered to myself, so fucking close yet so fucking far away!

" . . . *in five hours I will slay those who have mocked the teachings of* Yahweh, *who have defiled themselves by living among the dark races, who have given themselves over to the hated Jews whose plan is to destroy White Israel. The instrument given to me by the One True God is a tactical nuclear weapon taken by my brave and loyal followers from the powerless and corrupt government of the so-called United States. You cannot flee, you cannot escape, you cannot stop what has been prophesied. White men and women rise up! Rise up against the filth that lays claim to our future! Upon the destruction of this vile nest of unbelievers, prepare yourselves for the war that will cleanse America! You will not have to find us! We will find you! And together we will achieve the final victory and create the homeland we deserve!"*

"Fucking nuts!" I heard someone toward the front of the crowded room say. The angular face of a local newscaster replaced the messianic image of Blanchard. I heard her say the videotape we'd just watched had been left in the lobby of the downtown television station by an unidentified man just fifteen minutes prior to broadcast. Well, I thought to myself, if he's telling the truth, we've got five fucking hours left to find the bomb. After that it'd be kiss my butt cheeks goodbye as well as those of the Rose City's collective multi-culti, socially diverse ass. The television was now showing a live footage shot from a helicopter flying over downtown Portland. Looting had broken out in the downtown area near where the dirty nuke had been detonated, and it was reported that growing bands of gang members were roaming the city and the outlying urban residential areas mugging and thugging anyone in their path. Scattered shootings were being reported throughout the city as the police engaged random snipers, who were in turn engaging looters and gang members. All emergency services were "temporarily on hold until new priorities for response can be reestablished," and the National Guard was being pulled out of the city to be "redeployed where they might do the most good." I figured that would probably be about a hundred miles from Ground Zero so there would at least be someone around to seal off the crater Portland was doomed to become if I didn't get a fucking *break* sometime soon!

"Goddamn it Dick whatthefuckwasthat we just heard!" Danny Barrett bullied his way through the mass of military and civilian uniforms and charged up in front of me. I'd seen Danny pissed off before, even mad, but never Fucking-A Furious. He was shaking his big ham hock of a fist in my face and I had no doubt he'd have crushed Blanchard's skull like a ripe peach if it were at all possible in the here and fucking now.

"Danny," I said, "the bastard just started the doomsday clock's final countdown. I figure we got just three fucking hours to find the nuke and Nemesis. After that, we're gonna have to either keep searching for the device or go after Blanchard as he and Nemesis will be in their E&E net. We lose the nuke, we lose the city. We lose Blanchard, we still lose the city *and* we set ourselves up for a rematch whenever he chooses. He's got us by our furry little balls and he knows it. Now what did we get from the damn computer?"

Barrett cooled down immediately. Running a hand through his hair he shook his head from side to side. I knew he was frustrated. So was I. But time was not on our side and we had to keep focused and keep moving. Hundreds of thousands of lives depended on our staying the course and overcoming the truly shitty odds against us. Outside the PANG everybody and his mother was going nuts. We couldn't. We had to go *into* the city while everyone else was trying to get *out* of it. And we had to find a single shiny suitcase and the nutjobs who were probably right now putting it in position where it would do the most harm possible. How and where the fuck would Blanchard do it? The look on my face must have given my thoughts away as Danny punched me hard in the shoulder.

"Okay, ya hairy ass cocksucker! But you better get to the colonel before I do. If you don't, I'll leave you just enough to whet your whistle but not much fucking more. The egghead found a partially deleted file that cyber-shoved its way to a crack in the operating system. You can ask Bill Gates himself what that all means, I'm just telling you what I was told. Basically, the geek explained that the bit of information we recovered was supposed to have been flushed by Lassiter but somehow got stuck and he found it. It's the remainder of an e-mail message from Blanchard to Lassiter, possibly about the placement of the device. It's garbled, but the words 'Wind Storm' appear three times in what we got. No precise reference or linkage. Just 'Wind Storm.' It only stood out cause it came up multiple times. Whadda you think?"

I jerked my head to the door and we rumbled outside into the dark night air. "I think I need to see Lassiter and run it past him. He's in federal custody and I promised Karen I'd leave him in one connected piece regardless of the cost. Still, there's more than one way to skin a Tango. Find Paul and get gunned up. You and Trace are riding security on the birds when we go in. The platoon should be nearly here and ready to roll. Call fucking Clay and bring him up to speed. Tell him to see to it all civilian air is grounded over and around Portland. The Air National Guard guys have to have permission to shoot anything flying other than us outta the skies from now until further notice, including news choppers. I'm gonna go chat with the asshole and ask him about Wind Storm."

Barrett nodded. We briefly clasped hands and then he was gone. I stood for a moment and looked around me. I could see the lights of Portland International Airport just across the maze of runways from the PANG. A solid line of nonmoving vehicles stretched from the terminal and parking areas out toward Highway 205 running north to south. Poor fuckers weren't going anywhere unless it was by leather personnel carrier!

Blanchard was fucking smart.

Now the whole world was watching. News-hungry motherfuckers around the world would be able to watch Portland get blasted off the map and when that happened would come inflammatory commentary, promises of vengeance, and orders from the White House declaring martial law across the country. Known or suspected political and religious extremists would be hunted down and arrested at the point of a hundred guns in the search for Blanchard and his remaining "priests." Every agitator with a bullhorn and a voice would be in the streets screaming for justice and declaring America to be the most violent racist nation on the face of the globe. What worried me the most was Blanchard's promise to find those who he was relying upon to join up with him. The colonel was a master practitioner of both terrorism and guerrilla warfare. Were operational units and cells already in place around the country, armed, ready, and just waiting for him? Were there other targets out there that Nemesis and its underground army had reconned and were prepared to destroy after the Portland weenie roast?

Suddenly I realized why the bizarre five-hour warning had been given! After all, Blanchard only needed five minutes to place and arm the nuke. But he'd need at least two hours to get clear of Ground Zero, which meant he'd want to be at least sixty miles away and under cover when the SADM detonated. The extra time on the clock might mean he was en route to Ground Zero. But it could also mean he was giving a much larger army of zealots their marching orders. Get ready, the time is now, start doing those things planned, prepared, and rehearsed for long ago. After the colonel and Nemesis were clear of the blast site they'd move to link up with a much larger army, an army no one knew anything about.

I popped open my cell and punched in Karen's private number. When she answered, I ran my ideas past her so she could brief Clay and the president as she saw fit. Then I headed for the holding area where Lassiter, my only link to Blanchard and Wind Storm was waiting. I didn't know where the fuck we were going next, but I sure the hell aimed to find out. I'd have to play it cool, though. Very professional. I couldn't let my standard issue roguish personality get the better of me. Lassiter would have to be handled like a baby. I could do this. Yes, the new and improved Rogue Warrior could do this.

"Can I help you, sir?" the FBI agent guarding the outside of Lassiter's holding pen greeted me.

I gave him my friendliest smile and then hit him with a haymaker from hell. My fist connected with his jaw at the hinge point and he dropped like a sack of boneless chicken to the floor. I opened the door to the pilots' lounge and saw the little blond man sitting in the far corner of the room, hands in his lap. He was of medium build and not half bad looking. He looked up at me, smiled, and stood.

"Richard Marcinko, I assume? The colonel expected it would be you they would send after us."

I covered the distance between Lassiter and me in about two huge steps. Grabbing Lassiter by the front of his shirt with both hands I jerked him off his feet and head-butted him in the nose. I felt the fragile cartilage break and a sudden hot spray of his blood burst from it all over my face. Dropping my weight and centering it evenly on my feet I spun hard to the left. As Lassiter's body reached its full extension in the air I let him go. He flew across the room, arms flailing wildly, and bounced like a tennis ball off the far wall. I watched as he tried to push himself up with both hands, blood dripping from his crushed nose. I could tell his head was spinning and I'd probably cracked a rib or two playing "bounce the bad guy" with his body. But I wasn't finished.

Stepping over him I grabbed two big handfuls of hair and slowly pulled his head up and back. The acute extension of his neck vertebrae caused cracking sounds as I locked him up. A low howl began to rise up out of Lassiter's throat. I cut that bullshit short by slamming the toe of my combat boot up between his widely spread legs and into his nut sack. Held like this, he couldn't do anything but absorb the full pain of my attempt to pop his head off while his balls were exploding like fifty-cent cherry bombs on the Fourth of July.

When I felt him go limp I dropped him. His head bounced off the floor with an ugly *splat*. Rolling him over I could see he was semiconscious. Maybe we could talk now. I sidestepped to the table the FBI had used earlier during their nonproductive question and answer period. There was a pitcher of ice water on it and three empty glasses. I grabbed the pitcher, turned, and threw its contents—cubes and all—directly into Lassiter's bleeding, swollen face.

Gee, that woke him the fuck up!

Sputtering and swearing, he struggled to a sitting position then launched himself toward me, growling like some fucked-up junkyard dog. When he reached where I was standing I kicked him square in the top of the head. The blow pole-axed his dumb ass and he dropped flat on the floor yet again. I lifted my right boot heel over his open left hand and smashed it down for all I was worth. The brittle sounds of all five fingers shattering were quickly drowned out by his shrill scream. I watched his entire body as it retracted like a broken rubber band, curling up in a tight little ball, the broken and now useless hand hidden away between Lassiter's equally broken and now useless *cojones*.

"FREEZE! FBI!"

Nuts! Not this dumbfuck *again!*

As the seriously pissed off federal agent stumbled into the room, his Glock .40 in both hands and aimed at my black heart, he slipped on the combination of blood and ice water that now coated the floor. When the muzzle of his weapon came off line as he tried to regain his balance I stepped forward and to my left, closing the narrow gap between us. Grabbing the pistol in both hands I deftly twisted it to the outside and against the agent's wrist and thumb. It popped out like candy from a baby. I watched the agent's eyes widen as he realized what had just happened. Giving him what I hoped was an apologetic look, I backhanded the flat of the Glock's steel upper slide against his skull then threw the weapon into the far corner of the room. The poor bastard took two staggering steps back, looked up at the ceiling, and then fell sideways to the wet floor.

Well, I couldn't blame him for trying. Maybe they'd give him a medal or something after he got out of the hospital. Fuck, I'd even recommend him for one!

Turning my attention back to Lassiter, I reached down and jerked the silly fuck up to his feet. I threw him at one of the chairs at the table . . . and *damn it* if I didn't miss! Shame on me. Lassiter spilled sideways off the chair as he bounced off of it, throwing his broken hand out to cushion the sudden impact with the floor.

Now *that* had to hurt like HELL!

OOOOOOOOOOOOHHHHHHHHHH!

Lassiter began grunting and breathing like a schoolgirl in heat as he vainly tried to find his bearings. I hadn't said a word since coming through the door. By now, he was sure I was simply going to beat his ass to death. And he was right. I was. Unless, of course, he decided to cut the bullshit and *talkie-talkie* with me most ric-tic about Blanchard, the nuke, and whatever the fuck Wind Storm was. "*Stop! Please! Stop! No more . . . no more! Stop, goddamn you!*"

Ah, sweet words of remorse and surrender! Now we were getting somewhere. Lassiter, balled up in the corner of the room farthest from me, was eyeing the unconscious FBI agent. When he looked up at me I could tell he was 110 percent convinced I was stark raving insane. If I'd fuck up the FBI to get to him . . .

"You're crazy, Marcinko! Fucking crazy! Leave me the fuck alone."

I walked over to Lassiter and grabbed his right ankle. Dragging him out of the corner I let loose only long enough to reach down and grab up a handful of his pants belt. With a powerful jerk I lifted him off the floor and slammed him into one of the still-standing chairs. I grabbed his face with one hand and squeezed it until I saw tears forming in the corners of his eyes. Bringing my face an inch from his, I roared as loudly as I could directly into it. I then let go of the now totally cowed Nemesis operator, took two steps back, and waited.

"What . . . do . . . you . . . want . . . from . . . *me?*" he choked.

"Wind Storm."

It was like I'd fired a jolt of electricity through his body.

"How . . . ? Fuck, Blanchard will kill me."

"*You dumb motherfucker!*" I yelled, "*I'm going to kill you if you don't tell me what I want to fucking know right now and right fucking here. What is it you don't understand about what I just said? Wind Fucking Storm. What is it? Where is it? How much fucking time do I have? Talk to*

*me you cocksucker. Talk to me or I'll rip your fucking heart
out and eat it in front of your lying, dying eyes!"*

Remember what I said earlier about my bedside
manner? It sucks. But it does get results.

Lassiter's first response to my little speech was to
piss himself. A sure sign we'd made progress. Then he
started sniffling and whimpering. That I didn't need. I
hate whiners. Then his whimpering turned into talking. Now that was better, much better. I picked an
overturned chair up off the floor and sat down next to
him. For the next five minutes Lassiter babbled on
about mud races, the Phineas Priests, Blanchard's role
in starting the second American Revolution, and most
importantly what and where Wind Storm was. The
battered, bruised, and broken man had just finished
when I heard the sound of many feet running down
the hall toward the lounge. I stood up and met the
rush of FBI agents and Air Police, their guns drawn, as
they tried to crowd their way into the now destroyed
room. "The prisoner tried to escape!" I shouted above
the melee of officers, agents, and assholes all. "Thank
God I got here when I did! He damn near killed your
agent here! If I hadn't stopped him . . ."

The mob furiously fell on poor old Lassiter like
sharks on chum. I slipped past the beating in progress
and trotted back down the hall toward the great outdoors. "Sucks to be you," I murmured to myself as
Lassiter's screams and howls followed me outside.
Fuck him. I'd gotten what I needed and it was time to
go nuke hunting.

I saw a newly arrived transport chopper on the tarmac—the platoon from SIX had arrived. I'd found a
hangar to house them and I instantly started to jog in
that direction. I couldn't wait to get to where my pla-

toon of real-deal killer SEALs was waiting for its lead
dog. As I approached the hangar, I spotted Trace. Her
lithe figure was now encased in an OD green Nomex
flight suit and an M4A1 was slung across her chest.
She waved and pointed to the hangar. I raised a hand
in acknowledgment and kept on running. Barrett was
standing just outside getting a briefing from the crew
chief of the CH-47. He and his crew would be the cavalry who would take charge of the SADM once we
had it in hand, or try to pull our asses out of the fire if
we didn't get it in time. As I burst into the brightly lit
interior of the hangar I saw my boyz standing ready.
Paul was right in the midst of them, and he threw me
an enthusiastic thumbs-up.

They were the most beautiful bunch of lethal bastards I'd ever seen.

And I was about to take them downtown on a hot
load for the fucking ride of their lives.

I pulled up short and nodded once to the platoon.
They could see in my eyes and in the way I was standing like the Fucking-A God of War I am and have
always been that I was ready to lead them on the most
important mission they'd (God willing) ever face. As
one, they began cheering and waving their weapons
high above their heads. The SEAL war cry echoed
throughout the hangar.

HOO-YAHHHHHHHH!

It sent shivers from the top of my thick Slavic skull
down to the tips of my booted toes. "Saddle up, motherfuckers!" I yelled. "We're goin' downtown! *HOO-
YAH!*"

17

"This was our first chance to prove ourselves. If we blew it, it would probably be our last."

DANNY O. COULSON, *No Heroes:*
Inside the FBI's Secret Counter-Terror Force

ONE BY ONE I RECHECKED MY THIRTY-ROUND MAGAZINES. Each one held twenty-seven rounds of green-tipped 5.56 brain busters courtesy of Uncle Sam. The first two rounds loaded were red-tipped tracer so I'd visually know when it was time to change mags. The last round loaded was tracer, as well. I used that one to dial in follow-on fire and to freak the fuck outta anyone downrange looking to dial in on me! I *never* let anyone else handle or check my weapons for me, whether on the range, in training, or when going hot like we were doing now. I trust in *moi*, and encourage others to do the same. A bad mag at the wrong time will get you or a teammate killed. I've seen an operator lose a whole load of bullets out the bottom of his magazine at the worst possible moment because he didn't check the fucking base plate prior to mission launch. You learn from others' mistakes if you're

smart. You learn from your own if you're lucky. I was
taking in eighteen mags for the M4A1 alone. In
Vietnam I'd learned the value of having as much
ammo available to me as possible. As a SEAL going
up against the Viet Cong and NVA I carried *boo-coo*
bullets, grenades, commo gear, and water. That's the
shit that kept me alive. At most, I would shove one
issue meal ration into my jungle ruck for a foray into
the woodline. Food was not a priority for me in the
bush. Hell, there were things aplenty I could eat *in the
bush* if I got hungry!

After carefully inspecting each magazine from top
to bottom for serviceability and reliability I slipped it
into an ammo pouch on my rogue-black Tactical
Tailor–made Modular Assault Vest. My SEALs had
purchased a shitload of this outfit's custom-designed
tactical gear from the in-house manufacturing firm in
Tacoma, Washington. They'd raided the place while
working with the 2/75th Ranger Battalion, which was
practicing airfield seizures at Gray Army Airfield on
Fort Lewis prior to the emergency call-out to Portland.
The MAV two-piece modular vest rode high on my
upper body and allowed me the full range of movement I needed while still letting me ride easy in either
an aircraft or vehicle. Those shooters wearing body
armor could easily and quickly adjust the vest as they
positioned it over their ballistic protection. I had two
large utility pouches to act as drop bags for my 40-mm
munitions, extra thirty-round mags, and a few other
lethal goodies I just can't live without. I went with four
3-Mag 5.56 modular ammo pouches on the front of the
vest to handle my primary magazines. Two additional
utility pouches allowed me to carry an emergency
TalkAbout radio with a transmission range of five

miles, and an emergency trauma kit for patching my ass up if I got in the way of any heavy metal shit flying in my direction.

Like I said, bullets, bombs, and commo is all you need when it comes to kicking ass and taking names in my particular line of work.

I secured my new Glock 17 with night sights and TacLight in its modular SAS-style drop holster on my right thigh. Backing up its 17 + 1 high capacity magazine were six more fully loaded mags, all nicely secured on my left thigh courtesy of the modular leg mount that complements the pistol's carry system. Also attached on my left thigh was a Saber radio pouch for commo with the helos, a knife pouch holding my Wor-Tech tactical folder, a small utility pouch for my SOG Specialty SwitchPlier™, and a strobe / compass pouch for my emergency rescue items. Everything would be up close and personal once we went for the nuke.

The best CQB is based on the KISS principal. *Keep It Simple, Stupid.* Walking among the shooters from SIX, casually chatting and checking on their preparations, I was pleased to see to a man they followed the Rogue Warrior's formula for close-quarters fighting to the "K." Everything they were carrying was lean, mean, and strapped tight. The platoon leader was a savvy young pup named Fletcher with grit in his gut and steel blue eyes. As I looked over his people while they prepared their weapons and gear, I couldn't help but feel proud. They appeared fit, confident, and to move with a single purpose. Despite the Navy's attempts to "clean up" SIX, the come-and-go commanders after me hadn't weakened the resolve of each succeeding generation of shooters who came to the Team.

I'd designed SIX to be able to move from Point A to Point B with little more than a rucksack, a weapon, and the smallest amount of mission-specific equipment an operator needed to get the particular job done. Today, thanks to all the paperwork and signatures required even to take a crap in the Navy, a ludicrous amount of time usually elapses between the moment a call to action comes in and the time the operators ship out. But I'd noticed the operators—the shooters—the only ones that count when it gets right down to it—have improvised, adapted, and overcome the administrative obstacles placed in their way to an admirable degree. I knew that was true of this bunch. I'd kept in pretty regular touch with SIX's shooters since my "retirement," despite the Navy's black-balling my hairy ass from the compound. Blood *is* thicker than water, and it was blood that built SIX.

If I'd given them the green light my shooters at SIX would have busted me out of jail any time. That was the degree of loyalty we held—and still hold—for each other. There was no one who could have stood in their way. I could have gone anywhere in the world and found myself a new home. But I've never run away from anything in my life. And I'd never compromise my men to the degree such a gesture of brotherly love would have demanded. The brass were lucky I hung around for their little circus. Otherwise they'd have had to rely on the post office to bring me the results in the fucking mail!

I know for sure that there was nowhere else on earth I'd rather have been right at that moment. I was suited up, geared up, gunned up, and ready to roll. This is what I'd trained my entire life to do. This is what I'd trained my men and those officers under me to do. The ancient warrior ethic had been reawakened in me during the last year and I was now once again going to lead warriors, true warriors, into combat.

Understand, good reader, that what the Navy never could figure out was *why* my men could and would do the things I demanded of them. What Charlie Beckwith accomplished with his shooters at DELTA I accomplished with mine at SIX. I deliberately inculcated within the very souls of my operators a spiritual dedication and belief in themselves and their mission. They were modern-day warriors using modern-day weapons and equipment to accomplish an age-old task: hunting down those who were dedicated to terror and chaos.

I'd successfully bred into SIX the understanding that we were the most recent links in a long chain of warriors stretching back thousands of years. That they owed their very existence to all those courageous and honorable warriors who had come before them and laid down their lives for worthy causes. My shooters knew they were more than just the sum of their individual efforts. They were the living emblem of countless brave men who'd come before. Spiritually, mentally, emotionally, and physically linked to such a noble ideal, SEAL Team SIX became unstoppable. The most effective counterterrorist unit ever created. Such was the caliber of the twenty-first-century SEAL who I was preparing to lead into battle against Blanchard and his spiritually mutated Nemesis team.

We were taking four M240B medium machine guns in with us, three with the assaulters and one with the SAR team on the '47. The M240B is a gas-operated, air-cooled, linked belt-fed machine gun that replaces the tried-and-true M60 machine gun. Firing 7.62 rounds from the open-bolt position, the new gun has a maximum effective range of 1100 meters. I liked its new plastic buttstock and its improved M145 Flex Sight. We'd pulled the folding bipods off for this mission and each 240B gunner had slung his weapon with a Safariland cable sling for maximum support and flexibility in any firing position. I demanded 1000 rounds for each gun, the additional belts of ammo carried in the gunners' TT-3-Day Assault Plus packs. I wanted maximum firepower put down on Nemesis, and with the integrated weapons systems we were taking in with us I figured it was sure to be one hell of a firefight with the odds stacked in our favor.

I'd test-fired my rifle and pistol at the PANG's indoor range along with the rest of the platoon. Trace and Danny had squared their combat loads and gear away earlier and were now helping the crew chief of the CH-47 unlimber the two electronic mini-guns the big black Chinook from the 160th Special Operations Aviation Regiment commonly carry. The '47 would serve as an airborne gun platform for us as well as an SAR asset once we got on target. The minis could blanket an area with thousands of rounds of steel-core 7.62 rounds with exceptional accuracy. Trace would accompany the back-up team on the '47, with Danny handling overall Command & Control from PAVE Hawk #2. I'd be taking the first 'hawk in with its chalk of shooters, the second fully loaded 'hawk hot on our ass. We had to hit our target hard, fast, and perfect the first time out. My plan was audacious, risky as hell, and way outside the box, even for special operations.

"Dick?"

I looked up to find Lieutenant Fletcher, the officer in charge of the platoon from SIX, standing next to me.

Lieutenant Fletcher was an academy graduate. Since meeting him I'd been impressed with his easygoing manner and lack of bullshit when it came to turning his people over to me for the duration. The platoon's senior chief told me privately as we were drawing our ammo that Fletcher had proven himself a capable and flexible leader. The platoon had several classified flyaway missions under its belt and the young lieutenant had drawn first blood on one of these. He was cool, calm, and astute. I liked that in a young officer. "What's up, Phil?"

"The platoon is ready for final brief. Where do you want us?"

Fletcher was geared up much like I was with the exception of the M240B slung across his chest like some badass electric guitar from Hell. He had a black drive-on rag tied gypsy-style around his skull and a pair of Bolle assault goggles pushed up high on his forehead. His hands were encased in skintight black Nomex flight gloves, each index finger cut halfway back to give him maximum feel of whatever trigger he was pressing. He'd opted for Nike assault boots like those I'd first ordered from Germany when I'd stood SIX up so many years ago. The Nikes were light, well sewn, and their unique sole pattern allowed an operator to move with security on wet or slippery surfaces. I noted the lieutenant favored the SIG 226 9-mm pistol in stainless steel. A good choice of weapon.

"Tell 'em to bring their asses over here and to take a seat anywhere they can find space. Dahlgren and Barrett have their marching orders. We'll link up with them on the birds. You ready, Lieutenant?"

Fletcher gave me a sturdy smile. "Yes, Sir. We're all ready. We won't let you down, Captain. My boys are the best in the Team at what they do. If 160 can get us to the target, we'll do the rest. You can count on it!"

"Well Fucking-A Tweety," I replied. "Let's do it!"

Five minutes later I was surrounded by the best people Naval Special Warfare had to offer me. I waited as they made themselves as comfortable as possible on the hangar's cold concrete floor. Finally I felt I could hold my own against Blanchard's team of religious psycho-killers. I had sixteen go-to-war motherfuckers in full kit straining at the leash. Time was running out but the odds, at least in my book, were now at least even. I knew where Blanchard was, what he was doing, and where he was headed. I knew what *Wind Storm* was and I knew I could assault it with what we'd pulled, scraped, borrowed, and stolen over the last twenty-four hours. I also knew it was up to me to take the nuke away from Blanchard and then get it clear of the mainland if at all possible. I had a plan, but it was one I was keeping to myself for the time being.

"Lissen up!" I barked. "I'm only going to say this once. You got questions, you ask 'em! We got one fucking chance to do this right. One! We fuck up and a lot of innocent bastards are going to fry before the sun comes up tomorrow morning. I know what you fuckers can do, and you all know me. We're going in together, and we're coming out together. *Hoo-yah?*"

Their response was instantaneous and deafening. With a grim smile I nodded in satisfaction as each operator acknowledged the challenge I'd just thrown down. We were holding one-way tickets on this trip. Once airborne and over the target, there'd be no turning back and no giving up. Each and every man jack assembled in front of me knew about Nemesis. They were renegades, yes. But they were also first-class operators who knew our tactics and techniques as well as we knew theirs. Never had U.S. counterterrorists gone toe-to-toe with their own kind, on their own soil. Our prize would be much more than a recovered tactical nuclear weapon; it would be the continued safety and security of the nation.

Fuck it, I thought to myself. This is what I've trained all my life for. Time to see if Dickie can cut the mustard or if he's just been jerking off all these years.

"Our target is the *Wind Storm*, a 250-foot, three-deck seagoing pleasure boat. She was leased last year by Colonel Max Blanchard under a false name to make a trip from her home port in Seattle down the Washington coastline and up the Columbia River to Portland. It is coming upriver even as we speak. The SADM is onboard and under the direct control of the colonel.

"According to my intel, Colonel Blanchard split Nemesis up after the nuke was delivered to him. The fuckers we've been engaging around the city flew into Portland early and took up positions where they could guide and monitor the events leading up to the detonation of the device. What this means is that HRT and my people—until your arrival—have been bleeding ourselves dry taking on Blanchard's advance team. The remainder of Nemesis has been standing by to steam toward Portland from the Port of Astoria."

I paused, looked around at the intense faces of the men in front of me, and then continued.

"*Wind Storm* is the vehicle for delivering the SADM to Portland's doorstep. Blanchard plans to navigate the fucking thing center mass of where the Willamette River cuts the city in two, anchor the boat, then set the timer and boogie using two Zodiacs. He only needs sixty miles between him and the nuke to be in the clear, come detonation time. Nemesis has run the route several times over the past year from Astoria to the city under the guise of training exercises in support of the Coast Guard."

"How we going to hit this bitch, Skipper?" Kossens hand dropped as he asked the question I knew was on everyone's mind.

"Like a fucking freight train," I replied. "The assault team splits into two elements. I'm on the first bird; the lieutenant here is on the second. Six shooters go with Dahlgren on the '47. They will cover our asses as we go in. Their job is to take on Nemesis if they try to *dee-dee mau* by rubber raiding craft once the *Wind Storm* comes under fire.

"We're fast-roping onto the foredeck's helo platform. This is a fucking luxury boat so the landing point is going to be mighty fucking tight quarters! I'll kick the first rope and secure the deck with my team. Helo number two will be flying right up our ass and Lt. Fletcher will have to get his team on the deck most *ric-tic* so we can begin clearing the topside of Tangos.

"From that point on it's just us and them. Intel says there's no civilians onboard so collateral damage is a nonissue. You see it, you kill it. I don't give a fuck about the boat, either! We'll have to move fast and that means we break any and everything in our way. The objective is the device. You all know what it looks like. Do whatever is necessary to gain control of it. Once one of us has the fucking thing, don't you dare give it back! Questions?"

A sturdy older operator in the back spoke up.

"What if the motherfucker has armed the nuke, Dick? What's our contingency plan if the damn thing is wired hot?"

"Good question, sailor!" I responded. "We're not going to waste time checking the fucking case. Once we have control, the '47 is coming in and setting down just above the surface of the river next to the *Wind Storm*. I'll take the case and transfer to the Chinook. You bastards on the SAR team will stay aboard and act as a security element in case the '47 has problems and we go down somewhere between the *Wind Storm* and the mouth of the Columbia. There's a Zodiac aboard the helo. One sixty will take us at least twenty-five miles out to sea and then drop me and the nuke off in the Zodiac. Twenty-four hours later, if the bastard hasn't detonated and blown my sorry ass off the face of the planet, the Coast Guard will zero in on a signal from my Saber and we'll all enjoy a happy fucking ending."

"Who's staying with you on the water, Skipper?" asked Fletcher.

"Me, myself, and I, Sir. It only takes one to baby-sit a SADM, armed or otherwise. If it goes off, it'll make a helluva bang but loss of life will be kept to a minimum. Clear?"

"Clear, Captain," replied Fletcher. "But if you want some company . . ."

"No need to say it, young man. Message received. Now let's get moving, shall we?"

Someone pushed the massive hangar doors open and moving like one soldier my sixteen headhunters and I headed for where the helos were preparing to launch, their rotors spinning in the night, the sound of their powerful turbine engines washing over us with a hot wind. I bent low as I began jogging for the lead 'hawk. Behind me five other SEALs did likewise. As my team swiftly loaded our bird I watched as Fletcher's people clambered into the second 'hawk. The six-man SAR team swung around behind the CH-47 off to my right. The team struggled up its lowered rear ramp one at a time, the weight of their weapons and equipment making the short climb a challenge in itself. Danny waved at me from where he was sitting in the copilot's seat of the second helo. I waved back and gave the big bastard a thumbs-up. I then caught sight of Trace's lean, full figure. Her form made her distinct even in her flight suit, accessorized by the cross-slung M4A1. I watched the she-commando quickly kneel on the tarmac next to the Chinook and raise both hands skyward in an ancient prayer to her gods. A strange power surged through me as she lowered her hands and climbed aboard. In an instant she'd disappeared into the hull of the twin-engine assault chopper and its ramp gracefully swung upward and locked into position.

Son of a bitch, I thought to myself, that *is* one scary woman!

Two of my shooters scooted aside as I climbed into the 'hawk's main compartment. I took the headset handed me by the crew chief and tugged it on.

"Ready, Mr. Marcinko?" the pilot asked.

"Roger that," I replied. "Let's do it!"

"Tower, this is Red Flight Leader requesting permission to depart."

As the 'hawk began slowly moving forward I adjusted my ass on its aluminum plate deck. The pilot gave the bird its head and I felt a hard rush of adrenalin hit me as we gained altitude. I settled back and closed my eyes for a moment, taking it all in. There was no going back, no backing down, no giving up.

"Sir? We have the target's position locked in. The AC is race tracking at 4000 feet AGL. *Wind Storm* is ten nautical miles out from the city. I'm taking us down over her deck. Hold on, it's going to be a fast ride from here on out!"

18

" . . . to suspend a successful general in command of an army in the heart of an enemy's country . . . is to upset all discipline, to jeopardize the safety of the army and the honor of the country, and to violate justice."

AL KALTMAN, *The Genius of Robert E.Lee:*
Leadership Lessons for the Outgunned,
Outnumbered, and Underfinanced

"CLAY? CAN MARCINKO ACTUALLY PULL THIS OFF?" FROM behind his desk in the Oval Office, The president of the United States swung around in his comfortable leather chair to face the two advisers sitting across from him. The famous room was softly lit and its curtains were drawn to shield this daybreak meeting from the always prying eyes of Washington's competitive press corps. A gentle sprinkling of rain had accompanied the quiet, early morning arrival of Karen Fairfield and Clay Mulcahy at the White House fifteen minutes earlier. They'd gone directly to the president's office at his request.

Clay Mulcahy weighed his answer carefully. He'd

been working frantically for eighteen hours straight and the pace he was keeping was beginning to take a toll on the veteran crisis manager. "They're airborne right now, Mr. President. We redirected an AC-130 gunship from Travis Air Force Base in California up to Portland earlier in the day. The AC is over the target at this time and vectoring in the assault force. It'll paint the *Wind Storm* with infrared light so the helo pilots can make their final approach with as much visual clarity using NVGs as possible. Marcinko has sixteen operators from SEAL Team SIX, plus his own team and a fully armed CH-47 from the 160 SOAR. He's got the assets and the balls, that's for certain."

A former Air Force pilot, the president knew full well the air-to-ground support capabilities of the AC-130. Its twin Gatling guns mounted off the port side of the aircraft could lay down a cone of fire capable of devastating an entire football field in less than three seconds. Its 105-mm cannon was accurate enough to take out individual enemy vehicles and bunkers from 7000 feet, night or day, good weather or bad, thanks to its highly sophisticated computerized targeting and firing systems. Very little survived an aerial attack by an AC-130. It was the ultimate flying machine when you wanted something—or someone—on the ground turned to mush. "Thank you, Clay. I'll take your answer as a qualified maybe. Karen, your opinion?"

Karen Fairfield shifted slightly so she could try and get a better read on the president's mood in the dimly lit room. She'd been fending off interagency attacks on OISA's ability to manage the situation in Portland ever since Blanchard's video-recorded statement had been televised. The string of public gun battles her team in Portland was responsible for had not helped her from a political or public relations standpoint. The Army's senior leadership was pressing the president hard to allow DELTA to take over the operation, and the Navy's leadership was screaming to get its most elite platoon away from "Demo Dick Marcinko" and safely back under the authorized commander of SEAL Team SIX. Even the CIA was lobbying to get involved, although its paramilitary assets and track record were better suited to causing wars of ethnic cleansing than stopping them.

In light of the president's sarcastic response to Clay's hedging, Karen chose to tackle the question head-on and speak her mind. "Dick will pull through for us. Blanchard is reported to be within ten miles of Portland," she began. "Even if he detonates the device where he is now, the results will be catastrophic. However, we have no hard indicators he is aware of the air assault Dick is leading against him. Our security on the ground in Portland and here in Washington has for once been effective in this regard. I say odds are good that he and his force can accomplish the mission—if we don't interfere unnecessarily."

"Good odds, eh? You've seen the news I take it. Portland is a basket case! There are literally hundreds of thousands of Americans trying to get out of the city. The mayor is dead and its emergency services are useless. FEMA is fucked, if you'll pardon my French. They can't get close to the problems at hand.

"Worse, general panic is spreading throughout the Pacific Northwest. Seattle is reporting they're having problems keeping order, and San Francisco is even crazier than usual. My question for you is what's our backup plan if Marcinko fails? How do we stop

Blanchard from setting off the damn nuke if he successfully evades Marcinko's assault team?"

Before Karen could reply, Clay spoke up. "We're monitoring the assault effort from the command node at OISA. If the assault looks like it's falling apart, the gunship will be given instructions to sink the *Wind Storm*. We'll drop the vessel to the bottom and send in the Coast Guard to secure the site. I have a team of Navy hardhat divers standing by at the naval facility in Bremerton to recover the SADM from the river's bottom if we're forced to exercise this option."

Karen turned to Clay, but he continued to stare straight ahead at the president, refusing to meet her eye.

"Just who will give that order?" demanded Karen, unable to keep her astonishment and fury out of her voice. "And why wasn't I informed of this before now, Clay?"

"Like you, I work for the president, Karen. You know that. There are some things I am not able to share with you and this aspect of the operation is one of those. If the order needs to be given, the president will either issue it himself or delegate it to me. You are not, and need not be, in the loop on this one."

"Dammit, Clay! Does Dick know you're setting him up like this?"

"Control yourself, Ms. Fairfield!" ordered the president. "Mr. Marcinko knows what he needs to and nothing more. Thanks to you he's been well compensated, even given a presidential pardon for his past crimes as well as his current escapades. I've been told about the poor bastard he and that woman operator gutted just blocks from here. And I am aware that he beat the ever-loving shit out of a defenseless prisoner as well as the FBI agent responsible for protecting him! Between this renegade Blanchard and Dick Marcinko, I'm hard-pressed to decide which one should be put in front of a military tribunal first! Besides, with over thirty years in this business, I damn well think Marcinko understands his current position as well as ours. If it appears the raid isn't getting the job done, then we'll do the job another way, period. On some level, Dick and his people know that and expect it. I can get new SEALs. I can't get a new Portland or prevent widespread civil war as easily.

"Understand this, Karen. As president, I will not allow a racist maniac to use nuclear weapons against his own country. According to the FBI, their intelligence sources in the violent patriot and militia underground communities are reporting some pretty scary stuff is already taking place around the country. The radical agitators on the other side of the fence are likewise arming themselves and telling their people to get ready to fight in the streets against the white oppressor, whoever the fuck that's supposed to be. And in case you forgot, all our internal distracting chaos provides a great window of opportunity for some outside nation to strike a blow against us.

"Dick either pulls this off with a clear win or I will personally order the entire area to be sanitized with everything and everyone that gunship has onboard. I don't like it and I don't want to do it, but I will. Am I understood on this?"

Karen nodded curtly. "Yes, Mr. President."

He turned his attention back to Clay. "Have the FBI immediately begin detaining anyone we've identified as an extremist leader, regardless of race, color, or creed. We'll have to move quickly to take advantage of this situation, no matter how it ends out in Oregon. I'll announce a declaration of martial law only if it becomes absolutely necessary within the next twenty-four hours. I doubt that Colonel Blanchard considered that turnabout is fair play when it comes to cleansing the country of its undesirable elements, do you? He's given us the perfect opportunity to crack down on the radical fringe without having to ask 'Mother, may I?' of the courts."

Clay Mulcahy smiled. "No, sir. I'm sure he never considered it. We've needed a reason to go after our domestic problem children for some time now, and the colonel's extraordinarily good timing has provided it. We can begin sending the detainees to 'Gitmo within twelve hours of arrest. Per your directive, the Marine Corps has dramatically expanded Camp X-ray to absorb the anticipated additional population. We'll put the base off-limits to the press in the next twenty-four hours. National security concerns, et cetera."

Unable to sit still any longer, Karen gave the president her most winning smile and began to stand. "Mr. President, I need to get back to OISA. I have an operation to oversee. With your permission?"

"Of course, Karen. I'm glad we're all back on the same page. Trust me, Dick Marcinko will be given every opportunity to do his job. But it's only prudent to have a 'Plan B' in the wings, in the event he can't pull it off." With a casual wave he dismissed her.

After she'd left the room, Clay asked, "And what about Marcinko? I mean, what if he is successful?"

The president shrugged as he lit a cigar from the elegant wooden box on his desk. "I'll invite him out to Camp David for a weekend. There's nothing like a BBQ and a walk in the woods with the president of the

United States to make a man feel appreciated. Afterward he goes back under glass, where all good rogue warriors should be kept until they're needed. I'm sure I don't have to say this to you, but keep an eye on Karen, won't you? Don't want any of Marcinko's bad habits rubbing off on our good girl."

19

"I'm coming out so you'd better get this party started!"

PINK, "Get This Party Started"

MY FUCKING STOMACH WAS IN MY THROAT AS THE 'HAWK dropped like a gut-shot pigeon toward the darkness of the Columbia River. The pilot pulled the airframe up hard and leveled her out less than twenty-five feet above the water. The 'hawk's nose dipped slightly and I felt the helo picking up speed. We were now hauling serious ass toward where *Wind Storm* was reportedly making her way upriver. I knew Lieutenant Fletcher and his crew of pirates were stuck to our ass in the second 'hawk. Danny would be coordinating our assault as well as getting the '47 with Trace into a tight race-track 500 feet above us and over the target. Barrett was also in contact with the AC-130, now code-named "Heavy Dancer." Given the fucking *Wind Storm* cost about umpteen million dollars (to be precise) and made international trips year-round, I'd had a hunch the company responsible for leasing the boat might have had a worldwide tracking device secretly built into her hull. A honey like this was a prime target for high seas pirates and dope runners looking for an expensive cargo carrier to use, abuse, then pillage and sink at sea. An insurance carrier would want to save or recover the fucking thing if at all possible under such circumstances. With satellite tracking and GPS as sophisticated as it is today, I'd sure put one in. Hell, even piece-of-shit rental cars were getting planted with this technology these days.

Dickie's hunch paid off. Before we left the PANG, the boat's owners confirmed there were actually *two* such devices onboard. The first was standard issue and easy to find if somebody was looking for it. Apparently somebody had, because it was no longer operating. However, the second device was a sleeper and was actually built right into the hull itself. Only the owner and leasing agent of the *Wind Storm* knew of its existence. This device, the redundant system, was still operating perfectly. I'd shared my new intel with Danny who passed the information to the gunship, which in turn dialed in the homing device's radio frequency on the pilot's deck. This allowed the AC to vector our fast-flying asses right into the target zone with hair-splitting precision. Murphy was now fucking with Blanchard and I wasn't complaining a bit. Make a note! What goes around comes around in the Rogue Warrior's Book of Truths. Rogue Karma, you might say.

"I have her just off our starboard side! One minute!"

I pulled my headset off and handed it to the crew chief. Craning my neck, I could see the *Wind Storm* coming up fast. We were lining up with her bow for the final approach. The boat was lit up like Christmas. And why not? When I ran Red Cell and penetrated supposedly heavily guarded military bases, I'd soon learned that making a brazen and bold entrance was often a more effective strategy than trying to sneak in. Most people assume anything being done in broad daylight in the middle of the road is by definition not suspicious. Who would suspect a brightly lit, wildly expensive pleasure craft was the device smuggling in a stolen nuclear bomb? In the movies, it's always men in black in a rubber dinghy on a moonless night. Besides, I'd certainly learned Blanchard had a taste for the finer things, and the *Wind Storm* was a beauty.

There were a couple dozen other boats in the immediate vicinity, all heading away from Portland at varying speeds and degrees of maritime competence. I hoped none of these fleeing skippers got themselves right in the way of our landing party. We wouldn't be able to stop to explain to Popeye and Olive Oyl why they were suddenly getting pounded with more artillery fire than Omaha Beach. Why a boat like the *Wind Storm* would be heading *toward* a city about to be stir-fried into black glass might have raised an eyebrow or two, but we all know rich fuckers are crazy about how they get their kicks. Most regular blue-collar assholes were more concerned with saving their own asses than fretting over a pleasure cruiser chugging toward the City of Roses on an apparent sight-seeing tour.

"Thirty seconds!"

We were now skimming barely above the water's surface at high speed. I had my right foot buried deep in the thick black coil of rope positioned at the lip of the helo's flooring, holding it in place until it was time to kick it out and away when the helo flared to a momentary hover over the boat's foredeck. I'd directed the pilot to place us no more than fifty feet above the *Wind Storm* so the ride down the rope would be as fast as possible. By now Nemesis had to know we were inbound and a reception party was no doubt assembling to greet us. Blanchard would want to wax our uninvited asses before our boots hit the deck so I knew we needed to rip down the fast rope like chicken-lickin' raped apes if we were going to survive the first contact. On the plus side, it's harder than you might think to shoot a black blur dropping out of the night sky. At least, that's what I was counting on.

Shit! The 'hawk suddenly pulled pitch and shuddered to a crazy kind of stop over the *Wind Storm*. The change in "Gs" nearly blacked my ass out but I fought the wildly fluctuating pressures pounding against my brain and body and then felt the helo assume a bone-jarring hover. With a guttural roar I kicked the fast rope out and immediately grabbed a chunk of line even as it was free falling toward the hand-laid teak decking below. I threw myself out of the 'hawk and with a slight twist like I'd been taught to execute when inserting by FRIES, I began spiraling downward, holding the thick braided rope loosely between my Rogue-sized mitts. I wore my Hatch assault gloves with Kevlar palm padding to protect me from serious rope burn, but my descent was so fast and nearly out of control I still felt immense heat building up. I kept my boots completely off the rope since I had no intention of braking anytime soon. With my feet spread shoulder-width apart I slammed almost dead center on the ritzy little landing pad the *Wind Storm* had on its deck for hop-and-pop pleasure runs and catered partygoers.

Damn, I'm good!

My smug attitude was kicked right out of me as the SEAL only one boot heel above me on the line smashed directly into my fucking shoulders and upper back. I went flying forward and off the raised platform just as a stream of red tracer fire arced upward at the 'hawk. "GO! GO! GO!" I yelled at my operators as they came flying down the rope one after another. I landed hard on the deck hitting my face, hands, chest, and knees. *FUCK!* I rolled up into a kneeling position and swung my M4A1's muzzle onto a figure one deck above me. Slapping the selector switch to AUTO I pressed the little carbine's trigger and emptied my initial thirty-round magazine at the motherfucker who was trying to shoot down my aircrew.

Cocksucker!

The figure disappeared and I had no idea if I'd hit him or not. But at least his outgoing fire stopped and I watched as the lead bird slipped portside so the second chopper could maneuver into position and drop its load of operators onto the *Storm.* Off in the distance I could hear the distinct *thumpa-thumpa-thumpa* of the '47's twin rotor system as the 160 helo orbited above us. They'd be painting the *Wind Storm* with their onboard infrared capability allowing my airborne assets—especially the gunship high overhead—to monitor the action on the decks and in the surrounding water. We'd dropped in on Blanchard with our night vision goggles at the ready, but I knew Nemesis would be likewise equipped. They—like us—would take advantage of the IR spotlight Trace was now working the boat with. Sure as shit someone inside cut the electrics and the boat went dark from stem to stern. Goggles on, everybody. Now we were fighting in the odd green-black glow of night vision and that, dear reader, is some really weird outerspace shit.

"MOVE FORWARD AND PUT SOME FIRE DOWN ON THE UPPER DECKS, GODDAMN IT!"

Even as I gave the order, all three M240s cut loose from behind and beside me, their muzzle flashes near blinding as ribbons of tracer-led steel began chewing the expensive luxury boat apart. The noise was deafening and I thanked the war gods watching over us we were all using New Eagle International's most excellent facial bone tactical headsets. I could hear my operators despite the intense volume of firepower, and I could communicate with them and the birds simply by switching frequencies with the flick of a finger on my Saber. Make a fucking note! Commo in battle is key! It keeps a team shooting, moving, and thinking as a team. In my business, teams survive where individuals die. And I say dying is a fate reserved for the other guy.

"Dick! You've got movement on your left flank! On the main deck. He's moving fast."

I keyed my Saber. "Roger that, Danny! Trace, put some mini-gunfire down around this tub. Do a 360 and make it close. I want this son of a bitch to know we've pulled the fucking stops out on this one. It'll put the fuckers' heads down, too. GO!"

High above me and to my two o'clock I heard the buzz saw throb of a mini-gun. A solid sheet of fire lit the sky up as the '47 banked hard to port and began tearing up the river all around us. Through my NVGs I could see impressive geysers of water exploding into the air as hundreds of rounds slammed into the river's surface at thousands of feet per second. At the altitude

Trace was firing from and at the velocity of the incoming ordnance it was like shooting at concrete from an arm's distance away. I heard ricochets pinging and zinging over us, many of them slamming into the *Wind Storm's* hull. Suddenly the firing stopped and was replaced by a momentary weird-ass eerie silence.

I ended that little interlude by going after the man Danny warned me about.

Rolling over and over until I was looking down the long walkway on my left flank, I saw him. He'd gone to his belly when the mini-motherfucker had opened up and was just pushing himself up to his feet when I bracketed him with two rounds to the chest. Fuck me to tears if he didn't just stagger backward under the two hammerlike blows and then let loose with a 5.56 Squad Automatic Weapon, or SAW, on my big ass! I heard a grunt in my headset and knew someone behind me was hit. Shit! The Nemesis operator must have been wearing trauma plates inside his soft body armor, otherwise my two spine busters would have cut through him like crap goes through the proverbial goose. Fucking Murphy again! God, I hate that Mick! I willed myself to melt into the deck as a second long burst from the SAW roared over my back. I felt the TT-assault pack being ripped apart and then away by the angry little steel hornets my asshole buddy up yonder was sending in my direction. Suddenly a flash bang grenade went off between the shooter and where I was lying prone like a whore after a good hour's gangbanging. The *WHUMMFF-BANG!* of the diversionary device seemed to lift me off the deck. The SAW ceased sawing and I took the opportunity to roll an M26 baseball grenade down the passageway toward the Tango's last known location. When the fucking little ballistic globe went off, I heard a shrill scream followed by a series of grunts and sucking wheezes. I knew I'd nailed the bastard good and in an instant I was up and running toward him.

"GO—GO—GO!" I yelled into my voice-activated mike. I saw the downed man just as I was about to trip over his ripped-up body. The frag had torn one leg clean off below the knee and peppered the asshole's lower body with hundreds of shards of splintered steel wire. His head, encased in a black balaclava, was lolling from side to side as he continued to moan and gasp for breath. I hopped over him, landed in a growing pool of blood, slipped and fell to my knees, swore like the goddamn sailor I am, then pushed my M4's muzzle against the Tango's forehead as it lolled into view and pressed my goddamned trigger on full auto.

Adios, motherfucker. Better you than me.

Two SEALs darted around and past me. I could hear more firing coming from the other side of the fucking boat and then Trace was laying down a second ring of steel on the water. This one was so close I felt the spray coming off the boiling surface as she hammered away on the mini-gun now less than 300 feet above us. DELTA trained that bitch well, I thought. Fletcher appeared at my side.

"Skipper! You okay?" he asked.

"Right as fucking rain, Lieutenant! We got anyone hit so far?"

The young SEAL officer nodded quickly. "One dead. Simpson. Took a burst from the SAW amidships. Near cut him in half. I got another man down with a broken leg. Fast rope accident. He lost his grip and did a thirty-foot freefall to the deck. He's conscious and providing good cover on our six. Everyone else got in okay but Banner. 'Hawk #2 shimmied when it should have shook and he roped into the river. Cut away his gear and we fished him out using the fast rope the crew chief dropped before they pulled pitch. He's still in the fight. I gave him my 240 to play with."

I nodded. Teamwork. That was what had got us in here and saved a few of our asses so far. It was good to be back with my SEALs. "Let's start digging the bastards out! I'm going to have Trace hose this fucking boat from amidships to stern. Then we go below decks and root through each fucking nookie and cranny for the nuke. We brought plenty of flash bangs so tell the men to use them, and to use them a lot. The nuke is the priority. Fuck Blanchard! We'll deal with him only if he pops up on the radar screen. Copy?"

"Roger that!" Fletcher keyed his voice mike and relayed my orders exactly as I'd given them. I heard the '47 way out over the water as it swung around and prepared to carpet the unsecured portion of the *Wind Storm* with mini-gun fire. It was not in our best interests to fight these fuckers one-on-one. We were too evenly matched on all levels and time was working against me where the SADM was concerned. The boat was still making headway up the river and at a fair rate of speed, too. That meant someone was still at the helm and that meant the gap between Ground Zero and the bomb was closing.

This was a bad thing.

I kill bad things.

It's just my nature.

"Everyone down, we're hosing the stern and the wheelhouse from the air," calmly ordered Fletcher. He then slid down the inside bulkhead of the main deck and propped his Joint Service Combat Shotgun atop his knees. With a forty-meter effective range and seven-round, three-inch Magnum ammo capability, the new SOF 'gauge was a nasty little bit of hardware any way you sliced it. "Anytime now," mused the lieutenant.

No fucking shit! I instinctively tucked my chin deep into my chest as the mini-gun opened up just a hundred feet off the starboard side of the *Storm*. Everything from gigantic chunks to tiny splinters of deck, trim, and anything else the gunfire hit went spinning through the air and out onto the river like a Texas hailstorm. Trace was hitting the wheelhouse first in an effort to bring the *Storm* to a halt. Whoever was topside and sailing this poor bitch could not have survived the greasing she was applying in long, accurate, hellish hundred-round bursts. I heard the '47 moving forward and through my night vision goggles I could see my she-cat in the open gun window. The damn mini opened up again and this time it was the back half of the boat she was raking in long, lazy strokes. I knew Trace would rotate around the stern of this now seriously fucked-up pleasure palace and hose the shit outta the props. That would effectively disable the *Storm* and guarantee it would be here and now that this matter would be settled by *moi* and my chain dogs from SIX. Sure enough, I felt the vibrations of the pounding the screws and their shafts were taking as Dahlgren stripped them clean away from the hull. The '47 then moved again and Trace repeated the pounding of the decks, this time from the opposite side of the boat.

"All clear, Skipper! I'm outta ammo, so you're up!" she announced over my headset. The Chinook rose and lifted away into the darkness. Anyone who'd survived the scrubbing Trace had just given the *Storm* would have to have been holed up below decks. It was rat-hunting time for the boyz and me.

"Get 'em moving, Lieutenant!"

That's when my fucking cell phone rang. I couldn't resist—I fished the little fucker outta a utility pouch and punched the "TALK" button. Remember what I said about commo? "MARCINKO! GO!"

"Dick, it's Karen. Can you talk?"

The absurdity of it hit me like a punch from Mike Tyson. "Sure," I said, even as Fletcher fired off a short burst at someone I couldn't see, "just taking a fucking break when you called. Whazzzz up?"

I feared my attempt at humor had gone awry when Karen angrily replied, "Fuck you and listen up! I just left the president and that asshole Mulcahy. I'm at a fucking bar in Alexandria in the women's bathroom. I think that prick Clay is outside shadowing me!"

The stubby little black hairs on my ears stood straight up as I heard the venom in her voice. Warning bells were going off in my skull even as a bevy of automatic weapons fire rushed over and past me, the *craaak-THUD* of flash bangs accenting the ferocity of the combat now beginning to take place below decks. "Spill it. Shit's going down and I'm playing the backfield by myself right now!"

"Dick, you watch your six! Clay plans to order the gunship to sink the *Storm* with all aboard if he feels you're losing control of the situation. Worse, the president sees you as excess baggage and a possible political liability if what you had to do to get this far ever becomes public. Your pardon means squat right now unless you've covered your ass in some way I'm not aware of!"

Hmmmm, I thought to myself. The beltway bandits strike again. "Fuck him," I barked into the cell. "Anything else?"

"Yes. There's a plan taking shape to do an end run around the Constitution using Blanchard as the fall guy whether you get him or not. Telling you all this will probably cost me my career but . . ."

"I'll handle it," I told her, and I meant it. "Play nice-nice with Mulcahy. I'll deal with him when I get back. Gotta go, my long distance card is about to run out!"

I punched off and shoved the cell back into its holder. Fuck me to tears! Cross, cross, and double cross! I could handle the president because I'd followed his directive to the letter. By any and all means, he'd told me during our telephonic *chit-chat* at OISA. I love my microcassette recorder and use the little bastard all the time these days. You never fucking know when someone is going to say something you'd just dearly love to have available later on. I'd covertly taped the silly SOB and then made half a dozen copies and sent each one to a trusted friend—including my first editor who is now working for the FOX network—and my mean-ass Doberman of an attorney. If the president wanted to fuck with Dick, then Dick would fuck with the president—but in the public forum. I'd never brought down a presidential administration before but I'd always wanted to, just to say I did. Not a bad pickup line in a bar. As for Mulcahy, I'd deal with him in my own way and in my own time. You find rats everywhere. Karen had come through for me and at great personal and professional risk to herself. I wouldn't forget that. Loyalty is *Numba One* to me. She'd surely earned mine tonight.

"DICK! Need some help down here!"

Back to work.

"Whaddaya got, sailor?" I barked into my mike. I'd fired off half my magazines and was doing a hands-on check of my gear while I moved toward the sound of the action taking place. I stumbled over a body, or what was left of a body, on the rear deck. The minigun had hacked the pleasure cruiser's upper decks to sawdust. From the boat's slight list, I guessed we were taking on water. Trace had probably opened up the hull when she'd raked the screws on her last pass. Uncle Sam could pay for the damage; it'd be a bargain compared to rebuilding Portland. I took up a security position and scanned the decks and wheelhouse above me. The *Storm* was smoking from a hundred small fires, thanks to our ample use of tracer rounds, as well as the flash bangs my SEALs had been using in great numbers to flush any Nemesis rats out of the cabins below deck. "SitRep!" I barked into my mike.

Fletcher's voice came through my earpiece. "We've got two additional KIA. Another two with serious wounds and I need MedEvac ASAP off the foredeck. One with light injuries from flying glass but still operational. Three unhurt, including me. What's your status, Skipper?"

Damn it! My force of ten had been thinned out to four motherfuckers with all their eyes, ears, and fingers properly functioning. "What about Nemesis?" I asked the lieutenant.

"I think we got all of 'em, except the colonel . . . and the nuke. I haven't seen either down here but that's not to say he isn't curled up under a bunk somewhere with his favorite toy."

I shook my head like an angry lion. *Goddamn Blanchard to Hell!* Where was the fucker? Where would

I be if I were him? I'd keep the fucking nuke with me, that much was certain. No one reported seeing any one or thing leaving the *Storm* and with the amount of night imagery we'd laid down from both the '47 and the AC, I couldn't imagine Blanchard getting away from us unless he swam out using a Drager or SCUBA system. I hadn't given the rotten bastard enough time to do *that*.

"Trace?"

"Dahlgren here! Whatcha need, boss?"

"Bring the fucking helo down on the deck and drop off the security team. Fletcher needs shooters to secure this piece of shit, which is sinking beneath our feet thanks to your fine aerial gunnery skills!"

"Inbound, Skipper . . . and thank you. *I aims to please!*"

Christ, it was like having Jerry Fucking Seinfeld on the team. But much better looking.

"Danny! Get those 'Hawks in here. Have one hover off the foredeck so we can get our wounded out and away. Advise the PANG we got hurt people inbound. Then get the fuck outta here and call Karen on her secure cell, the one *I* gave her. She's got some info you need to hear."

From off in the distance I heard the two PAVE 'Hawks pounding the air toward us as Barrett complied with my orders. I wanted my wounded SEALs off the terminally damaged *Wind Storm* before it went belly up. I'd seen ships go down before and I knew that when it happened, it happened fast. No five-minute warning bell.

It was high time to find the nuke, and maybe in the process reintroduce myself to Colonel Max Blanchard. I checked my M4 and switched out a half-empty mag for a full one. Slamming the clip into the carbine's well, I jacked the slide to the rear and extracted a live round, replacing it with a fresh one from the new mag. I let the bolt fly forward and hit the forward assist for good measure. The little rifle was once again locked and loaded.

Okay. Where would I take the nuke? Where would I go if I were in charge of this sack of shit outfit?

To beat a terrorist you have to think like a terrorist.

My eyes roamed over the shattered upper decks finally coming to rest on the badly mauled wheelhouse. Who'd been steering this ship when we'd come up on her? Who'd kept her on track during the initial assault and firefight? *Who'd leased the bitch to begin with?*

I began climbing over small mounds of burning debris and headed toward the wheelhouse. Through its shattered windows I could see flames licking away at its interior. Someone had been up there doing his job and I was betting that person was none other than my MIA crackpot colonel. Find the colonel, find the nuke. It just made good sense. Behind me I could hear the sounds of the '47 maneuvering into position and dropping off the six-man SEAL reaction force. They'd bolster Fletcher's thinned out assaulters and help load the wounded and the dead.

I couldn't wait for the cavalry to ride in. I crept past bits and pieces of something vaguely human and scooted up next to the blown out doorway leading into the once super-luxurious control room. Remind me never to let Trace do my interior decorating, unless I'm looking for sawdust everywhere. Pulling my last flash bang from the drop pouch on my assault vest, I gave a quiet warning to anyone listening on the radio that I was about to make some unpleasant noise top-side. I worked the safety pin free, dropped it to the ruptured decking, and tossed the grenade into the gutted wheelhouse. It never hurts to be sure.

As soon as I heard the *KA-WHUMMP* of the little banger and saw the momentary bright flash of light it emitted upon detonation, I pulled my goggles off and let them fall against my chest on their dummy cord. Rather than bursting in with my normal roguish flair, I slipped quietly inside the cabin area, the muzzle of my M4 sweeping from left to right, my trigger finger poised above the smooth steel lever, ready to apply instant pressure if necessary. A small blaze crackled near the center of the cabin, providing a hellish kind of illumination to the scene. Fire and brimstone, pre-sent and accounted for. But was Blanchard here or not? It was a damn good thing I was playing it coy since the sound of a handgun going off to my right reached me a split second *after* the bullet it fired took off the lower half of my right ear! I dropped to one knee and fired the M4 on full auto into the cabin, try-ing to aim in the general direction where I thought the bullet had come from.

I stopped shooting and waited, holding my breath and trying to discern any movement or sound in the cabin. Out on the deck I heard the '47 pull pitch. Its roar was replaced by the PAVE 'Hawks I'd ordered in to get the wounded to safety. With a sudden lurch I felt the *Storm* begin to keel over on her starboard side. Time was running out. I had to search the cabin and hope to *fuck* I'd killed whoever had fired at me. If I really hit the jackpot, it would have been Blanchard! If I were lucky, if I were truly blessed, if Murphy had forgotten about his old pal Demo Dick, I'd get my bad guy, get my nuke, and get my frogman's ass off this fucking tub before it went to the bottom of the river!

Crouched just inside the doorway, all my senses strained to the max, I tried to detect any movement or sound in the wheelhouse that would tell me where my opponent was taking cover. I didn't need to work so hard; from across the cabin, a voice suddenly called out my very own name.

"MARCINKO! I figured it'd be you who'd come."

Blanchard's smoke-filled, rasping voice sent a chill up my spine. Sounded like a dead man talking. But maybe that was just wishful thinking. . . .

"Where's the nuke, colonel? Neither one of us has time for small talk."

"Oh come now, we've got all the time in the world. And I'm so enjoying getting reacquainted with your little Jew friend here. That ugly bit of gunfire you just sent in here almost deprived me of his company. How sad that would have made me."

There—in the corner—I could just make out two figures. One had to be Blanchard, partially protected behind a massive, solid brass table that had been turned on its side. The metal tabletop, pocked with scores of bullet scars, must have acted like a wall of armor and allowed him to survive the assault. But somewhere along the way the fire had obviously gotten to him. His uniform was badly scorched and I thought I could see places where actual bits of skin were peeling from his body. Fine. He deserved to burn. What concerned me was the man on his knees next to him, gagged and blindfolded, totally exposed. Blanchard held his gun directly against the man's handsome, blond head. Paul Kossens.

Fuck, fuck, fuck.

"Blanchard, you piece of shit. Let him go and deal with me like a man. I'm the one you want."

"Sorry to disappoint you, Dick, but I don't give a fuck about you. Believe it or not, this is bigger than either you or me. And I'll be rewarded in the next world for all I've done in this one."

"Newsflash—*you failed, asshole*. You completely and utterly failed. There's no reward coming to you anywhere. You're going straight to hell."

"If that is the case, I'll expect to see you there. After all, we're much the same Dick. I just got tired of taking orders from men I couldn't respect. You're too pussy-whipped by the machine to understand."

"Maybe we are alike, except for one big thing. I'm gonna be alive tomorrow, and you're not."

Another sudden lurch. I felt the *Storm* beginning to keel a bit farther over on her starboard side. I could see Paul's jaw working madly against his gag. If Blanchard could just be distracted for a moment and take his gun away from Paul's head, I was pretty sure I'd be able to get off a round or two without signing Paul's death warrant. Time to use that famous Rogue charm.

"Blanchard, there's something I've been meaning to tell you. I just want to be fucking certain you appreciate the fact that you and your pathetic team of lady golfers have been taken down by a gang of true, out-and-out mongrels. A Jew, a Black, and an Apache, along with Yours Truly, kicked your tender white ass. Oh, did I mention the Apache is a girl? I think your kind of inbreeding must be overrated."

I felt his contempt as I spoke and I was sure he'd swing his gun in my direction and give me my chance to take him out. But instead he just took a deep breath and replied in an almost pitying tone, "Marcinko, I don't blame you for what you've done. I understand you're just a servant of the Satanic government that employs you. I understand that your brain isn't big enough to fully comprehend the importance of what I'm doing here. I am a true warrior, fighting for the only things that matter—blood, homeland, destiny."

"Cut the shit, Blanchard. Your destiny is to be the prettiest bitch in the prison yard. You'll have a swell time."

"Dick, I want to help you. I want to pray for your soul and see if we can't both find some peace. Come here, let me lay my hands on you just for a moment and say a prayer for our wounded nation. Don't deny me something you can give so easily. Then I'll let your friend go and together we can decide what to do about the bomb."

Before I could respond, a terrible and primal roar erupted from Paul's throat, surprising me as much as Blanchard. Still blindfolded, he sprang upward with all the power his legs could muster and managed to throw himself right at Blanchard's head. The colonel's gun went off. I heard myself scream in fury as I watched the back of Paul's head explode in a blur of blood and bone. My own gun barked to life, sending a withering hail of bullets at Blanchard's makeshift hiding place. He'd completely disappeared behind the big wall of metal and I couldn't know for sure whether I'd managed to hit him or not.

The sight of Paul's blood running dark and red across the deck from his shattered skull filled me with the kind of pure, burning anger and hunger for revenge that I've only experienced a few times in my life. In that moment I became a machine with just one single, all-consuming thought—*Max Blanchard is a dead man.* I no longer cared a rat's ass about Portland, about the nuke, about Karen, about anything but finding and destroying the man who had just killed my friend and teammate before my eyes. Paul had sacrificed himself to even out the equation. That final act of heroism wasn't going to have been in vain. Blanchard was mine.

Fuck caution. Without pausing to seriously consider what I was doing, I ran directly toward the overturned table barricade. Using my shoulder like a battering ram, I slammed into it as hard as I could so that anyone behind it would be knocked over and pinned between it and the wall. The table slid a foot or two before it crashed hard against the bulkhead. I could tell by the way it struck the bulkhead that there hadn't been anyone behind it.

What the fuck?

I grabbed the table and hurled it aside. There, behind it, a piece of the floor in the wheelhouse cabin's corner had been neatly cut away, providing an escape route down into the lower decks. Of course Blanchard wouldn't have allowed himself to get caught like a rat in a hole. He'd always plan an alternate way out for himself.

Given his weakened condition, that SADM had to be feeling awfully heavy by now, but even at this point I doubted he'd be willing to let it out of his hands. It was the last and most powerful card he had to play. He'd be moving pretty slowly, probably trying to get to a place on the ship where he could arm it. Even though he'd miss the heart of the city, he'd figure blowing it up here was better than not using it at all. Since his escape route was taking him to the lower decks that were filling with more and more water, he didn't have many options left.

Not knowing what was waiting for me, I lowered myself through the hole in the floor. The ship's emergency lighting was still turned on down here and I found myself at one end of a fairly long inner passageway that had several doors opening from it along both sides. Here, closer to its belly, the creaks and groans of the vessel were unmistakable. Probably only a few minutes remained before it would capsize. The handsome wooden doors leading to the staterooms up and down the corridor banged open and closed as the ship lurched about in agony. All except the last one on the starboard side, which remained conspicuously shut. Blanchard.

I darted down the corridor and quickly blew the doorknob and lock to bits. Crashing into the room, I saw Blanchard hunched over an all too familiar looking titanium suitcase. He was fumbling with its locks, muttering distractedly to himself. Praying or cursing, I couldn't tell. My finger lovingly caressed the trigger of my Glock as he turned toward me—and for an instant I was stunned by the hideousness of his face. Or what used to be his face. His entire forehead and scalp were peeling away in thick, fleshy ribbons. He seemed confused by what was happening, like he wasn't really sure if I was there or not. That's when I realized it—he was blind. His facial wounds had oozed and bled so severely that his eyes had gradually been turned into useless sacks of fluid. Paul's last-ditch attack had probably done the rest. Motherfucker. A blind man trying to arm a nuclear bomb.

"See you in hell, Max," I growled and sent every

last bullet I had into him. Each one had Paul's name on it.

I walked over to his body and pushed my gloved hand into the mass of pulped and seeping flesh that was his corpse. There wasn't any head left, which kinda fucked up a down and dirty facial feature ID, but I was betting he was wearing his dog tags out of habit. I was right. I felt the steel chain with its two oval-shaped steel disks right where I knew they'd be. Jerking the ID necklace free, which is pretty fucking easy when there's no head to deal with, I wiped bits of bone and flesh away from the stamped metal and read "Blanchard, Maxwell, Col." With a sigh, I dumped the tags into my fatigue shirt breast pocket. Then I fished out my Wor-Tech knife from its pouch on my left thigh. With two quick cuts I removed the index finger and thumb from his right hand. I wrapped these in the OD drive-on rag I was wearing around my throat and dropped my little treasures into my left drop pouch. Nothing quite says *you* like your fingerprints and I wanted incontestable proof that I'd killed Blanchard before the river rushed in and washed what was left of his body out to sea.

I felt the *Storm* lurch farther sideways and start to slide into the river's depths. Time was not on Dickie's side any longer. Within seconds I'd have to get out of here or risk being trapped with Max's evil corpse as we went down to Davy Jones's Locker *conjunto*. Not my idea of a happy ending to what had been a great party so far. Besides, I had a president and a helluva woman both waiting for me back in D.C.—and I was gonna fuck them both, although in very different ways.

Behind Blanchard's corpse was one badly battered

titanium-cased man-fucking-portable nuclear weapon.
Come to papa, baby!

I holstered the Glock and grabbed the case and
leaped out of the cabin just as the *Storm* gave a mighty
groan of agony and began her final voyage. From my
headset I could hear my teammates' voices urging me
to get clear. No shit, I thought to myself as I tripped
and bumped and fell down the passageway, then
heaved myself back up into the wheelhouse, relieved
at least to be out of the certain deathtrap of the lower
decks. I could hear the helos roaring around overhead
and I figured *somebody* had to see me given all the high
speed IR we'd been using with such abandon. All I
had to do was keep my cool—and a firm grip on the
nuke. I'm a fucking SEAL and water is my natural
habitat. I just needed to get my ass clear of the suck-
hole the *Storm* would create as she went down. The
rest would be a piece of cake.

Unless the nuke detonated, of course.

And if *that* happened I wouldn't give a fuck either
way. At least it would be quick and I would have
accomplished my mission. Well, sort of.

I made a break for it and jumped as far out and
away from the doomed vessel as I could. As I hit the
surface of the river and sank below I used my free
hand to unclip my M4, which sank immediately. The
case was weighing me down but with the rifle gone I
could drag the fucker behind me while swimming my
ass off and push-pulling with the one arm I had available. SEALs are trained to swim in any circumstances
and I'd started my career as a frogman. Old habits die
hard and old rogues die even harder. I was not going
to lose the case or my life. Not now. Not after good
men had died in the process of getting me to my objec-

tive. My ear would be an "easy fix" for my friend and personal plastic surgeon, Mark Zukowski. He's now in private practice in Chicago. I keep him close at hand; he knows Rogue Manor and all of its sins well.

My shaggy, bleeding, one-eared head finally broke the surface and I sucked in as much oxygen as I could get. Reaching down I snagged my emergency strobe light from its pouch and activated the little fucker. Holding it as high out of the murk as possible I kicked for all I was worth to remain above the surface. I heard the '47 coming in and soon great swells were washing over me from its beautiful, beautiful prop blasts. I saw the rear ramp come down and the crew chief and Trace, both tethered to the interior of the airframe by long, supple safety lines, scooted out to the ramp's edge, now just inches above the river. I kicked with all I had left in me and felt strong hands grabbing at my uniform, and then hauling my tired ass up and into the Chinook. I kept my death grip on the case and nodded to Trace that I was okay. As the '47 lifted off I dragged myself deeper into its hull, finally collapsing on the fully inflated Zodiac I'd ordered to be stowed there.

I'd made it.

"Get us at least twenty-five miles out to sea," I croaked to no one in particular. "You're gonna drop me and the case off in the Zod and wait exactly twenty-four hours before picking me up. I don't know if this fucking thing is armed or not. Let's roll!" With that I fell backward into the rubber raiding craft, placing the nuke beside me on its hard-ribbed flooring.

Damn, I reminded myself, *I am so fucking good!*

20

"I am the War Lord and the wrathful God of
Combat and I will always lead you from the
front, not the rear."

COMMANDER RICHARD MARCINKO (ret.),
The Real Team

THERE WAS NOTHING MORE I COULD DO, NEEDED TO DO, OR
wanted the fuck to do except lie in that fucking Zodiac
and catch my goddamned breath. What about the
nuke, you may well ask? The damn thing hadn't gone
off yet so—for the time being—life was sweet. On the
other hand I could feel every fucking bump, blister,
scrape, bruise, and cut my roguish body had sucked
up during the last two days. Two fucking days? That
was all? When this was finally over I'd be gargling
down Dr. Bombay's mighty fine Sapphire by the canteen cup and popping 800-milligram hits of Motrin
(known in the Teams as "SEAL candy") for weeks. I
felt as if I'd been tossed into the world's biggest rock
polisher and tumbled for hours on end. I was not
happy about Blanchard's having blown most of one of
the only two fucking ears I came into this world with

clean off my fucking skull, either. I had to give it to the miserable bastard. He'd hung in there long enough to take his shot. Trouble was, he'd missed and I hadn't. He'd gotten my ear but I'd gotten his head—and I'll take getting head any day of the fucking week!

I pulled myself up and grabbed hold of the fucking case so many men had died for. I knew these hellish devices like the back of my callused hand. Nuclear nightmares in a convenient travel size is what they are. The damn Russians built an unknown number of SADMs and then went and lost, misplaced, or sold a shitpot of them when the Evil Empire caved in on itself. We weren't much better at keeping track of our own, as I'd proven at Red Cell. Hell, looking at the battered thirty-pound world-ender, I remembered getting ahold of a similar device simply by kidnapping a senior naval officer who had access to such things and threatening to rape his tight little ass with a fucking banana! Funny how patriotism, loyalty, and the Honor Code of the Academy go out the window when someone you don't know starts working a long, thick hunka something up your shitter while you're blindfolded and bent over a nice soft piece of furniture. It hadn't taken but two well-measured inches of yellow fruit and some graphic pillow talk to elicit the necessary access code to the storage facility where the nukes were kept. And I wonder why some of the Navy brass don't love me like a son . . .

Sleep well, America. Your guardians are more concerned about the sanctity of their pinkie-tight assholes than they are about your collective buttocks when it comes to the security of the most devastating weapons on the face of the planet.

Trace squatted down in front of me. She'd stripped

off her M4 and heavy aviation flak jacket after pulling my beat-to-shit hide out of the river. I had to lean in close to hear her over the racket the Chinook was making as we hauled ass for the Pacific Ocean. Her scent filled my nostrils, driving out the pungent, biting odor of burnt cordite, human flesh, and my own roguish stink. Ah, women. Can't live with 'em, can't live without 'em. Just because you've heard it before doesn't mean it isn't true!

"Shouldn't we open the case and see if he armed the device?" she asked.

I shook my soggy, aching head in the negative. "Remember what happened to George Moore. We gotta figure these bastards set anti-disturbance devices on everything, especially the fucking nuke! If it ain't broke, we don't fix it. As long as the pilot can get me out to sea for a twenty-four-hour solo cruise with no boom-boom, we'll be good to go."

Dahlgren nodded, although I could tell she didn't really agree. She'd done a hell of a job for us tonight. Without thinking, I reached out and cupped the side of her face with my hand. For a moment she closed her eyes and nuzzled my paw, then pulled away. We looked at each other in mutual understanding and respect. "You *do* like having me around, don't you Dick?"

I nodded once in the semidark of the goddamned noisy-ass helo. "Yeah, you're okay, Dahlgren. For a girl."

We both grinned as she flipped me a very professional bird.

"Where's that asshole Kossens?" she shouted over the whine of the turbine engines. "He kicked some serious ass tonight, too!"

Fuck, I hated to tell her, but I couldn't put it off. "Blanchard got him. He was a brave kid, right to the last. Went down fighting."

Trace's expression changed from mirth to a kind of blank mask that I'd seen way too many times in my career. *GODDAMN IT!* I willed myself to remain where I was seated on the Zodiac's gunwale.

"Last I saw of him, he was coming back to check on you right before I made my first gun run," Trace said.

The kid had been coming back to check on me when Blanchard nabbed him! I suddenly felt very old and used up. I'd not only lost a SEAL in action but I'd lost one of my kids, one of the new team.

"I'm really sorry, Dick. Paul was the best, you know I loved him, too. He wanted to be right where he was tonight, in the thick of it with the rest of us." Trace put a hand on my shoulder and squeezed. She then stood up and made her way forward to talk with the crew chief. I was alone. Alone and angry. Alone with a fucking maybe hot and maybe not nuke. Alone with fresh good-bad-painful memories of a go-to-hell young SEAL who'd faced danger with me shoulder to shoulder. I shook my head like a bull who'd been skewered in the middle of the ring. Maybe I'd grieve later, but for right now I was furious! Before this was over I'd see to it Paul's memory and family were taken care of by my government. He'd saved at least a hundred thousand lives tonight at the expense of his own. I'd not forget that, and neither would those who'd sent him into harm's way.

The crew chief's voice interrupted my thoughts. *"We're about ten minutes away from where we can put you down, Captain. Are you sure you have to do this? If it hasn't blown yet . . ."*

I looked him dead in the eye and nodded. "This shit may still be hot, no way to know but wait. Hell, I'm an old black-shoe sailor. A little time on the ocean isn't gonna hurt me one way or another. Just toss me an MRE and some water before you pull pitch. Another radio would be good, too."

The special-ops aviator nodded once and gave a thumbs-up. Twenty-five miles out at sea is one long ass way from shore for anyone to be bobbing around alone for twenty-four hours. Especially in a rubber boat no bigger than a 1960s Volkswagen van. I didn't want to risk the '47's crew any more than was necessary. I knew they'd burned a shitload of fuel already and there was no reserve bladder onboard to draw from if we went any farther out. I also knew there was a Coast Guard station at the mouth of the Columbia that could spare at least one ship to chop in my direction after the mandated twenty-four-hour waiting period was up. The fuckers had seagoing SAR aviation assets, as well. As long as Max hadn't armed the nuke when our attack started, the most I had to worry about was one night on the open seas. For a SEAL, and especially for *moi*, one night was nothing to get fussed up about.

I felt the chopper beginning to lose altitude. Looking over at the chief I saw him say something to Trace, who nodded once and then disappeared up toward where the pilots were flying the fucking eggbeater. I grabbed the nuke's case by its handle and clambered into the Zodiac. Swiftly and precisely, I lashed the nuke to the Zodiac using 550 para-cord I'd brought with me for that very purpose. Double-checking my knots I was satisfied the fucking Zod could do rollovers all day long and the nuke would remain secure. I then pulled a homing beacon I'd bummed off one of the PJs before leaving the PANG and taped it tightly to the case's dinged up side with good old-fashioned hundred-mile-an-hour tape. Hey, I never leave home without 550 cord and hundred-mile-an-hour tape! Whaddaya think I am, a fucking moron? If Moby Fucking Dick gobbled my ass up before the Coast Guard found me, at least they would be able to track and recover the device . . . unless of course it blew the fuck up between now and then.

Satisfied with my handiwork I made my way over to a starboard-side window of the helo and looked out across the vastness of the ocean. God, I love the sea! It had been years since I'd served a duty cruise. For a moment I recalled my last time on waters like these. I'd drowned two goddamned terrorists then. Now I was right back where my trials and tribulations had begun a year ago. The fucking irony was not lost on me!

But before I could start acting out the title role in *The Old Man and the Sea,* I had a few quick phone calls to make.

Digging around in my assault vest I found my cell. Mumbling a quick prayer, I punched the "ON" button and was rewarded with a green signal light! Somebody must have bought this shit from the highest bidder, given the beating the little phone had taken. I auto-dialed Danny first. He answered on the second ring and although I had to yell to be heard, he acknowledged my instructions and then rang off. Next I called Karen. That conversation took all of sixty seconds. I told her to keep it warm for me and I'd see her soon. It was now time to call the president of the United States.

Clay answered the Oval Office phone. I grinned as he recognized my voice. "How the FUCK did you get this number, Marcinko? And where the fuck are you? I can barely hear you!"

"Put the big man on, you rat-breath, low-life, cocksucking, back-stabbing motherfucker! I'll be dealing with you in person when I get back to Washington. And back the fuck off Karen. I find out you've been back-dooring her sweet ass, you'll find my ten inches buried to the hilt in yours. Now, put the president on, asshole!"

Remember, good reader, what I've told you about my bedside manner? It really does *suck*, doesn't it?

"DICK! ONE MINUTE OUT! MAKE IT QUICK! WE'RE RUNNING LOW ON GO-FAST JUICE!"

I waved an acknowledgment to the crew chief, then fished my waterproofed microcassette player outta my right breast pocket. I'd wrapped the little fucker in a watertight baggie before the mission. There was a cassette loaded and it was a motherfucker!

"Dick? This is the president. Congratulations on your success. I understand you have gotten our device back, yes?"

My lips curled back like a rabid wolf with a hard-on and no place wild enough to stick it. "Yes, Mr. President, I've got the fucking nuke. Now listen up. Paul Kossens, one of *my* SEALS, died helping me get your precious bomb back. A man named Danny Barrett is going to drop by your office in a few days to pick up Paul's posthumous silver fucking star. You're going to ensure all the paperwork is squared away and I'm going to personally give it to his next of kin when they bury him at Arlington. Am I understood, Mr. President?"

There was a half-second's silence on the other end before the president replied, or tried to, I should say.

"Goddamn it, Marcinko! I'm the fucking president of the United States! *Your* commander in chief! I can't believe I'm hearing you speak to me in this manner!"

"Believe it." I paused a moment for effect. "And I'm not done. Karen Fairfield is off-limits. She did her job and that's more than I can say for some of the rest of your ass-wipes. I want Master Sergeant Trace Dahlgren promoted ASAP to sergeant-major. Get some dumbass colonel over at the Department of the Army to handle that before I'm on the ground at Dulles.

"I have to go now and baby-sit a nuclear bomb, but before I do, I want you to hear something. You can presume there are many copies. You can presume that no matter what happens to me, *someone* will make these available to the press unless I get what I want. When I want it. Have a great day, sir."

I held the cassette recorder up to the cell's mouthpiece and punched the PLAY button. Watching the numbers spin on the triple-digit counter, I punched off when I knew the president had heard what I'd wanted him to—his absolutely clear and explicit orders to me, given over phone at OISA. Like I said earlier, good and faithful reader, I'd learned to play hardball along the beltway a long time ago. The only rules I play by today are my own, and I play damn hard and only to *win!*

The ramp began to drop and soft, early morning light reflecting off the ocean flooded the gloomy hold of the '47. Trace, the chief, and I all grabbed the hard rubber handholds on the Zodiac and pulled it toward the ramp. I tossed a paddle in, as well as the emergency kit the chief had assembled for me. I nodded in appreciation as he handed over his Nomex flight jacket. I'd appreciate its warmth while I waited on the Coast Guard to show up.

"We'll hover about ten feet off the deck and then bring her nose up. It'll just take a good push and you should roll right off the ramp and safely down. Good luck, Captain. See you soon!" The crew chief scooted back and gave a hand signal to Trace. I jumped into the Zodiac and prepared myself for the short drop to the ocean's surface. Someone pulled my frazzled ponytail and when I turned around it was Dahlgren.

"Sure you don't want any company, skipper? I'm available."

"You stay with the bird," I yelled over the increasing roar of the chopper's engines, "I've already lost one teammate I care about. I don't want to lose another one. You understand me, *Sergeant-Major?*"

Trace's eyes widened for just a moment. Then she hopped out of the Zod and joined the chief where together they could push my big ass into the water. I turned around and stared out the back of the Chinook. I could see nothing before me but the smooth surface of a calm sea. Fuck it if I was alone for a while! Loneliness builds character and I'd been on my own since I could remember. Besides, I needed a break. I couldn't remember the last time I'd slept. Big ocean, little boat, warm sun, gentle waves, tactical nuclear weapon that may or may not go off at any moment . . . what more could a simple man like me want from life?

"GO! GO! GO!"

I felt the Zodiac begin to slide as the helo dropped its ass toward the now churning waters below me. Holding on tightly I willed myself to keep my eyes open. As planned, the rubber raiding craft dropped free and pancaked bow-first into the ocean. For a moment I bobbed and bounced and wobbled like a motherfucker. As the '47 pulled pitch and roared up and away the little boat steadied itself and instantly the world was quiet and peaceful. I waved a hand up toward the Chinook as it grabbed altitude and thought I saw someone waving back. I'd check the radio comms in a moment or two . . . or maybe three. Shit, I was in no hurry to talk to anyone. The sound of the helo faded into the distance and I made a quick check of my gear. The nuke was intact and happily cinched into the Zodiac for the remainder of the exercise. The homing device I'd activated was steadily blinking away so I knew my signal was going out to whoever was monitoring it back on the mainland at the PANG. I stretched my tired old carcass and took off my assault vest. Checking my drop bag I was pleased to discover I still had the colonel's little dick skinners available for the FBI crime lab to fuck around with once I was on dry land again.

The morning air was cool, so I peeled off my soaked fatigue shirt, laid it over the gunwale to dry, and shrugged into the waterproof flight jacket the chief had given me. Then I took a long swig of cool, fresh water from one of the three two-quart bladders in the Zod. Looking around, I marveled at the sheer beauty of my surroundings. First and foremost I am a Navy man and going to sea is what real Navy men do. Satisfied with my current situation, I leaned back and closed my bleary eyes.

Exhausted, I fell almost instantly into that peculiar state of semiconsciousness that's not quite asleep but not quite awake either. The rocking of the boat, the sounds and smells of the ocean, gave me a strange sense of dislocation and I had the overwhelming feeling that the last year of my life had been nothing but a long, intense dream. I swear, for a little while I had the idea that I was floating in a different Zodiac after a different mission, somewhere between Portugal and Hell, having just consigned the Kelley brothers to a life sentence (admittedly, a very short one) at the bottom of the sea. Surely I'd open my eyes and see the night sky above me, the constellations strung across it, showing me and my crew of hardass warriors the way back home. Any second I'd hear Mick Owen's saying something in his distinctive Welsh accent like, "Wake up, Dick! I can't take another cock-up today."

I opened my eyes.

No stars—morning sun. No fellow teammates—me all alone. No Kelley brothers—just a suitcase that could take out a city in a heartbeat. Guess it wasn't a dream.

From thinking about the Kelleys, I found myself wondering more about Blanchard. How did a guy like him get so far offtrack? In some ways, our backgrounds and training weren't all that different. Hell, people were generally crazy; I'd long ago reconciled myself to that simple fact of life. The more important question was: How did he manage to put together his psycho team within a team without anybody ever getting the least bit suspicious? From what Paul had told me, I knew Blanchard had been looking for recruits for his band of sick fucks for years; this wasn't something that just popped into his head after one too many drinks at a retirement party a few months ago. And I was supposed to believe that *not a single person* in the entire U.S. military organization had a goddamn clue that something was seriously off about the guy?

What was it Blanchard himself had said to me on the *Wind Storm*? Something about this being bigger than him or me. Maybe I hadn't understood his real meaning at the time . . .

I didn't want to jump to conclusions, but it seemed as plain as the shiny suitcase sitting next to me that he'd had help somewhere along the way. Granted, maybe Blanchard was a charismatic leader to his men. Maybe he could hypnotize his followers into doing whatever he wanted with some magical spell or a sprinkle of fairy dust. But I'd been around the asshole enough times to know that he didn't possess the sheer imagination, the balls, or the patience to have single-handedly planned and carried out this whole mission.

It was like I'd been kicked in the stomach when I realized the simple truth—THIS WAS NOT OVER. I didn't know if he'd had help from people in our own government, or if he'd been the agent of some outside group. It had been clear for a long time that gangs of thugs like Hamas, Hezbollah, and Al Qaeda were quietly on the lookout for strategic forces already in place inside the U.S. that they could use for their own purposes. There's some unverified but believable intel suggesting Tim McVeigh had the benefit of foreign assistance in his Oklahoma City job. That would have been a mosquito bite compared to the pain Blanchard wanted to inflict.

I tried to slow my brain down. If I kept on like this, it was going to be a helluva long twenty-four hours alone in this boat. Why the fuck didn't I bring a deck of cards, a bottle of Bombay, and an ice bucket?

"Hey, sailor! Looking for a good time?"

What the fuck was that?

A jumper gracefully suspended from a HALO canopy sailed right over my head about a hundred feet above the deck. Now Appearing: Trace Dahlgren starring as Wonder Woman. I watched as she made a nice turn into the wind and splashed down just short of the Zodiac. She cut loose the 'chute as she hit the water and swam down and away from the harness to avoid getting tangled up. As she reappeared on the surface the parachute disappeared beneath the waves as the weight of its harness pulled it under.

"What the hell are you doing here?" I barked at Trace as she began swimming toward me. "Didn't I order you to be somewhere else?" I held my paddle out when she was close enough to grab it and pulled the little bitch into the Zod with one good heave-ho! Sitting back down, I put on my best war face. Trace ignored me, shaking her pretty head back and forth and then unclipping her hair and letting it hang. Standing, she unzipped her Nomex flight suit and stripped it right off. Underneath it she was wearing a black sports bra and matching black thong. I'd seen Dahlgren stripped down before at the Manor after she, Paul, and I had finished a butt-busting workout and were sweating ourselves silly in the wet steam bath, drinking beer and swapping lies. But somehow she was looking way fucking different now than I remembered her.

My reliable ten-inch companion began to rumble around between my hairy frogman's thighs, as if he wanted to see what all the fuss was about.

"I'm here because I want to be and the chief had a 'chute that needed jumping," replied Trace as she sat down on the gunwale facing me. "And yes, you *did* order me to be somewhere else and *yes*, I've willfully disobeyed that order! Now, with that said, you've got a choice. Are we going to waste this time talking, or are we going to fuck?"

"We're going to fuck," I growled as I made my way to her side, "until otherwise directed."

Never, ever let it be said that the Rogue Warrior hesitates when it comes to making the *really* important command decisions.

Index

AC-130 (Heavy Dancer), 247–48

Andrews Air Force Base, 115, 137

AR-15 carbines, 43

Arlington National Cemetery, 18

Barrett, Danny, 44–59, 87–88, 114–15, 119, 121, 122–23 152–61, 183, 202, 211–12, 214–15, 217–19, 232, 233, 238, 248, 252, 260, 276, 277
  background of, 44–45
  and explosion at PANG Op-Center, 196–99
  in Hotel Campbell assault, 166, 169–80
  in Hotel Fitzgerald assault, 136–51
  Marcinko's strategizing with, 189–95

Barrett, Ev, 153

Barrett M82A1 rifle, 33, 41, 51

Beckstein, Samuel, 98, 109, 191

as enemy of white supremacists, 72–82

murder of, 1–7

as presidential advisor, 65–66

pursuit of killer of, 43–59

Beckwith, Charlie, 203, 231

Blanchard, Max, 109–12, 115, 116, 124–25, 135, 137, 154–55, 180, 184–85, 187–88, 190–91, 192–93, 198–99, 201, 202, 209, 213–20, 235, 241–45, 271–72, 281–82
  attempted recruitment of Kossens by, 120–21
  death of, 267–69
  as former Army colonel, 109–10
  Kossens killed by, 263–66
  nuclear destruction threat of, 215–20, 241–42
  in *Wind Storm* battle, 248–70

Blue Light (Special Forces Group Counterterrorism unit), 203

Bolle assault goggles, 233

Bowden, Mark, 210
Bureau of Diplomatic
    Security, 31

Cambodia, 18
Camp David, 245
Camp X-ray, 245
Carley, Norm, 204
Carl "the Troll," 71, 74–84
Carver, John, 123
CCSP/OOO (Coordination
    Center and Special
    Projects/Office of
    Overseas Operations), 31
Central Intelligence Agency
    (CIA), 13, 45, 46, 242
CH-47 Chinook helicopter,
    212, 226, 232, 238, 270
Chinatown, 157, 192
  dirty nuke blast in, 183–85
Christian Identity Movement,
    88, 131
Clausewitz, Carl von, 42
Claymore antipersonnel
    firing device, 40
CNN, 125
Coast Guard, U.S., 236, 237,
    243, 275–76
Cold War, 66–67
Colt M4A1 assault rifle, 37,
    142, 211, 212, 226, 228, 238,
    251, 273
Colt rifle, 5.56-caliber, 211
Columbia River, 126, 183, 187
Coordination Center and
    Special Projects/Office of
    Overseas Operations
    (CCSP/OOO) 31

CORDS program, 44–45
Coulson, Danny O., 29, 88, 227
Curry, Ed, 1–7

Dahlgren, Trace, 8–14, 30–31,
    42–59, 60, 62–64, 86,
    114–16, 118, 119, 121, 123,
    185–86, 189, 199, 211–12,
    219, 226, 232, 233, 236–38,
    261, 272–75, 278–79,
    283–84
  background of, 12
  Chihuahua Apache heritage
    of, 12
  in Hotel Campbell assault,
    154, 156, 158, 159–60,
    165–80
  in Hotel Fitzgerald assault,
    135–36, 138–51
  injury of, 159, 176–80,
    185–86
  Karras interrogated and
    tortured by, 94–113
  in Karras pursuit, 50–51
  in Wind Storm battle, 247–61,
    270
Domestic Terrorism squad
    (FBI), 190

Eagle Industries, 123
Energy Department, U.S., 70,
    77

Fairfield, Karen, 30–31, 50,
    122, 157–59, 185, 191–94,
    196, 198, 202, 209, 220,
    257–58, 266, 276–78
  description of, 64–65

Karras's torture and, 114–19
OISA and Marcinko's
    meeting with, 64–94
in Operation Velocity
    meeting, 85–93
President's meeting with
    Marcinko and, 240–46
FBI, 124
Domestic Terrorism squad
    of, 190
Fletcher, Lieutenant j.g., 229,
    232–33, 236–38, 247
in *Wind Storm* battle, 254–57,
    259, 261
Fort Bragg, 95, 109
Fort Lewis, 28, 228
Frederick II (the Great), King
    of Prussia, 85

Galco shoulder rig, 43
Gehlen, Reinhard, 13
German Naval Intelligence, 13
Gray Army Airfield, 228
Green Berets, 28
Guantanamo Bay, Cuba
    (Gitmo), 245

Hamas, 282
H&K 10-mm MP-5 machine
    gun, 38, 123, 124, 144
H&K USP .45 compact, 43
Heavy Dancer (AC-130),
    247–48
Hezbollah, 282
Hostage Rescue Team (HRT),
    88, 115, 123, 124, 165, 167,
    170, 171, 174, 179, 201, 202,
    235

in Hotel Fitzgerald assault,
    136–51
Hotel Campbell, 155
    Laski assault at, 164, 167–80
Hotel Fitzgerald, 154–55
    assault at, 135–51
House Intelligence
    Committee, 78
Ho Yen-hsi, 94
HRT, *see* Hostage Rescue
    Team

Jackson, Andrew, 71
Jeet Kune Do, 12
Joint Service Combat
    Shotgun, 255
Joint Special Operations
    Command, 204

Kaltman, Al, 240
Karras, Tony, 60–62, 64, 74,
    86, 116, 117, 119–20, 122,
    125, 135–36, 155, 209
    interrogation and torture of,
    94–113
    pursuit of, 50–59
Kelley, William and Gerry,
    15–16, 281
KelTec .32-caliber pocket
    pistol, 124
Kimber Compact .45 auto,
    43
Kirby, Irene, 125
Kossens, Paul, 8–14, 30–31,
    42–59, 86, 94, 96–97, 118,
    122, 138–51, 154, 156,
    158–61, 187, 199, 210–13,
    219, 236, 281, 283

Kossens, Paul (cont.),
Blanchard's attempted
recruitment of, 119–21
death of, 263–66, 267–68,
273–74, 277
description of, 13
in Hotel Campbell assault,
165–68, 174, 175, 179–80
in Hotel Fitzgerald assault,
136, 138, 140–51
in pursuit of Karras, 50–59

Langley Air Force Base, 150
Laski, Jack, 155–56, 161, 189,
192, 195, 197
in Hotel Campbell assault,
163–80
Lassiter, Richard, 190, 192,
197–99, 202, 210, 212, 218,
220–25
Leo (police officer), 47–48
Leupold & Stevens Mark IV
M-1 scope, 10X, 23–26, 33
Little Creek, Va., 18, 162
"Little Ensign" (SEAL
officer), 17–22
Los Alamos, N.Mex., 66
Lyons, James "Ace," ADM
USN, 60–61

M4 see Colt M4A1 assault rifle
M-9 Berettas, 200
M60 machine guns, 39, 231
M145 Flex Sight, 232
M203 40-mm grenade
launcher, 37, 211
M240B machine guns,
231–32, 233

McChord Air Force Base, 187,
201
MacDonald, Ken, 204
Machiavelli, Niccolò, 152
McVeigh, Timothy, 282
Magnum, .41-caliber, 123
Magnum Winchester, .300-
caliber, 141
Marcinko, Richard, 152–61
Beckstein murder
investigated by, 42–59
in combat with Nemesis,
135–51
in discussion of Blanchard,
114–21
early career of, 8–31
Fairfield's meeting with,
60–70
in final assault preparations,
227–39
healing arts knowledge of,
28–29
in Hotel Campbell assault,
162–80
in Hotel Fitzgerald assault,
135–51
in Karras interrogation,
94–113
in Laski pursuit, 162–80
in Lassiter pursuit, 210–26
Mulcahy and President's
conspiracy against,
240–46
naval career of, 21
nukes stolen by, 68–70, 81
OISA meeting with, 71–84
Operation Velocity assigned
to, 85–93

in Oregon assault plans,
    122–34
at PANG Op-Center, 189–98
and Portland dirty nuke
    explosion, 181–88
presidential pardon of,
    90–91, 93
SADM rescued by, 270–84
in *Wind Storm* battle,
    247–70
Marine Force
    Reconnaissance, 61
Meinertzhagen, Richard, 135
Minot, N.Dak., 26–27
Modular Weapon System
    assault rifle, 211
Moore, George, 194–97, 215
    death of, 197, 273
Morgan Gregory, 155–56
Mount Hood, 126
Mount St. Helens, 126
MP-5 10-mm submachine
    gun, 38, 123, 124, 144
Mulcahy, Clay, 83, 85–93, 112,
    119, 124, 158–59, 187, 201,
    219, 220, 257–58, 277
    background of, 85–86
    in conspiracy against
        Marcinko, 240–46
    in Operation Velocity
        meeting, 85–93

Napoleon I, Emperor of
    France, 8, 60
National Guard, 68
    Oregon, 157–58
    see also Portland Air
        National Guard

National Security Agency
    (NSA), 77–78, 80–82, 83,
    84, 95
NATO ball ammunition, 7.62-
    caliber, 39
Naval Amphibious Base,
    U.S., 162
Naval Special Warfare, 234
Naval Submarine Support
    Facility, 79
Nazi Naval Intelligence, 120
Nemesis, 95–97, 100, 109,
    112, 116, 120–21, 136,
    137, 141–51, 154–56, 175,
    186, 190, 199, 211, 213–14,
    217, 220, 231, 235–36, 251,
    259
NEST team, 66, 70, 81, 87, 89,
    115, 124, 157, 191
    attack on, 32–41, 49
New Eagle International
    tactical headsets, 247
New London, Conn., 79
Nike assault boots, 233
Nomex:
    balaclava, 2
    flight gloves, 233
    flight suit, 226, 283
Noriega, Manuel, 13
NSA (National Security
    Agency), 77–78, 80–82, 83,
    84, 95
nuclear power plants, 181–82

Office of Internal Security
    Affairs (OISA), 30–31, 47,
    49, 59, 71, 72, 77, 86, 94, 115,
    118, 122–23, 186, 241, 243

Oklahoma City bombing, 282
Op-Center, at PANG,
    189–209, 215–18
    explosion at, 196–98
Operation Velocity, Marcinko
    assigned to, 83, 87, 91–93
Oregon National Guard, 157
    see also Portland Air
        National Guard
OSS, 13
Owens, Mick, 281

Panama, 13
PANG, see Portland Air
    National Guard
ParaRescue unit (Portland
    Air National Guard), 136
PAVE Hawk helo, 136,
    138–40, 151
Penetrator slug, 33–34
Persian Gulf War, 94
Phineas Priests, 109, 131–32,
    225
Portland, Oreg., 111, 112, 113,
    114–15, 117, 124, 183–88,
    213–19
    aftermath of dirty nuke
        explosion in, 216–17, 219
    dirty nuke destroyed in,
        180, 183–85
    Marcinko briefing on,
        125–34
Portland Air National Guard
    (PANG), 136, 148, 157,
    179–80, 183, 186, 213, 218,
    219, 232, 248, 260, 276, 280
Portland International
    Airport, 187

Portland Police Bureau, 210
President, U.S., 87–93, 118,
    240–46, 257–58, 276–78

Qaeda, Al, 282

rail adapter system (RAS),
    211
Raufoss .50 BMG M903,
    33–34
Red Cell, 27, 31, 54, 77, 79, 95,
    166, 181, 248–49, 272
    mission and purpose of,
        10–11, 60–62
Reich, Judith, 78, 82
Rickover, Hyman, 206
Ridgeway, Mathew B., 1
"Rocket Man" (terrorist),
    32–41
role playing, 166
RPG, 32–33

Saber radio pouch, 229
SADMs, see special atomic
    demolition munitions
Safariland cable sling, 232
Safariland thigh holster, 123
S&W Model 13 .357
    Magnum, 2–3, 4–5
Scholtes, Dick, BGEN USA,
    204–05
SEAL Beach, Naval Station
    at, 81
SEAL Team ONE, 13, 29
SEAL Team TWO, 204
SEAL Team FIVE, 29
SEAL Team SIX, 14–15, 19,
    27–29, 54, 77, 92, 95, 123,

139, 166, 200–01, 225, 242, 256
creation of, 9–11
invincibility of, 229–34
mission of, 202–09
Secret Service, 124
September 11th attacks, 26, 62, 185
SFOD-DELTA, 12
SIG 226 9-mm pistol, 233
Silicon Forest, 164
Smith, Clint, 29
snap links, 167–68
SOG Specialty SwitchPlier, 229
SOS TEMPS, 44
Special Air Service, British, 203
special atomic demolition munitions (SADMs), 77, 82, 83, 89, 95, 96, 109, 111, 116, 155, 180, 226, 243, 266, 272
    Portland explosion of, 183–88
    as "suitcase nukes," 66–69, 81, 96
    terrorists' capture of, 32–41
Special Boat Service, British, 204
Spetsnaz soldiers, Russian, 96
Squad Automatic Weapon, 5.56-caliber (SAW), 253
State Department, U.S., 30–31
Stoner .308 battle rifle, 23–26
"suitcase nukes," 66–69, 81, 96
Sun Tzu, 94, 122

SWAT team (Department of Energy), 70
Sword of the White Race, 72–84

TacLight, 229
Tactical Tailor combat sling, 211
Tactical Tailor Modular Assault Vest, 228
Tigard, Oregon, 155, 160
Togo Heilhachiro, 181
Travis Air Force Base, 241
Ts'ao Ts'ao, 189
TT-3-Day Assault Plus packs, 232

Velocity, Operation, Marcinko assigned to, 83, 87, 91–93
Vietnam War, 18, 45

Willamette River, 126, 235
Wind Storm (boat), 218–19, 220, 224–25, 234–37, 239, 241, 243, 282
    battle on, 247–70
Worden, Kelly, 27–28, 154
World War II, 13
Wor-Tech tactical folder, 229

Zodiac, 212, 236–37
    Marcinko's escape in, 271–84
Zoryoa, Gregg, 210